# Free City

OTHER WORKS BY JOÃO ALMINO
AVAILABLE IN ENGLISH TRANSLATION

*The Five Seasons of Love*
*The Book of Emotions*

# Free City

João Almino

*Translated by*
Rhett McNeil

DALKEY ARCHIVE PRESS
CHAMPAIGN / LONDON / DUBLIN

Originally published in Portuguese as *Cidade Livre* by Editora Record, Rio de Janeiro, 2010

Copyright © 2010 by João Almino
Translation copyright © 2013 by Rhett McNeil

Almino, João.
[Cidade Livre. English]
Free City / João Almino ; translated by Rhett McNeil. -- First edition.
pages cm
ISBN 978-1-56478-900-6 (pbk. : acid-free paper)
1. Brasília (Distrito Federal, Brazil)--Fiction. I. McNeil, Rhett, translator. II. Title.
PQ9698.1.L58C5313 2013
869.3'42--dc23
2013025983

Partially funded by a grant from the Illinois Arts Council, a state agency

Obra publicada com o apoio do Ministério da Cultura do Brasil / Fundação Biblioteca Nacional / Coordenadoria Geral do Livro e da Leitura

This work published with the support of Brazil's Ministry of Culture / National Library Foundation / Coordinator General of the Book and Reading

MINISTÉRIO DA CULTURA
Fundação BIBLIOTECA NACIONAL

www.dalkeyarchive.com

Cover design and composition by Mikhail Iliatov

Printed on permanent/durable acid-free paper

# CONTENTS

Yes, Brasília.
I marveled at time
which is already covering with years
your flawless mathematics.

—Paulo Leminski


And in his memory they remained, in perfect purity, castles armed and ready. All of it, which would be duly revealed in its own time, had been, at first, strange and unknown ... This great city would be the most elevated one in the world.

—Guimarães Rosa


Just like the migrant workers of Brasília, I, too, considered myself to be a "builder of cathedrals."

—Juscelino Kubitschek

# Introduction:
## Seven Nights and a Burial

At one point I thought about throwing out everything that I'd researched and written, setting aside my memories, fears, and anxieties for a volume of memoirs in which I would recount not only my childhood in the Free City, the city that came to shatter the silence that had dominated that plateau for millennia, but also my interest in journalism, the story of how I met my current wife, and the birth of my three children, relegating my research to newspaper articles and concentrating on the words of my father, words that I'm still revising after a conversation with my aunt Francisca during his burial.

But no, my narrative remained a mixture of my memories, those of my father, my research, and aunt Francisca's observations, and I made the mistake of handing it over to a writer who rid it of all its commas and periods, filled it with slang terms and scenes of violence, informed me that it would be necessary to add a moral and philosophical dimension to it, and even asked me if it contained some sort of lesson, which I found absurd. Because of this I decided to send it to the publisher straight away, even though it lacked a moral element, a philosophy, and a lesson, only to get upset later on when I received the polite response that it didn't fit in within the guidelines of the publishing house.

I considered selling my car to finance the publication of the book, cut out all the florid prose, and reinstated my periods and commas, since I didn't have time to waste on stylistic ornamentation anyway, and I also consider it to my advantage that I'm a journalist: describing Lucrecia, who is looking at a bird, I would never say that the wind wafted tenderly against her visage, nor that her beauty was adorned with amorous smiles, nor that her eyes gazed upon the boundlessness of the savannah or that they fluttered like the wings of a bird over scarlet fields. When I was halfway through, a critic who called himself my friend criticized not only my style but the content as well, Your experiment is going to be a disaster, he predicted, and I attributed this prediction to a difference in our politics, since we were on opposing sides, he considered me a reactionary and even now he walks past me without saying hello, but I owe to him the suggestion to create this blog and publish the story little by little here, like a nineteenth century serial—as such I was able to keep my car.

I don't presume I know everything that happened back in those days, I may have made some mistakes, written too much or too little; you all know that memories and research projects are flawed and incomplete, so it's best to confess right up front that I've forgotten a lot of the facts, and that, of the ones I remember, I don't always remember them accurately or precisely, and for that reason this is a text to be modified by its readers, as if I'd created a Wikipedia for this story, with the only rule being that I'm the only one who is allowed to meddle with my memories and those of dad and Aunt Francisca. As for the rest—the description of events that gives us the impression of belonging to the spirit of the times—you readers of this blog can revise as you will, and if you have any incident to relate or commentary to make, don't be shy.

Throughout the process, I added a personal opinion here and there and amended what I know with what had already been published about Brasília up to the current year, 2010, thus becoming greatly indebted to Isaías P. Ferreira da Silva Junior, whose work examines in minute detail the flora and fauna of the region as well as its first inhabitants, and follows the details of the construction of the city, a task that is at once that of historian, anthropologist, and sociologist. And he is even more indebted to many, many others, who, through historical accounts, sociological and anthropological analyses, memoirs, testimonies, statements to newspapers, reports, chronicles, poems, short stories, and even novels, sought to paint a picture of the Free City, also known as Pioneer Camp during the period of Brasília's construction.

My father remains the source of inspiration to publish this book, since, when he was attempting to reconcile his growing interest in the construction of the city with his journalistic activities, he told me that writing was also a type of construction, that one went along laying brick upon brick, and with that lesson in hand I have spent many years carrying his journalistic torch forward, and it is because of this same lesson that I am now arranging the bricks of this story into their present shape.

Finally, I would like to thank João Almino for his revisions. I met him in 1970 when he first set foot in Brasília, and he was the one who first encouraged me to start writing this story. Up to this point, this is the only paragraph that you all, the readers of this blog, have commented on, since you all just have to know what my name is, or at least whether or not I'm João Almino, as if the import of the story could change depending on who its author is, but never mind all that, I'm maintaining my anonymity for the simple reason that it gives me more freedom, most importantly the freedom to be honest.

JA

*First Night:*
*From A to Z*

"Brasília is a novel worthy of being told," a phrase that I pulled out of one of the many notebooks that Moacyr Ribeiro, my father, buried inside a box on the day after the city's inauguration, was uttered at a time when my father was collecting statements made by foreign visitors to the city under construction. On the cover of the notebook there was a landscape in green, yellow, and blue, with the word "Onward" in red across the middle of it, with beautiful palm trees and five boys running off to explore it, knowing just where they're headed, wearing cowboy hats and red bandanas, knee-high socks, long-sleeved shirts with the sleeves rolled up above their elbows, broad leather belts, each with a canteen of water, and the one in the middle holding the Brazilian flag, its pointed pole ready to be planted squarely in the future, and two stripes at the bottom of the picture and another, thicker one below them, off to the right, where Dad had written "Construction of Brasília 1956-1960" and, on the last two lines, "Comments by people from around the world."

I had to get Dad's statement before he died, which was also a way for me to patch things up with him during the delicate period he was going through and right the wrong of having been estranged from him for so long, actually, ever since I'd walked away from him, six years after the Valdivino incident, in the middle of an argument that I'm still trying to understand and that started when I told Aunt Francisca the things I'd heard about Dad, and, even so, she still didn't refuse to marry him, It's all a lie, she said, Well then, tell me the real story, No, I've got nothing to tell you, she replied. It was then that I, using as a catalyst a disagreement we had over an article I'd written, left home ranting against my father and moved into Aunt Matilde's apartment, but always remained uncertain and needed to know what truly happened before he died.

These days, months after the seven nights I spent with him and the seventh night, the night of his death, I wonder if I was his murderer. Maybe it's in order to redeem myself that I combine phrases from his buried papers with stories that I've read and heard, especially the ones that I heard from him starting the moment I noticed the joy in his eyes when he saw me at his side, for joy is sometimes expressed with tears, such as when we encounter beauty, justice, or kindness in their purest state. Weariness of this world and acquiescence to the approaching hour of his departure from it were transformed, little by little, by the pleasure he took in my conciliatory gesture. I couldn't believe everything that he told me, and that "everything" seemed insufficient, but I recognize that, in his tremulous voice, he spoke quite a bit, as if he needed someone on whom he could unload the stories that he'd always kept to himself. During the day he was quiet and sometimes I'd leave to have lunch with my wife and kids at our house in Lago Sul, meet up with my friends at the newspaper, or go to the University of Brasília library to do research, but at night I'd read aloud to him and he'd revise a sentence here or there and tell me lots of stories, sometimes until the wee hours of the morning, about Valdivino and the crime that possibly never happened.

Given the state he was in and his eighty-two years, whenever Dad would forget a detail he'd just invent another or even fabricate exact dates, but I, too, had witnessed quite a bit when I lived in the Free City from ages six to ten, before I moved into one of the houses in the W-3 South section of the Pilot Plan with Aunt Francisca, and, thus, I was able to complement and amend my Dad's memories with those of my own. All I had to do to start constructing the story was fill in the dry sentences he told me with sunshine, dust, tears, and fear, as well as everything else the story of the Free City should be made of: machines and tractors, cement mixers, excavators, bulldozers, steamrollers, asphalt plants, cranes, pile drivers boring into the ground, simple slats of lumber, as well as nights, bars, and prostitutes. A story that I could turn into an epic poem about men and machines creating a new city, migrant workers, tons of them, especially men who arrived without their wives, hoping to land a job with a construction firm, carrying their wooden trunks or bundles of clothes, an aluminum mug and a knife hooked to their belt, just like Valdivino used to have.

It's been six months since Dad died and I decided to finish the book, months that have, at times, shrouded these words in mourning clothes, and, at other times, helped me unearth some flashes of life from my forgetfulness, as I search for phrases in the desert. I am so preoccupied with this that my friends at the paper have noticed my indifference to the current political debates— me, who used to be so nonconformist and combative. My life is passing by on two separate planes: I take the kids to school, call the plumber to fix the kitchen sink faucet, clean the pool, and, at the same time, it's as if I've been living in another world, with a single, eternal history, which I don't yet completely comprehend, and which I myself am attempting to compose.

I'm sitting at the table on the porch with this nearly-complete chapter and others that are underway, full of notes and sections already written, my elbows on the glass tabletop, smoking my pipe, drinking coffee or a Campari, listening to the frogs in the early evening, thinking back on other frogs, and suddenly a shroud covers everything, even the beautiful landscape in front of me, and this story starts to turn sour. I stop, take a breath of fresh air, look out at the city lights shining on the lake, rummage around in another corner of my memory and work late into the night, blazing trails of disquietude, sometimes for hours and hours without writing a single line. At other times I struggle to restrain the flood of words that flow chaotically from a powerful memory, like when they told me the details of Valdivino's possible death, and I felt betrayed by Aunt Francisca and left the house upset with my Dad. The worst is that until now this blog has been completely useless, there hasn't been a single follower, a single useful comment, perhaps because I want to hide the real motive for writing this, a motive that's mine alone, the motive of someone who seeks to disguise human suffering and martyrdom with words, of someone whom the gods have abandoned and yet still hopes to be reborn and discovered, of someone who still feels guilty for the death of his father. But I don't want to talk about myself, I'm not as crazy as the doctors say, I'm not paranoid, nor am I just imagining things, my madness was only temporary, and that was many years ago anyway.

There was a time when I was eight years old and Dad was my idea of a great man, severe and just in his decisions; a time when he was cultured, intelligent, knew everything, and treated me as if I were his real son, his authority manifested in his powerful gestures and terse speech. The misfortunes that had befallen him before he came to the Free City hadn't yet made him bitter. But I didn't get to know him all at once; the image that I have of him was formed over the course of many years, and even now, after his death, isn't complete. With novels, one would expect that there wouldn't be any doubts about the moral makeup of the principal characters or the crucial facts of their lives, so it's a good thing that I'm not writing a novel and should just be content with the things I know. Why try to correct on paper something that was wrong in life? Why try to fabricate an answer to something that only and always presents itself as unknowable?

If I could, I'd continue my conversation with Dad. I miss him, and my heart keeps combining feelings, of tenderness and hatred, that shouldn't be mixed together, as I mull over his words and a strong breeze beats against the palm trees, whispering conjectures in my ear and helping me pound the keyboard of the computer.

I look out at the other end of the garden, where, in the darkness, small trees that I planted a year ago shake nervously. I see a figure out there. Dad! I call out. Silence. I can still hear his voice, like an echo, down in the depths of my fear. What is he saying? He's repeating Íris's version of the story: Valdivino never died. I no longer object to this; that old anger, revisited, is merely a memory of anger, and I accept what he tells me in his fragile, sickly voice, carried by the wind. Dad! I call out once more, and tears fall from my eyes while a maelstrom of contradictory images, ideas, and feelings whirls around in my head, and then I see myself as a child, the little crybaby whom Aunt Francisca would scold, then caress on her lap.

As soon as the lights from the generator were turned off, I'd close my eyes, but I was never able to see the beast of slumber that Aunt Francisca told me would come to put me to sleep, and I was afraid that Valdivino would appear to me and blame me for his death. Children are like that, he would appear to me in moments of fear, in his timid, superstitious manner, asking questions that made no sense, crying about something or other, crying so much in my dreams that a pool of tears formed around me, and even so I wasn't moved. But was he dead?

My present-day insomnia is an extension of those hours when, in the darkness of night, I heard sounds of drunkards out in the street, my dog Typhoon barking, macaws that lived out behind the house or a lone owl, and I'd open my eyes to the kaleidoscope of grays and blacks that turned into monsters on the walls.

To give the story some life, all I had to do was transport

myself back to a day from my childhood, imagine myself in the middle of an avenue in the Free City, and then I could see my aunts sporting fine figures and scowls, Valdivino seated at a table transcribing letters, Dad talking with someone in the doorway of a bar, a little girl with braids and dark eyes riding a bicycle, Typhoon following behind me, and I could see the colors of the shops, the wooden buildings, bulky black cars parked on the side of the street, their white-wall tires exposed, and then the smell of gasoline would emerge, the smell of oil, the smell of trash heaps and horse manure, and the stories of crimes, sins, despair, and grandiose futures would appear on an enormous, colorful screen.

I look out upon a day from my childhood and see three male characters conversing in front of our house, where Aunt Francisca has just set out some chairs, and I don't even need to describe to you the wooden house with no sidewalk, identical to all the others that you see in photographs from that era, in front of which, as I was saying, the three characters were having silent conversations, communicating phrases in gestures, uttering words that I can't hear, or, if I do hear them, that I can't understand, and which, if I understand them, don't interest me, one of them with an oval face, white and freshly shaved, a trace of displeasure in it, a sharp, playful look in his eyes, the expression of a very successful man, one who had accumulated many experiences throughout his life. Typhoon is sitting beside him, listening to his conversations with ears perked up. This is Dad.

The second one, whose hands hide his hat as he doffs it, has a muscular, well-formed body, a strong, straightforward look on his sunburned face, a well-trimmed moustache, and anyone who looked upon him would envy his felicitous appearance. This is Roberto, back when it wasn't yet clear whether he'd be the boyfriend of Aunt Francisca or Aunt Matilde.

The third one, of an unpolished simplicity, with a hat that's much too big for his small head, is a talker, looks intelligent, and is the only one with spurs on his boots, having arrived on the back of a mule, but if he garners my attention, it's because of his fragility. When he takes his hands out of his pockets, he gesticulates endlessly, swaying forward and back on his chicken legs, and gives the general impression that he'd be blown away if the wind were to catch him. The other two look him up and down when they pass by him. From this description, you will have already guessed it: This is Valdivino.

What feelings of longing are these that emerge from a happiness invented by memory? No, neither my mistrust nor doubts are of recent vintage, they were already present back when I was a boy, I just had to wait a few years to be able to perceive them. My desires have changed, my aspirations are different, I was successful once, before losing almost everything, but the hours pass just the same on different clocks, and the sun, facing the construction projects that filled the landscape, paints the morning with the same colors and conceals them, as always, at dusk. You, my lone, faithful follower on this blog, are right, why disturb what is quiet and forgotten?

On that first night when I met with Dad to clear up my doubts, he denied that he murdered Valdivino, it was a delicate thing for me to resurrect those old suspicions, and he told me that it was best to believe in the version told by the prophetess of the Garden of Salvation, Íris Quelemém, according to which Valdivino hadn't died at all, and perhaps never would, he had always been an insomniac and a sleepwalker, and was still walking around aimlessly, walking day and night through the forest in search of Z, the lost city. Leave it be, João, those waters have passed us by.

Sometimes, as I was wrapped up in a daydream, our life in the Free City would invade my memory, a life made up of places and scenes, as well as Dad's stories, and those of my aunts and the other characters around us—and of those others, mainly

Valdivino's—the things, facts, and people from my childhood arranged as if they were in an enormous family photograph, or on a chessboard in the distance where the distinctions between the pieces had dissolved into a uniformity imposed by time. Only Dad could, for the first time, reorganize the pieces on that board, and liberate my memory from that immobility. Fact is, he's not dead, nobody killed him, Dad replied, he's traveling or merely asleep, like Íris said.

A few years had passed since the incident occurred, when Dad returned to the Garden of Salvation, entering it anonymously, the Garden overgrown, and saw Íris enveloped in her white garment—long and wide, with puffy sleeves—flowing hair, blue ribbons running down her shoulders, beads around her arms and neck, big hoop earrings in her ears, and scarlet polish on her long fingernails, preaching at the top of Battle Hill, already with the bearing of the prophetess Íris Quelemém who would become famous throughout the Central Plateau, an indeterminate age in her round, wrinkle-free face and big, sharply radiant eyes, with the pensive air and unhurried voice of someone who was, at that moment, searching for inspiration for each of her words: From your venom shall flow the balm that will cure you; evil shall not grow within you, unless it be the evil that grows out of the conflict of your virtues, but if you're lucky, you shall only have a single virtue; may it be tolerance or patience or love—words in which Dad could identify echoes of words he'd already read or heard. After everything that happened between Íris and Dad, it was to be expected that, at the very least, she would feel troubled by his presence. She looked at him at length and stopped speaking, thus creating a long, compelling silence.

On that first night, between four dingy white walls, Dad recounted the conversation he had with her. I came to talk about Valdivino, What took place is what was written, and Valdivino didn't die, he's still alive, she replied, Well, then, where can I find him? He is Karaí, the holy blessed Lord Master, but Taú and Keraná had seven children, the seven afflictions that shall fall upon the earth, and Valdivino's wanderings are only the beginning of one of them; he is in the jungle, searching for Z.

On the day of the incident, April 22, 1960, the day after the inauguration of Brasília, Dad was urgently called to the Garden of Salvation, I remembered it well, since my memories of that day were very present for me, not only because of something that had happened earlier between me and Aunt Matilde, but also because Dad had traded his blue Willys jeep for a black '46 Ford Coupe Convertible, in which he'd sped off that morning.

I distrusted what Dad told me on that first night, closed in between four walls, that Valdivino didn't want any doctors to come, that it had to be him, Dad, he trusted Dad and nobody else, and that, when he arrived in the bedroom of a plywood shack in the Garden of Salvation, Valdivino was lying on the red dirt floor, wearing canvas pants, bracelets on his wrists, naked from the waist up, he had bruises on his head, perhaps from blows from a cudgel or something even heavier, he was delirious and stammered out a bunch of words that Dad tried to interpret. On the table there was a photograph of an adolescent girl whom Dad thought he recognized and a postcard from the city of Salvador, and a bottle of booze at the edge of it—oddly enough, since Valdivino didn't drink. Nobody had seen or heard anything, He came to the Valley fleeing from creditors, said a stranger. Dad noticed that they were calling him Abel, He fell and hurt himself on his own, Sir, he drank too much of the ceremonial liquid, not sure if he did it on purpose, said another stranger, sticking his head in the window, then taking off soon after, and Dad never saw him again. Seems like you people around here are always just falling and hurting yourselves, Dad commented with a touch of sarcasm, recalling that he'd recently, at Valdivino's request, come to Íris's aid there in the Garden of Salvation and found her in a similar situation.

Dad suspected that the attacker was there in the room, he glanced around for anything that could serve as evidence, or at least a clue, all he found was a Continental cigarette butt on the ground, then he went over to Valdivino as he tried to utter a few words, delicately cradled his neck in his hands, and tried to lift his head. At that point it appeared to him that Valdivino had passed away, so he checked for a pulse and removed all doubt. That's the first sin ever committed in the Garden of Salvation, an old man said to Dad, You mean the first crime?

Dad stayed a while longer in the Garden of Salvation, waiting for Íris Quelemém to receive him, until they came to tell him that Valdivino was still stretched out on the floor, Some say he's dead, others that he's still alive, so Dad started back towards Valdivino's shack, but someone gave him a message that the prophetess requested that he leave, that she'd send for him if he was needed.

When Dad returned to the Garden of Salvation two days later, Íris told him, He's a saint, to explain why Valdivino's body wasn't rotting. It will never rot, she prophesied, and she later spread word that Valdivino had been resurrected, that he was alive, although neither Dad nor anyone else at the house ever saw him again.

When she began to have her first visions, confirming the prophetic gifts that a *mãe-de-santo* had recognized in her, back when she still lived in Bahia, Íris had a revelation that Don Bosco had given her the mission to travel to the Central Plateau to help establish a new civilization, and she finally found her true path when, in November of 1959, she paid a visit to the widow Neiva Chaves Zelaya, better known as Aunt Neiva, a thirty-three-year-old truck driver who had recently founded the White Arrow Spiritist Union in the Gold Mountains, near Alexânia in the state of Goiás.

Bernardo Sayão is at the origins of many things, Dad told me, enclosed within four walls, for if it wasn't for him, Aunt Neiva would never have come here, and we wouldn't have either.

I'd like to thank my only follower on this blog for informing me that, in 1941, during the "March to the West," President Getúlio Vargas had invited the agricultural engineer Bernardo Sayão Carvalho de Araújo to modernize agriculture in the Central-West, founding the National Agricultural Colony of Goiás in the São Patrício Valley, and Sayão had started from scratch, learning things there that he'd later employ in the creation of highways and the construction of Brasília. He brought machines and people from distant places to the uninhabited banks of the Das Almas River, which flows into the Tocantins River, built a highway connecting the Colony to Anápolis, a city of fifty-thousand people back then, a hundred and forty kilometers away, and built the Colony in the face of opposing bureaucrats, unafraid of inspections or administrative lawsuits, the city of Ceres eventually emerging out of the Colony, named as an homage to the goddess of grains.

None of this is actually of interest, that Aunt Neiva lived on a farm in Jaguará, a city near Ceres, in the state of Goiás, and later lived in Ceres, and that Bernardo Sayão had been the best man when she married one of his trusted associates. If I include these details here, it's only in order to satisfy my lone follower, who thinks the historical information he sent me is of fundamental importance. Maybe I'll take out all this information when I reread this and just jump right to May of 1957, when Aunt Neiva, already a widow, was living in Goiânia, and Sayão invited her to join the others who were building Brasília. And it was the same with us, it all began with an invitation from Dr. Sayão, The story of Ceres explains a lot about Brasília, João, Dad told me, enclosed within four dingy white walls.

When Dad was a student in Belo Horizonte, my grandmother ran into serious financial difficulties and was unable to support him, but Dad didn't abandon his studies and get a job because he received help from my other father, or rather, my biological father, a middle-class cousin who owned a farm near the Das Almas River in Goiás.

In Brazil in the Fifties, there were very few places that granted degrees in psychiatry. For people from Minas Gerais, after training in the hospitals and clinics of the capital, Belo Horizonte, the best option was to leave the state. Dad obtained a residency at the National Center for Mental Illness in Rio de Janeiro, where his younger sister, Aunt Matilde, a determined, fearless young woman, had just moved to start a job in one of the ministries of government.

When I lost my entire family—biological father, mother, and two older siblings—in a terrible accident—a subject, like many others, that I'd rather not discuss—Dad wrote to Aunt Francisca, my mom's sister, to tell her that he wished to raise me. Aunt Francisca was against it, she didn't want me to go to Rio, she knew that Dad had struggled with alcoholism since his failed marriage, she'd been raised to have rigid moral and religious principles and worried that an atheist like Dad would raise me with no religion, but the fact is that in a short time, at the age of six, I found myself living with Dad and Aunt Francisca, not in Rio de Janeiro, but in Ceres, in the state of Goiás. I'll reveal only the ingredients of this long story: the end of Dad's residency at the National Center for Mental Illness, my family's farm near the Das Almas River, which Aunt Francisca had inherited, Dad's bitterness, his desire to hide himself at the far ends of Brazil—despite the protestations of his sister, Aunt Matilde—and his ability to persuade Aunt Francisca that he had overcome his drinking problem and wanted to live a peaceful life managing the farm and helping to raise me.

After deep reflection, Aunt Francisca decided to take the risk, telling Dad in a letter that there'd be no lack of work for him in Ceres, that if he didn't want to set up a psychiatric practice he could dedicate himself to another branch of medicine, since from the start the city had supported the healthcare industry, workers received free health care and the city already had two hospitals, with a third under construction, she didn't care that others might think that they were living together as husband and wife, she was a righteous, principled woman and answered only to God. She only imposed one condition: that I be raised in the Catholic religion.

I reciprocated Aunt Francisca's affection for me, and, at the beginning, Dad did more than just take on paternal authority, he was a companion to me, taking me on walks and talking to me about life.

Thus, we were living in Ceres when, one day, news spread that Dr. Bernardo Sayão, already vice-governor of Goiás and one of the directors of Newcap—the Company for the Urbanization of the New Capital of Brazil, which had been created through legislation on September 19th of that year, 1956—needed people to grow and cook food for those who were coming to build Brasília. He knew the disposition of the inhabitants of the Agricultural Colony and the experience they'd acquired in the production of foodstuffs, and for that reason he believed he could convince some of them to move to Brasília, together with people from Anápolis and Goiânia.

Aunt Francisca was the first to get excited about the idea, then Dad became convinced that it was an opportunity that couldn't be passed up, and both of them spoke to me of a future that seemed to signify nothing less than happiness. The word "moving" danced endless, magical pirouettes through the skies of the future, but at first it didn't capture my interest, perhaps because in Ceres— setting aside the great tragedy of my childhood—Aunt Francisca and Dad had shielded me from suffering, which I had heard about more than I'd actually experienced personally. I had everything and felt grateful for everything I had.

However, since the best thing I had was the love of Aunt Francisca, if she thought it good to leave, then I was delighted to accompany her. It was fortunate that Dad had wanted to live with us and take care of me, and that he'd instilled in me, at an early age, the notion that I should open my eyes to the vastness of a world that was much bigger than Ceres. The move was a door to that much vaster world, where wealth and happiness awaited us.

On this point I disagree with João Almino's revision, with which he imbued our journey to the Central Plateau with too much wishful thinking. Therefore, I'm cutting out everything he added and retaining my original text, in which I merely state that, for Dad, the move would put his sense of adventure to the test and demand of him greater exertion than he'd ever before mustered. He thought about traveling through Goiânia or Anápolis, which was then the end of the line of the railroad that led to the southern half of the country, but at the time, as one of you readers of this blog astutely remembered, the Araguarina Company didn't yet offer daily service between Goiânia and Anápolis, one hundred and thirty kilometers from the location where Brasília would be built, and even much later, up until the paved highway was inaugurated in 1958, the trip from Anápolis to Brasília was twelve hours through potholes and dust. We got there after a few days in Dad's blue Willys jeep, sometimes cutting across terrain with no road, first heading towards Cabeceira Grande, where the Preto River serves as a border between the Federal District and the state of Minas Gerais, and from there we took the road to Unaí.

We found a plot of land when we got there, but there was a misunderstanding. Aunt Francisca was qualified to prepare food for the workers, but Dad wouldn't be able to perform the tasks of an engineer that were wrongly expected of him and, although he could diagnose an illness here and there and care for the insane—after all, he'd spent two years in a psychiatric residency after he graduated—he decided that he didn't want to dedicate himself to medicine. Unfit for the challenges of the times, yet conscious of the magnitude of what was being created on the Central Plateau, two days after we arrived he made a proposal to Bernardo Sayão, who, although he didn't yet live in Brasília, was already directing all the principal operations there.

At the entrance to the land where the first campground was set up for the construction of the new capital, Sayão, stout, with a square, manly jaw, big ears, sharp eyes, a big, straight nose shaped like a perfect triangle, sweaty-faced, sunburned, expressively handsome, with voluminous hair parted at the side, seemed to my dad to stand two meters tall—later on Dad would come to find out that he was exactly one meter and eighty-six centimeters tall—and his fifty-five years didn't show. Dad told him that he wasn't an engineer, but that he would like to accompany the construction of the Goiânia-Brasília project, that he would dedicate himself to observing and recording everything, so that a detailed account of that epic endeavor might be published on the day of Brasília's inauguration, written from the point of view of someone who lived the day-to-day of it, an official history of Brasília, which he called "The Golden Book," from the start of construction up to its inauguration.

Sayão didn't see any utility in the work of a scribe, since he had an aversion to idle chatter, I want practical people, ready to take on the jungle, look, Dr. Moacyr, it's like I always say, all that's possible to do has already been done, so we'll do the impossible, but, perhaps even because he preferred action to chit-chat, he ended up pragmatically accepting the presence of Dad and his notebook, not for the Goiânia-Brasília highway project, but during the construction of the two thousand-meter provisional runway of the future city, Just stay out of the way, he ordered.

When he revealed to Dad that President Juscelino Kubitschek was going to land there in a Brazilian Air Force plane on October 2 to visit the site that was selected the year before by the Commission for the Localization of the New Capital, Dad asked permission to record the visit in his notebooks. Sayão once again showed contempt for that inferior task, But come anyway, you can accompany the delegation, he said.

Dad carefully prepared for the visit, since he wanted to win the president over with his knowledge of the land and, thus, secure his position for good. At great cost, he acquired from Newcap a copy of the report that, towards the end of February in 1955, Donald J. Belcher had delivered to the Commission for the Localization of the New Capital, in which he read that "Brazil should be praised for the fact that it is the first nation in history to base the selection of the site of its capital on economic and scientific factors, as well as qualities of climate and beauty." He drove his jeep to the Brown Ranch—which was called that because the location had been given the code name "brown," which had beat out green, red, yellow, and blue, but which mainly corresponded to the Bananal Farm, which was adjacent to the Gama and Vicente Pires farms—and there sought out the junction with the existing roadways, the Anápolis-Planaltina road, which ran east-west through the proposed ranch, and the highway that connected Cristalina and Formosa to the south, verifying what Belcher had indicated in his report: "The distinguishing topographic feature is a triangular-shaped dome delineated by Deep Creek and the Bananal Stream where they come together to form the Paraná River, which then runs east toward the São Bartolomeu River."

When the president, who had brought with him architect Oscar Niemeyer, was received by the governor of Goiás and Bernardo Sayão, Dad had already explored the vastness and transparency of that valley and accompanied them out to a cross that Sayão had fixed in the ground, and out to the Gama farm as well.

The president is the new Tomé de Sousa, Dad commented to Bernardo Sayão, referring to the first Governor-General, who, upon disembarking at All Saints Bay on March 29, 1549 initiated construction on the nation's first capital, And you are going to go down in history, Dr. Sayão. Look, Dr. Moacyr, I'm not interested in publicity or posterity, I'm interested in doing, Sayão replied, his broad-brimmed hat in hand, as always.

At the Brown Ranch, they passed by Camp Creek—which had earned that name since, in 1893, members of the commission presided over by then director of the National Observatory Luiz Cruls had camped there in order to demarcate and study that valley of severe, majestic tranquility—as a botanist on the Cruls mission described it—and Dad mentioned, loud enough for the president to hear, that he'd been taking notes on everything and discovered that JK had his own "Golden Book" of Brasília, an official history of the place, according to what he related those present, paying no mind to what Dad had said. Only much later would Dad read the famous phrase that one of the two followers of my blog sent me, which the president recorded in his book that day: "From this central plateau, this secluded place, which will shortly be transformed into the brain of the nation's most important decisions, I cast my eyes once more upon my country's future and foresee the new dawn, with an unbreakable faith and limitless confidence in its great destiny," also adding—the blogger is certain of this—that, having put an end to the separation between the coast and the interior, Brazilians will no longer live the way Friar Vicente de Salvador described in the seventeenth century, that is, like crabs, cleaving to the coast.

I've reinstated this paragraph, which had been eliminated in João Almino's revisions, to affirm that the visit came to an end without the president even noticing that Dad existed, but there would soon be a new opportunity to meet him, when Dad managed to accompany closely another of Bernardo Sayão's bold efforts: the construction, at the Gama farm, in only ten days— from the 21 of October to the 31—of the first official residence of the president, a wooden structure built on stilts, designed by architect Oscar Niemeyer, which only avoided being called the

Palace of the Dawn because JK liked the name so much that he resolved to save it for the definitive palace. Two days after the start of construction, on October 23, according to what I read in the papers that I dug up, Dad accompanied Sayão to Luziânia to receive the first trucks carrying material for the construction of the city, which had left from Minas Gerais and Rio on October 18. Ever hopeful that the president himself would show interest in his writings, he took daily notes—up until the end of the month—on the construction of the Catetinho Palace, the record stating, in the first of his many notebooks, on a date near that of the construction of Catetinho, that the wood from Goiânia took five days to arrive, since the sinuous roads had to pass through Campo Limpo, Corumbá, and Brazlândia, as a new, attentive blog reader—not yet a follower—confirms.

When Catetinho was inaugurated on November 10, the president spoke to my father for the first time, asking him what he did for a living, and upon hearing Dad's explanation he affirmed that during the years of Brasília's construction he would receive innumerable visits from distinguished people, that's all he said, but Dad took those words as acknowledgment that the president indeed needed someone to take notes for his "Golden Book" of Brasília, and this was more, much more, than Dad had hoped for. From that moment on, whenever allowed, he was seen with his notebook accompanying Bernardo Sayão everywhere, in broad daylight, two great men side-by-side, Sayão even taller than Dad, who inquired about everything that took place and compiled an almost daily chronicle, which he kept in a cardboard box. Dad even witnessed something that was said to be a regular occurrence, which one of the followers of my blog reminded me of: that Sayão, a man of action, averse to routines, formalities, paperwork, and cabinet members, authorized requisitions for materials on the back of scraps from packs of cigarettes, and that, whenever a machine operator didn't understand his orders, he'd take control of the machine himself, demonstrating how it worked, sometimes even finishing the job. Dr. Sayão, I'd like to write an article about you, the most daring of Goianos, Dad proposed to him, I'm not a Goiano, Dr. Moacyr, I'm a Carioca from Tijuca.

It was merely a trial run, on June 21, 1957, Sayão had managed to get Dad a few hours at Catetinho and afterwards at the lobby of the Newcap offices where the civil servants were receiving General Craveiro Lopes, the president of Portugal, the first foreign head of state to visit Brasília, and thus, for the first time, Dad felt entrusted with the task of accompanying illustrious visitors and recording, for History, their observations about the new capital.

Never forget this date, João, that phrase, and not much else, is all I remember about that event, which is, nevertheless, narrated in detail in the notebook that I carefully read before my conversation with Dad, confined within four white walls, on that first night, and in that notebook it's written that Dad showed up late at Newcap, and that he didn't witness a single conversation at Catetinho, that he was only able to see, from a distance, the general accompanied by his wife Berta, aside from hearing a serenade in the middle of the frigid night, when the temperature got down to three degrees celsius. It didn't work out this time, but one day, my son, Dad told me, this box is going to be valuable, they'll have to rummage through it when they want to find out how everything began.

On the day of its inauguration in February of 1957, Dad, Aunt Francisca, and me—as well as Aunt Matilde, at that point—were among the four hundred people living in the city that was coming into being, on lands parceled out from the Bananal, Vicente Pires, and Gama farms, and whose principal avenues were opened by Newcap just a few months after we arrived. In 1957, Dad started training me to be a tour guide in that city, the Free City—"free," mainly because its merchants were exempt from paying taxes.

Visitors found me amusing because I knew everything about the city, by the beginning of that year I knew each one of its three hundred and forty buildings, its houses and stores, both dry goods stores and groceries, and in time I'd come to know its restaurants, fabric stores, barber shops, dye houses, carpenter's shops, butcher shops, pharmacies, its two schools, its movie theaters, its bars, its wooden pension houses and hotels, which advertised the comfort of their spring mattresses, and then the Baptist, Kardecian, and Presbyterian churches, as well as, in the central plaza, the São João Bosco Catholic church, which Valdivino helped build, where a vigil would one day be kept over the body of Bernardo Sayão, and where I confessed my fantasies about Aunt Francisca to Father Roque Viliati.

I knew the name of every hotel in the city, from the first, Hotel Brasília, which Dad told me brought back memories of his encounter with Lucrécia, the famous prostitute, to the ones that were built later on, Paradise Hotel, Dom Pedro II on Central Avenue, the Portuguese Pension House on Third Avenue, the Normandie, the Wine Palm, the Jurema, and the Santos Dumont.

Dad said that in this last one, which was owned by a former Polish refugee, the young and attractive Countess Tarnowska, he had met two foreign writers, the poet Elizabeth Bishop and the novelist Aldous Huxley. The countess owned a movie theater in Anápolis and decided to open another one in the Free City in its early days. The movie theater, where Dad would sometimes take me, against Aunt Francisca's wishes, was initially housed in a building that looked more like a wooden barn than a movie house, but later on it moved to a new location in one of the biggest buildings in the city, a structure made of corrugated iron, where they played slapstick comedies from Rio starring Oscarito and Grande Otelo, films produced by Vera Cruz starring Eliana Lage, Marisa Prado, Anselmo Duarte, Ilka Soares, and Alberto

Ruschel, as well as many foreign films, like *An American in Paris* with Gene Kelly and the Italian neorealist films of Rosselini and Vittorio de Sica. I didn't see all these as a kid, but I saw them later, or at least heard about them, recognized their posters, vaguely recalled comments that Dad or Aunt Matilde made about some of them, or else they were seen by the three readers of this blog who commented on my post this week and are primarily culpable for any imprecision therein.

The countess was just one among many foreigners, whose names I've forgotten, names that were Arabic, Jewish, Portuguese, Spanish, Italian, German, Belgian, French, Russian, Greek, and Polish. As Dad declaimed, reading from a foreign newspaper back in those old days: "it doesn't matter where they hail from, whether they are Brazilians or foreigners, because no matter who arrives here, they soon partake of the enthusiasm they live with in this city, suddenly aware of the fact that something grandiose is being created here."

The Free City also attracted people from all over Brazil, with a preponderance of people from Minas Gerais and Northeasterners. When the workers couldn't live with their families in the work-camps, they moved to the commercial areas, which were dominated by Arabs and Northeasterners, or to the squatters' villages that were going up: Vulture Hill and Kerosene Hill, Hope Town, Tenório Town, IAPI, Divineia, Vincentina, and Sarah Kubitschek. Just eight years old, I would explain in detail, to the astonishment of the newly arrived, that the lots were distributed in a program of commodatum, and since the deeds were not definitive, they would be returned to Newcap at the end of 1959; that permits were not granted for the houses, which would all be destroyed when Brasília was inaugurated—the first disposable city, the Free City was built to be destroyed. I knew what a commodatum was because Dad, at the same time that he was just getting on his feet with the unprofitable activity that was something like that of a historian or journalist, was also dedicating himself to a more lucrative field, for, as one of the first to arrive in the Free City, he had obtained "Brasília Obligations," which gave him priority and advantages in the purchase of land, and little-by-little he became a commodatum merchant.

At the beginning, Dad was pretty much my only companion, I loved and admired him, I must admit, I liked to watch him organize his papers, which were stowed away like precious stones, You're a real Mineiro, Dr. Moacyr, I heard people say, and I understood that it was meant as a compliment about Dad's talents, he was a genius in both letters and business and knew how to talk to everyone without committing to anything, always making the best of the circumstances. Sometimes he'd take me hunting, and it was on a hunt out near the Descoberto River, in the year we arrived, that we first met Valdivino. I later made friends with some of the kids who came there with their families, or parts of families, like mine, I passed the time putting collectible cards into albums, leafing through comic books, playing table-top button soccer or real soccer, I'd discuss the stories of Batman, Popeye, Captain Marvel, and Robin Hood with the few friends I had while we listened to *Geronimo, Hero of the Backlands* on the radio and were moved by this hero's defense of justice in the fictional city of Cerro Bravo in the state of São Paulo, alongside his beloved, Aninha, and his sidekick, Kid Saci, fighting against Colonel Saturnino Bragança and the bandits—One-leg, Skull-Face, and Sparky—and sometimes we'd venture out in search of cashew fruit and pequi fruit, returning home with our legs and feet yellow with mud. Get straight in the bath, young man, Aunt Francisca used to command.

Back then she seemed taller than she is in fact, her average height in just the right proportion to her full-figured body. No other woman had such beautiful black hair, and I liked her round face, her small, thin-lipped mouth—from which emerged a voice that, although mild, was clear and confident, from which I heard sobs and laments, never screams—and her sharp, black eyes—at times serious—which knew how to smile and enchant, and explored everything they encountered with curiosity, above all looking upon me with tenderness. She showed me how to press the keys of her accordion, I would take a seat on a chair, as if I were in a movie theater, to watch her in front of her sheet music, picking out the notes, my eyes and lips showing my happiness, and then a desire within me would cause me distress, a desire to play the accordion and embrace that soft, dark flesh, but soon I would control myself, reined in like a trained horse. The rain also played its music on the zinc roof-tiles, at first like the soft sound of a piano, later rich in percussion, as if the poured sand of the construction companies were falling down on our heads, and then a full, rhythmic orchestra, with no lack of roaring thunder, came upon us suddenly, the loud splashing sounds coming through the window, and the wind entered to caress the legs and thighs of Aunt Francisca. She smiled at me and at the accordion, always playing, and the rain bathed her smile in melancholy, further exposing her gentleness and tender heart.

The rain brought with it a slightly chilly breeze, I rested my eyes on Aunt Francisca and tried to straighten out my crooked thoughts, which I sought, in vain, to correct with teachings from the church, but my imagination rebelled and, with the wind, traipsed along her face, her entire body. Suddenly, footsteps could be heard, and a drenched figure approached the door, it was Valdivino, who would visit with us for a while, admiring Aunt Francisca's talents, same as me, then leave for more hours of work, for I had the impression that Valdivino did nothing but work, worked ceaselessly, and that when he had a few minutes for a break he came to our house, where he also worked, fixing pipes, installing a new showerhead, building a wall here, painting another one there.

Aunt Francisca's gaze kissed me as she stroked her accordion with a flannel cloth, leaving it radiant, the way she did with the furniture in the living room, which she polished with peroba oil, bending down or shaking her hips, as when, in the kitchen, she made sweets out of caramel, coconut, and papaya. She was always active, didn't stop moving from morning to night. When she wasn't busy at the restaurant of the Social Welfare Alimentation Service, known as SWAS, she took care of the house, going from one end to the other, making sure the living room never got messy, the sinks never got grimy, the furniture never got dusty, and the wardrobes never got moldy. Sometimes I couldn't control myself, and my affection for Aunt Francisca would come out as pinches on her arm or tugs on her hair, my amusement complete when she'd take off her sandal and run after me with it, never able to catch me.

She expressed an opinion about everything around us, especially Dad's tastes and decisions, Why don't you have a linen suit made, we have a good tailor here in the Free City now, you need to look more refined, Mister, For walking around in the mud?, he'd reply.

On Sundays, Aunt Francisca would paint her fingernails and toenails, wearing a nightgown with buttons in the front, which allowed for a glimpse of her bra, she'd come out of the bathroom smelling of perfume, plucked her eyebrows with tweezers in front of the mirror, and painted her lips red, then put on a modest dress and went to Mass with a scarf about her head and rosary in hand. Upon her return, she'd mention a possible girlfriend to Dad: Today at church everyone was staring at Mr. Ferreira's daughter, beautiful yellow dress, matching shoes and handbag, a fine young lady, don't you think?

She and Aunt Matilde couldn't have been more different, a difference that I noted on the clothesline, where I observed the colored panties of Aunt Matilde and the white ones of Aunt

Francisca; Aunt Matilde's large corsets and Aunt Francisca's smaller ones; the sleeved dresses of Aunt Francisca and Aunt Matilde's sleeveless ones; Aunt Francisca's petticoats and Aunt Matilde's shorts.

I'd leave early for Mass with Aunt Francisca. She was the one—never Aunt Matilde or Dad—with whom I'd pray the rosary at nine o'clock at night, before going to bed. She was the only one who praised me for wanting to be an altar-boy, and for thinking about entering the seminary, during a period when I even desired to be a saint, capable of improving the world through my virtues and example, earning a guarantee of free entrance to heaven in the bargain. Valdivino is a saint, Aunt Francisca used to say, and I at least wanted to be his equal.

On Sundays, while Aunt Francisca got ready to go to Mass, always wearing long-sleeved dresses, Aunt Matilde would put on a pair of tight jeans or a pair of shorts that showed off her long thighs and plop down in front of the hi-fi, a big, wooden piece of furniture supported by matchstick legs that took up almost half of the side-wall of the living room, beneath the beautiful pendulum clock that we'd brought from the farm at the Das Almas River.

When we returned from church, she'd still be there listening to the latest hits, either on the radio or the phonograph, where she'd play the new records she received from Rio over and over again, to the point of driving Aunt Francisca mad. At such times I identified more with Aunt Matilde than with Aunt Francisca. While Aunt Francisca liked to listen to romantic songs, with a touch of melancholy—"Goddess of Asphalt" by Nelson Gonçalves, "Loneliness" by Dolores Duran, "Sorrowful Ballad" by Angela Maria, or Maysa singing "I don't exist without you"— Aunt Matilde had a more diverse taste, and would listen to "All the Way" by Frank Sinatra, an album of Nat King Cole performing "Ansiedad" and "Cachito" in Spanish, and she discovered João Gilberto's bossa nova through songs like "Bim Bom" and "The

Morning of Carnival," as well as the new, lively rhythms of Celly Campelo in songs like "Stupid Cupid" and "Pink Ribbons."

Their tastes also differed come Carnival. I recall that during Carnival of 1958 Aunt Francisca's favorite song was the samba "Madureira Wept": "Madureira wept/ Madureira wept in sorrow/ When the voice of destiny/ Obeying the divine/ Called for her star . . ." But Aunt Matilde had her fun listening to the Carnival march by Dircinha Batista: "Mommy, I failed/ Mommy I failed the test/ For the very first time/ Little daughter, little daughter/ Little daughter dear/ Was it French?/ Was it Portuguese?/ I don't know, mommy, I can't even suspect/ The test was so tough, mommy/ That I shipwrecked!"

In the Free City the Carnival celebrations weren't as fun as the São João festival later in the year, and to me they didn't mean anything more than playing around with a plastic bottle that looked like the ethyl chloride sprays of Carnival, which I filled with water so I could soak the neighbors. I'd also sit on the sofa in front of the hi-fi, listening to the Carnival hits, along with Aunt Matilde, Aunt Francisca, and some of my friends who lived on our street: "He dresses like a Bahian girl to pretend he's a woman/ You'll see that he's a . . . / You'll see that he's a . . . / At the ball at the theater he claims he's Salome/ You'll see that he's a . . . / You'll see that he's a . . . "

I hoped that at this point one of the readers of this blog would remind me of the many, many other songs that I can no longer recall, but over the weekend these pages weren't accessed a single time. I make brief note of this not to complain, it's pointless to waste time complaining, and I'll quickly change the subject to say that at home there was only one pleasure greater than listening to hits on the radio, which was to explore every gap between the wooden boards of the wall when Aunt Matilde and Aunt Francisca were together in their bedroom, or when Aunt Matilde, light-skinned and tall like Dad, with a full-figured beauty that intimidated me, ensconced in dresses that traced her backside, left for her job as a civil servant. Then I could spy on Aunt Francisca as she changed clothes or took long baths, I would listen to her undress, the sound of her clothes being hung on the hook on the door, the splashing of water against her body, the swish-swish of the soap in the recesses of her body. In my daydreams I could see her pitch-black hair fallen about her shoulders, the soap bubbles sliding down her shiny skin, the curls frothy as a cotton ball down where her thighs met, and then I'd fantasize about us bathing together, I could hear Aunt Francisca's prolonged urination into the toilet and I'd imagine her sitting in there nude, I could hear the sound of her brushing her teeth and then I'd reckon that, if I were to open the door, I'd see her directly before me, with her back to me, and perhaps she wouldn't even notice that I was watching. One time, as I lay on the floor, I pushed the bathroom door open slightly, and Aunt Francisca, naked and wet, covering herself with a towel, opened the door and shot me a severe look, So it's you, you shameless boy. I promised myself that I'd never again perform that vile act, but the temptation was great because the house was small, Aunt Francisca's butt was desirable, and the gaps between the boards were plentiful.

As a child, I wasn't afraid to be at home alone with the door and windows open, or walk about nearby, pointing out hotels, stores, bars, and restaurants to the newly arrived. I'd take my faithful mutt Typhoon—white with black spots, the delight of all the boys—with me along the smoothed dirt avenues, turned to mud by the rain, listening to the crude, rhythmic music of the generators, which ensured the lights would stay on while the construction at the Saia Velha Hydroelectric Power Plant still remained incomplete. A powerful generator here, a weak one over there, further on a house lit up by oil lamps, another by gas lamps, and thus the colors of the lights painted the shadows, now blue, now various tones of yellow, white, or grey.

Especially in the early years, since there were few buildings and, thus, few lights, which were only illuminated by the generators for a few hours, their owners generally turning them off before ten at night, and since not all of the buildings even had generators, the sky was a field of stars whenever there was a new moon. Don't point with your finger, it'll cause warts, Aunt Francisca warned me, and then showed me Orion's Belt and the Southern Cross.

I remember the times when I would walk through the streets late at night, back when the Free City didn't sleep, its stores open, selling wares into the wee hours, since Brasília was built at a frenzied pace, and it was at these times that I'd watch guitar players or drumming in bars or even serenades out in front of houses on moonlit nights.

Sometimes Typhoon would lead the way, and I'd follow him through the open-air market and avenues, hearing advertisements for films and job opportunities, folk music—both *baião* and *xaxado*—and sermons blare from loudspeakers. When he was a pup, Typhoon liked to visit the shoemaker, Mr. Albuquerque de Pinho, because he could smell the leather, glue, dye, and polish, and much later, at the beginning 1959, he invariably wanted to go inside the Bom Jesus Butcher Shop to try to snatch a piece of meat.

The city's biggest attraction, and a source of pride for me, was that it gave the impression of being the Wild West, a city straight out of American movies, which, as Dad used to say, didn't exist in other parts of Brazil. Since it was meant to be provisional and would be destroyed once Brasília was inaugurated, all the houses and shacks—usually with roofs made of asbestos or zinc tiles, sheets of aluminum, or straw—had to be made of wood. Hence, all the conflagrations, which spread rapidly, and which I also witnessed out in the fields, where every year, a freak occurrence, the vegetation would catch fire and then shamefully sprout forth again, afraid to grow.

Back in 1957, Dad enrolled me in a class of thirty-three students at the Baptist Institute, a building made of horizontal slats of wood, with a two-tiered roof, and a single classroom, the first private school in the Free City, but he soon transferred me to a public school, the much larger Scholastic Group Number 1, or SG-1, located in the residential and administrative center, which, since it had been the first location of Newcap, came to be called Oldcap, and which also housed the SWAS restaurant—where Aunt Francisca eventually became caterer—and the headquarters of the PD, the Police Department of Newcap, later called SPB, the much-feared Special Police Force of Brasília, which, according to one version of the story, could have been responsible for the death of Valdivino, if it were indeed true that Valdivino was dead.

Dad was filled with pride about the fact that the school was a project of the architect Oscar Niemeyer, completed in just twenty days, a long, raised shoebox on stilts, inaugurated on September 21, 1957 by JK himself, who, a month later, planted a *cabralea canjerana* in the backyard, just a stubby thing back then, which I worshipped as if it were the god of an indigenous religion. At the time, I didn't notice how barren the schoolyard was, that place where we had our little parties, perhaps because the sun often gave life to its colors and illuminated its sparse foliage. I woke up at six-thirty in the morning to go to school, taking my drowsiness and ignorance along with me, and when our hijinks—tossing paper airplanes and passing doodles and notes—weren't enough to jolt me awake, I'd nod off on my desktop in the back of the classroom until it was time to head back home at two o'clock.

I made some friends, whose names I omit so that you all, the few readers of this blog, don't waste your time with people who won't reappear in this story. Suffice it to say that they had varied builds, abilities, and temperaments. One of them, a large clown who largely just clowned around, didn't even need to speak, he could crack us up with just a facial expression, formed by his toucan eyes and nose. Another came to school in starched clothes and brilliantine in his well-combed hair, and I tried to imitate him at home whenever we expected a visit from Aunt Francisca's friends, all much older than me, whom I hoped to woo. Another still was a dark-skinned kid who liked to show off his vast knowledge of curse words. To my astonishment he could list off a dozen different names for the genitals of both men and women, and would draw a triangle on the cement with chalk, with streaks all over it, like sunrays, It's a pussy, he'd say. A teacher noticed one of these chalk drawings one day and wanted to know who had done it, at which point I believed that the drawing faithfully represented the female genitalia, since even the teacher had recognized it. There was also a violent sort, always ready to stir up a fight, who gave everybody nicknames and once yelled at me, Come here, Joli, gesturing with his fingers as if he were calling for a dog. I slapped him square in the face and threw him on the ground, we scuffled and dirtied ourselves in the mud, his nose was bloody and his shirt ripped, and instead of him having to explain himself, I was the one who was sent to the principal's office. I'll never forget the chubby, nervous, effeminate kid who liked to recite poems, rolling his eyes and gesturing exaggeratedly with his arms, nor the big fat boy with a baritone voice who sang at school festivities, a talented student in every subject and the teacher's pet, always protected and praised by her. I even have recent news about that guy: he became a lawyer. My best friend was a sports star, strong and tall, with a wide face and big ears, who always wanted me to play soccer with him in the afternoon. I didn't trust any of them, except for him. He's an engineer now and lives in Goiânia. I don't remember anything about anyone else. As for me, I was always out on the streets and only stood out because of my knowledge of the city's avenues, and also because I was the smallest of them all. Even though I never studied, I wasn't among the worst in the class and I'd cry in secret whenever Aunt Francisca saw my report card and complained about my grades.

The blog reader who objected to this new paragraph will note that, for the most part, I've incorporated the revision he suggested. I agree that I don't need to go into detail about my childhood imagination in regard to the female sex, especially if I'm unable to treat the subject delicately. However, I'll retain the basic observation made: since there were more families in Oldcap, I saw more women and kids out on the street than I did in the Free City. On account of the girl with black braids who rode around on a man's bicycle, I began to dream of owning a bicycle. If I were to pedal beside her on Central Avenue in the Free City, she would look at me with her black eyes and smile at me, I would embrace her, she was so pretty, and she would be my first girlfriend. So I asked Dad to get me a bicycle as a present; I'd ride to school all by myself and cross paths with the girl with braids, I'd heard that women could reach orgasm rubbing their privates on the bicycle seat, and I would be right beside her, pedaling, pedaling away, she would smile at me again, and we'd get off our bicycles and kiss passionately like they did in the movies that Aunt Francisca forbade me from seeing.

Whenever I got good grades, I'd ask Dad again to buy me a bicycle, as a present, a present that never came, but in recompense Dad rewarded me by taking me to the National Radio amateur talent shows on Sundays, where we'd watch the stage show from the packed auditorium, or else we'd go to a football game and cheer for Guará, a team that competed for the championship against various other teams that were named for construction firms, and after the game we'd go see a movie at the Brasília Cinema, located on the central city block, or else at the Countess Cinema or the Trailblazer Cinema, which was past the market and close to the end of one side of the city.

On the exact opposite end, a little removed from the city

proper, was a place that existed only in my imagination, for going anywhere near it was the biggest of the various prohibitions that Aunt Francisca had decreed for me. I knew that Dad sometimes frequented that red-light district, known as Placa da Mercedes, and had become the associate of a corpulent, mustachioed man who did business out there. How can you go into business with a guy like that?, Aunt Francisca demanded of him one day, He gave up the brothel a long time ago, Francisca, he's in the construction business now, I don't know about that, sounds fishy to me. I suspected that Aunt Francisca was right and later on I also thought that that guy, in one of the possible scenarios, had some involvement in Valdivino's murder, if it really was a murder.

For me, one of the differences between the region of the Das Almas River and Brasília was that here there weren't any *almas*, any souls. Dad was the one who explained it to me. Dad, are dead souls going to appear here in our house?, I asked him. What souls, child, are you going crazy? The kinds of souls that used to appear in Ceres, that Aunt Francisca once said she saw. Have you ever seen one? Not me, but Valdivino said he did. It must have been back in Bahia, because they don't exist here. But you've never seen one, Dad? No, and you're going to be disappointed: dead souls don't exist in Brasília. Is it because they don't like new cities?

I was no longer afraid of dead souls, but when they said that Valdivino had possibly died, I feared that he would appear to me late at night or that he'd come pay a visit to Aunt Francisca, passing right through the zinc roof-tiles or wooden walls.

Amid much forgetfulness, these were some of my memories, but none were so present for me as the ones that Dad called to mind when he spoke, between four walls, about the suspected murder of Valdivino around the time of the inauguration of Brasília and the dazzling story of the Prophetess of the Garden of Salvation, according to whom Valdivino hadn't died and perhaps never would, that he was wandering aimlessly around the Central

Plateau, in search of Z, the lost city. Well, that's not true, more vivid than these memories was the recollection of that episode with Aunt Matilde, during the wee hours of the morning on the day before the inauguration of Brasília, parading around her bounteous breasts and backside in the room where I slept, thus beginning a story that would only be carried to its conclusion many years later, as I'll have the opportunity to discuss further on. I felt more distance between the two of us than between me and Aunt Francisca, she had taken on some of the mannerisms of someone from Rio, said things that I didn't understand, and maybe for that reason I was afraid to approach her, I never dared play with her, pinch her, or pull her hair, as I did with Aunt Francisca. I had always slept there in the living room in a hammock, but on that night, for the first time, I was sleeping on a new mattress that had been placed on the floor, one of four mattresses that had arrived at the house that day, since, as there were no vacancies at the hotels, Newcap had bought twenty thousand mattresses to give out for free to residents who would accommodate visitors, and Aunt Francisca had made up a story about receiving three nieces from Minas Gerais.

Aunt Matilde came in from the street—she had gone out with her boyfriend Roberto, an engineer friend of Dad's—everyone was already asleep and she opened the door slowly, trying not to make any noise, then appeared like a dream from the other side of the china cabinet in the darkness of the living room, still within my field of vision. I heard the sound of her hands pulling off her tight skirt, and I leisurely examined her silhouette from bottom to top, from her pointy-toed high-heeled shoes—their red color tinted by the darkness—her silk stockings rose up her long, shapely legs, and her skirt had already started to slide down, tight against her buttocks. Did she notice that my eyes were half open? I remained motionless, only adjusting the position of my eyes and head to better see the dance of her body, which went a few steps forward, then a few steps back, as in a square dance, now displaying her stomach, now her back, I was afraid she'd hear my heavy breathing, sometimes part of her body would disappear behind the hi-fi, and I had to strain my neck to see the gauzy shadows of another article of clothing as it fell from her body, her thighs came in and out of my field of vision, I saw her arms raised to the roof as she took off her blouse, and then her slender waist came into view, a little later her hips joined the playful game of revealing then hiding themselves, just to torment me, Get naked, completely naked for me, Aunt Matilde!, I screamed silently in my reverie, and suddenly, liberated from the tight fabric, her hips came into plain view, and my eyes slid down her thick thighs, which turned into stick-thin legs by the time they reached the ground, just like furniture legs, she was barefoot at this point, her shoes tossed to the right side of the living room, then she bent over to pick up her shoes, and two mountainous buttocks raised up majestically right in front of me. I held my breath, but opened my eyes wide to see that butt, which had grown larger along with my desire. Shh! I saw Aunt Matilde in front of me, naked, with her finger on her lips, telling me to be quiet, whispering to me, Don't look, little boy, and there came those thick thighs walking towards me, my eyes fixed on her darkened sex, on the breasts that Aunt Matilde's curvy body seemed to be offering up to me. Shh! she repeated, a shiver went up my spine, my heart pounded, I could smell her perfume, Aunt Matilde naked, completely naked, right in front of me, and what if Dad woke up? What if Aunt Francisca walked into the living room right then when Aunt Matilde, naked, completely naked, was leaning over me with her ample breasts? But Dad and Aunt Francisca were asleep, and the silence of the house was only broken by the sound of my breath. I sat up, opened my eyes, saw close up the large, white thighs of Aunt Matilde, who was squatting beside me, her knees now grazing the mattress, my eyes bulging, as if they wished to read, study, and never forget every millimeter of that body. Shh! Flustered, I rubbed my eyes, Aunt Matilde even closer now, the smell of her skin more powerful, the air rarefied, and then Aunt Matilde's pointy breasts lightly touched my face, going up and down along it, palpitating. I could smell alcohol, and Aunt Matilde looked beautifully timid, her hair disheveled and down around her shoulders. I was useless, I wanted to grab Aunt Matilde, attack her like a fierce lion, grab her sex, suck freely on those tits, which were pointing toward my lips. She was wildly beautiful, I sat up on the mattress and timidly stared at her; then I looked more, my gaze traversing the grey color of the night, it was the first time that I had seen nudity so close up and amplified. Aunt Matilde then backed away, standing up, her thighs rising like tall trees, and then she again leaned over me, all of a sudden, put my hands on her breasts and whispered, That's what you want, isn't it, you shameless little boy, that's it, isn't it? She pulled my head forcefully onto her breasts and demanded, Go ahead, suck! My lips barely grazed the nipples of those fleshy breasts, I wonder if milk will come out of them? That's what I thought, but I didn't have the guts, and I stayed awake all night yearning for Aunt Matilde's tits and feeling the pleasure of sin. In the morning, Aunt Matilde sternly told me, You'll be sorry if you tell your dad what you did. I hadn't done anything, and I didn't intend to tell Dad anything about it, ever, but I understood that I had sinned, that I had started down an evil path and that a terrible punishment awaited me. I hoped that there would be time for the priest to forgive me before I died, and suddenly hell appeared before me, complete with caverns, serpents wrapping themselves around my legs, and cauldrons, their enormous flames consuming me, demons stirring them with iron tridents that were glowing hot, a massive sense of guilt burned as hot as that fire and took charge of me, I remembered what my friends used to tell me as we left our catechism classes, about the host that transformed into a bloody piece of flesh when it approached a sinner's tongue, the wrath of God unleashed on those who took communion without confessing, or in even more drastic fashion, as in the case of the boy who was run over by a tractor.

On Sunday, in the confessional of the São João Bosco Church, I omitted, in a whispered voice to Father Roque, the most sinful details: "I saw Aunt Matilde . . . " I was going to say "naked," but the priest found my hesitation sufficient enough for me to pray a few Ave Marias, through which God forgave my various sins, that of sight, of touch, of taste, and, most of all, the sin of the imagination.

One day Aunt Matilde came into the bathroom while I was finishing up my bath, You like to look at other people, don't you?, let me see if it's true what they say, that really is a big cock for your age, you're going to be happy, João. I know I'd be eliminating some suspense if I were to say that I think that this was the reason that, years later, when both she and I were on the run from the police, I had the courage to remind Aunt Matilde about that episode and invite her to experience some of my happiness, but it's still too early in the story for me to go on about her reaction or defend myself, which I'll leave for another chapter.

*Second Night:*
*With Body and Soul*

On the second night, when I sought out Dad to complete my story about the Free City, he reminded me, between four dingy white walls, that a few days before the inauguration of Brasília—and therefore a few days before the supposed murder of Valdivino— he had gathered all that he'd written since we arrived in 1956, including statements he had collected from famous people about the city under construction, and wrote an article, his first, with which he intended to commemorate the occasion.

He figured that, with Brasília, his moment of glory had arrived, especially because, since April of the previous year, and after many frustrated attempts, he had finally managed to get some recognition from the president's entourage for his idea to accompany illustrious visitors, receiving authorization to do it on two occasions, during the visits of the Cuban Prime Minister, Fidel Castro Ruz, and the French writer and Minister of Culture André Malraux. He prepared the article—which, years later, I found on yellowed paper among the documents I'd unearthed—and sent it to a newspaper in Rio, as well as *The Tribune*, a newsweekly that had been founded in the Free City in 1958.

Dad hadn't been able to get a single phrase out of the conversation between JK and Fidel Castro in the library of the Palace of the Dawn on April 13, 1959, and the basis of his article ended up being JK's account of it, which he had heard from a third party and meticulously transcribed in one of the "Onward" notebooks that I leafed through. And right he was, said Aunt Matilde assertively, in regard to Fidel, upon reading that JK hadn't been able to discuss Operation Pan America with him, because Castro, in JK's own words, "doesn't understand dialogue," "he's a man of monologues," and had spoken for two hours straight without stopping, and when the Brazilian president tried to interrupt him for lunch at one in the afternoon or attempted to get up out of his chair, Fidel grabbed him by the arm and spoke with even greater vehemence, which made it so that they didn't finish lunch until three hours later. The president should have taken advantage of the opportunity to learn at least the basics of communism and the Cuban Revolution, said Aunt Matilde provokingly, to which Dad objected, But I heard on the radio that, a week after Fidel left here, he went to the United States and cleared up the misunderstanding, telling Vice President Nixon: "I know that the world thinks we're communists, and I have stated clearly—very clearly—that we are not communists"—Dad changed his tone of voice to emphasize the words "we are not" and "very clearly," But that's all ancient history now, retorted Aunt Matilde.

I think that it was around this time that Aunt Matilde started to take a liking to the idea of revolution, due to Roberto's influence, and to the news about the Peasant Leagues in the Northeast, and although back in those days I didn't understand her points of view, they would one day solidify my ever-closer relationship with her. Aunt Francisca sought to change Aunt Matilde's mind on the subject, They want to destroy everything, to take from some people and give it to others, And you, who are so religious, should be in agreement, since that's what religion teaches, Not through destruction or violence, not by taking things from people by force, I'd like to see a revolution, I said, to which Dad retorted, Don't talk nonsense, João, that's just one of your aunt's crazy ideas, the law should be respected, no one is going to take what's mine from me, that's why we have a right to private property, But you're not a landowner, you have nothing to worry about, Aunt Matilde asserted, In a revolution not even Roberto would be spared, he'd be guillotined, the way they did in France, Aunt Francisca predicted, This is a different era, said Aunt Matilde, Ok, he'd be shot, amended Aunt Francisca, This is all just lip service, just theories, she can't really be serious about it, she's just doing it to tease us, she has a comfortable life and would never want to lose all her comforts, said Dad, provocatively, Roberto's family owns land, so this position is just for show, he wouldn't want to lose his inheritance, he just wants to amuse himself and us with his ideas, added Aunt Francisca.

When he talked about revolution, Roberto disagreed with Aunt Matilde, for him the economy wasn't crashing and the State wasn't completely bankrupt, we weren't living through the final crisis of capitalism, nor was the corruption as bad as all that, he had sympathy for the government, You can't go believing in every rumor that gets floated around here, Matilde, tell me, who are the corrupt ones, specifically? We're in a leaking canoe, Roberto, insisted Aunt Matilde.

It's certain that, sooner or later, we're going to have a revolution here as well, concluded Aunt Matilde. It would be a disaster, asserted Aunt Francisca. Capital would disappear entirely, industry would come to an end, then the economy would really go to hell, what's the point of spreading poverty?, argued Dad, for whom what really mattered were his own accounts: if he was making money, then the economy and the country were doing well. That might be true at the beginning, but progress would follow, as happened in the Soviet Union, responded Aunt Matilde. Communism would never prosper in Brazil, our temperament isn't suited for it, countered Aunt Francisca. At the time I felt closer to Aunt Francisca than to Aunt Matilde and I thought that Aunt Francisca, not Aunt Matilde, was right about this, the exact opposite of what took place years later when, as an adult, I ran into Aunt Matilde in circumstances that the child could not yet have imagined.

Dad's article, which didn't reflect all the richness of that discussion, reproduced the phrase that Fidel, according to what JK recounted, had spoken with some emotion in the helicopter on the way to the airport, upon seeing the city under construction from above: "It's a very happy thing to be young in this country, President." As for the speeches delivered by André Malraux, on August 25 of the same year, 1959, Dad was able to transcribe them almost in their entirety, citing from them that Brasília was "the most audacious city ever conceived by the West" and "the first capital of the new civilization." In the same article, Dad insinuated that he had accompanied Georges Mathieu on the visit this French painter made to Brasília on November 17, 1959, when he referred to the construction of Brasília as "the birth of a miracle" and "one of the greatest epics in the history of mankind, maybe the greatest . . . If Valéry had seen Brasília, perhaps he would have doubted the mortality of civilizations. After seven centuries, during the course of which the search for evidence hid the truth from us, the West has rediscovered the path of its true calling, by way of Brasília. The world has never had so many reasons to be hopeful as it has today with you, Brazilians!" Lastly, Dad closed his article by quoting the words that art critic José Guidol had delivered in September of 1959: "Brasília isn't merely the greatest endeavor undertaken in our world, it's a laudable attempt to find the path to the international freedom of the human race." That was the larger objective, Dad would repeat to Aunt Matilde, whenever she provoked him with her criticism: the international freedom of the human race. Oh I believe it!, she'd reply ironically.

The article didn't make much of a splash, but it explains why

Dad managed to get invited as a journalist to the inauguration of Brasília's first major newspaper, as well as the party that was going to be held at the Planalto Palace on the night of April 21.

A day before the inauguration, on the morning that I woke up dreaming of Aunt Matilde's breasts, Dad made me read his article and told me, João, one day you'll understand, you have to attend the celebration of the inauguration of Brasília, history is being made here. And then he gave me a present, a white linen shirt and a watch, my first watch—a Swiss Bulova with a second-hand—so that I could remember the exact time at which each ceremony took place. This is never going to happen again, pay attention to everything that's going to take place over the next two days, you'll understand it someday, this present is better than a bicycle—with this I immediately imagined myself showing it off to the girl with braids on one of the streets in Oldcap.

On other occasions Dad had suggested that I remember the dates that he considered milestones in the construction of the city, or else he'd say to me, João, remember this story, and then he'd narrate some facts that had come to his attention, like when Sayão told him that the United States had asked Newcap for an exception to be made so that their parcel of land, lot number 1, could be bigger than the others, and that, to avoid any resentment, it was decided that not only would all the lots be the same size, but also that lot 1 would go to the Holy See, since Brazil is a Catholic country, lot 2 would be allotted to Portugal, which discovered and colonized Brazil, and lot 3 would go to the United States, the first country to officially recognize Brazil as an independent country.

This time, Dad wanted me to make note of the time of the parade of events over the course of the day. Can I take Typhoon? No, there was going to be a large crowd, and Typhoon would get lost, it was best to leave him at home, where we'd leave out food and water for him, I shouldn't worry, he wouldn't run away.

My memory may be imperfect, but on that day, April 20, I can recall Valdivino down to the smallest details, down to his gentle voice and his delicate, courteous manner of being. At five in the afternoon I went with him, Dad, Aunt Matilde, and Roberto to attend the ceremony in which the president of Newcap, Israel Pinheiro, would hand over the keys to the city to President JK. Valdivino was restless, awaiting the arrival of the love of his life, surrounding whom he always created an air of mystery and about whom he wouldn't stop talking, a woman who was more important than the Pope, and the only person able to consecrate the birth of this new civilization. If his girlfriend didn't come it would be a disaster, for the future of the city depended on her. I figured that Aunt Francisca had stayed at home so she wouldn't have to meet that woman, since at the time I suspected that Aunt Francisca had fallen in love with Valdivino.

While we waited for the president to arrive, we remained in the Three Powers Plaza, amid hundreds of migrant workers, listening to Valdivino's stories, which entertained us with their details about the construction of the Palace of the Dawn, in which he'd had a hand, after the church beside it was completed. Talkative and happy as always, in spite of his weary eyes and almost sickly skinny figure, he recounted, in his gentle voice, The president's bathroom in the Palace is black and the First Lady's is pink, Mr. Moacyr, one of the laborers slipped and fell and broke the pink toilet he was carrying, and the president and Dona Sarah were set to arrive two days later and it was absolute chaos, then the new toilet came in from Goiânia by plane, fastened into a seat with a seatbelt, as if it had bought a ticket.

We all laughed, except for Aunt Matilde, who had little patience for Valdivino's stories. More people arrived. The authorities took their seats. The president must be arriving soon, said Roberto, who was holding hands with Aunt Matilde. The president is a courageous man, Mr. Roberto, as you know, one night, the pilot of his plane said that they wouldn't be able to land in Brasília on account of bad weather, recounted Valdivino, the radar at the airport was even on the fritz, but the president had never been afraid of flying and told the pilot to circle around until they could land—that's what they told me, anyway—and later the Willys jeep that he was riding in got stuck in the mud, and you know how the president is, Mr. Roberto, he's a simple man, so wouldn't you know it? he popped his hat on his head, put on a rain slicker and galoshes, and got out to push the jeep. His driver is the one who told me. And one time he suddenly arrived during a rainstorm, noticed me hammering away, wearing my plastic poncho like everyone else, then caught my eye and asked me, How late are you working tonight? I'm working through the whole night, President, it'll be twenty-four hours straight, and it was true, it had been like that for a month, I worked twenty-four hours then rested twenty-four hours, and it would be that way until the Palace was inaugurated.

The afternoon drew on perfectly, and what remained of it would be no less perfect. The autumn rays no longer burned our heads, and our shadows began to stretch along the ground. There were still a couple of hours before the sun would disappear behind the National Congress building and the Ministry buildings, The worst thing about being isolated out there is that I never see the president anymore, Valdivino continued, but in return, Mr. Moacyr, I'm no longer paying off my debt, see if I'm not in the right here, Sir, after I stopped working construction on the Palace of the Dawn, I put together my savings and caught a twenty-eight passenger DC-3 plane on Real Airlines to Fortaleza—with stops in Bom Jesus da Lapa, Petrolina, and Crato— where my brother, who'd gone there from Bahia, was hiding from the rest of our family—this brother, who died, as you know, Sir, was the only one who accepted me, the whole rest of the family is on the outs with me—ok, well, I came back here to Brasília with my brother on a 16-day trip, because I didn't have money for an airplane ticket and we weren't able to hitch a ride on any of the NIIC trucks—he was referring to the acronym of the National Institute of Immigration and Colonization. A businessman had organized a caravan made up of two Fenemê trucks, Valdivino continued, and a wealthy landowner financed tickets for me and my brother. I had to sign promissory notes valued at twenty thousand *cruzeiros*, sixteen for the tickets and another four because the arrangement came with a guarantee of employment. Right in the middle of the trip, we discovered that, for anyone who wanted to be sold, prices went from five-hundred to two thousand *cruzeiros*, depending on the physical state of the individual. The truck driver then handed over the documents of the sale to the buyer: birth certificate, identity card, worker's permit . . . That's absurd, said Aunt Matilde, do you know about this, Roberto? Those who were buying didn't even pay a salary, Dona Matilde, since the ticket had already been paid for, the workers had to work to pay off the debt first, but of course, that wasn't the case with me, nor my brother, nor many of the people who came here in the trucks. An employment agent received us when we arrived at the Free City. He was supposed to know the necessities of the construction firms and arrange job placements for us, but the only thing he cared about was collecting money from those who owed it—which wasn't the case with us either. So the truck dropped us off in front of the NIIC, and the rest of the story you already know, Mr. Moacyr, since that was when we met up and I was working as a waiter at the Brasília Palace, so I'll ask you, Sir, do you think, given all that, that I still had the obligation to pay that debt, Mr. Moacyr? Those people don't mess around, Valdivino, it could be dangerous . . . Dad was familiar with those abuses. They made business arrangements to finance the tickets of the migrants coming to the Free City, then employment agents sought them out wherever they were, even in the remotest corners of the backlands, and they, fleeing the drought-stricken region, allowed themselves to be seduced by the promise of work in Brasília, submitting to whatever the conditions might have been. It was a lucrative business, which Dad even considered at one point, but gave up on that notion in favor of more lucrative ones.

Of all the dangers I face, this is the least of them, Mr. Moacyr, the landowner can search high and low, but he'll never see me around in the commune, and in my case he can't harass my family, the way he does with other people, because I didn't leave any family behind, clarified Valdivino, and then quickly got back to his story, I don't know why he did it, but when we got to NIIC, my brother asked: Do you need a carpenter? They said they did, and my brother had never worked as a carpenter, but he was a handy guy. Would you like to take the test? And my brother: Sure. He grabbed a crooked piece of cedar and made it nice and straight. Do you have a worker's permit yet?, they asked. No? Well, find a place to live and then come back here.

When the president took his place on stage at five-thirty in the afternoon with the first lady, Dona Sarah, his two daughters, Márcia and Maria Estela, the vice-president, João Goulart, and the president of Newcap, Israel Pinheiro, all I could think of were the scenes from the night before and was unable to look at Aunt Matilde, or her boyfriend. She seemed more elegant than ever to me in her white spaghetti-strap dress with black polka dots, full below the waist, descending halfway down her shin, her high-heeled sandals also white, with a braided front, which made her taller than Roberto, a black and white purse in her hands, with a gold snap and a thin black strap.

We stayed there until dark, listening to speeches by Israel Pinheiro, by a barber who wanted to speak in the name of the people, and by the president, and the mysterious woman never made an appearance, a woman whom I visualized as luminous, wearing flowing garments, a saint upon an altar. According to what Valdivino was saying, without her presence, the day would be a waste, completely purposeless. If only the president could at least make up for her absence somehow ... I had a special memory of him, since on one of the three hundred trips that he made to Brasília during its construction—and there had been forty-one months of construction—he had driven to the Free City in his Romi-Isetta, accompanied by his daughters, Márcia and Maria Estela, to attend a circus performance, and he had shaken hands with a number of kids, although I wasn't able to get close to him, but during the performances I kept my eye on his Cheshire cat grin, which made his face wrinkle all over whenever the clown pulled some prank, or when the chimpanzee rode a bicycle or a tricycle or walked around on stilts or balanced on the slackline, or even when the trapeze artists amazed us as they flew from one side of the ring to the other. I ran into him on other occasions and saw hundreds of photos of him, but none of these images ever supplanted that scene, forever stored away in my memory like the final scene of a film or a painting on the main wall of a museum. Even when he was being serious, for me he was always that same grinning Cheshire cat that I'd encountered on that day long ago.

Imagine my expectations at that moment, the pleasure I felt in seeing him again, in the possibility of getting to shake his hand, less out of vanity than out of genuine admiration, a sense of admiration that could only be compared to Aunt Francisca's veneration of the saints. Judging from what I heard, Dad, Valdivino, and Aunt Matilde's boyfriend all knew him, and it seemed possible that he would come over to talk to us. But no, that was but a sweet illusion, the ceremony ended without him even deigning to shake our hands.

Walking through the Three Powers Plaza, we looked out towards the Esplanade of the Ministries. It's like the president says, Roberto observed, this is the first capital built from scratch, in an uninhabited place, without the support of any village or town.

It's all because of you all that I was able to work on the construction of that building, the twenty-eight, said Valdivino, pointing to the National Congress building, with its two "washbasins" (one right-side up and the other upside down), which the workers called "twenty-eight" because of the number of floors it had. All the thanks goes to Roberto, said Aunt Matilde, I guess that now you also owe me thanks for the fact that you're always on the run and have to live in hiding, commented Roberto, What happened later isn't your fault, Sir, but I've been thinking: this trouble never would have happened if I'd kept building churches instead of working in that building. Always talkative, but with a timid, polite manner about him, Valdivino told us that at first he'd lived in the construction firm's camp close to the iron buildings—"that's what we called the Ministry buildings"—and later moved to the Planalto Villa, "over there on the other side of the Planalto Palace." I started as just a laborer, carrying bags of cement in wheelbarrows, we worked both day and night because we had to meet the deadlines for the inauguration, Oh you poor thing, said Aunt Matilde, that's a form of slavery, You should have told me, said Roberto, with his arm around Aunt Matilde's waist, you should have started out in a better position, I don't complain, no sir, Mr. Roberto, they paid well, and I had that debt from the trip here, since I brought my brother with me, sometimes I also worked weekends and holidays, when they paid us double, and while on other jobs I'd been paid eighteen or at most twenty-five *cruzeiros* an hour, when we went up in those tall buildings of the "twenty-eight" that you see over there, they paid me up to fifty *cruzeiros* an hour, which was my way of making that little double-pay that you all got, he said, referring to the doubled salary which Aunt Matilde had a right to, just for having moved from Rio to Brasília. But the salary should have been even more, Mr. Moacyr, I'm all about work, not about accepting rewards for things I should be doing anyway, a worker has to be serious, efficient, honest, and has to be paid well for what he does, don't you think so, Mr. Moacyr?

It was already seven o'clock, Dad was getting impatient and left in a hurry for the inauguration of the *Correio Braziliense*, the first newspaper in Brasília, and he wanted to be there at seven-thirty when the first lady arrived with her daughters, Wait for me here, he requested.

She's still gonna come, she promised me she would, Valdivino said after Dad left. We were silent, Valdivino suffering because of his friend's tardiness, and me measuring the passing of time by the second- and minute-hands of my new watch and watching the night fall upon the Ministry buildings, while Aunt Matilde and Roberto exchanged smiles and whispers.

Now, it was definitely dangerous, said Valdivino, taking up the subject once again, that's why they paid more, Mr. Roberto, there were fatal accidents, because they hired people with no experience and there were no safety measures, when one person fell, they'd cover him with a tarp and take him away, there was one day when seven people fell all at once, six of them died and one was maimed, and it wasn't just here, the coffin-maker in Newcap stayed busy all the time, there were days when twenty or thirty people died, from accidents or sickness, the bodies taken to the cemetery in Luziânia; the migrant workers really are heroes, warriors, Dona Matilde, they deserve that bronze statue, he said, pointing at the sculpture by Bruno Giorgi at the far end of the Three Powers Plaza.

It was already dark, and the temperature slowly began to drop, I'm going to turn into a popsicle, Aunt Matilde complained, This is the perfect temperature for me, said Roberto, It's strange, I think something changed when I told her that Mr. Moacyr was coming, said Valdivino, But didn't you work here as a master-builder, Valdivino?, asked Aunt Matilde, continuing the earlier conversation, as if she had doubts about the stories he was telling.

I was only a laborer in the beginning, I'd help out with whatever was needed, I even worked as a framer, which means I set up the steel rebar frames of those two washbasins, the one that contains the Chamber of Deputies and the one on the right, the one that's upside down, which holds the Senate, but what I really wanted to be was a mason or a carpenter, a profession that has good job security, and then a guy walked by who recognized me from back when I was building Mr. Bernardo Sayão's house and he asked me, Hey aren't you Valdivino?, Yes, I am, Well, Mr. Sayão used to speak so highly of you, and you're still just a laborer? I still am, But you could be working as a foreman, that's what he said. And it was true, because I pay attention to details and demanded that each piece of material be cut very precisely, when there were really careless people out there who only got their job because they knew someone from back home. Mr. Sayão never found out about this, but I owe my promotion to him. It was then that I found a place in Planalto Villa, where they'd gathered people from the Pacheco Fernandes labor camp, which was in charge of the construction of the palaces, and the Rabelo, Pederneiras, and National camps as well. More than three thousand people lived there. Since I was by myself, they didn't want to give me housing on the other side of the parking lot and soccer field, where the foremen and master-builders and engineers lived with their families, but I was able to escape the bunkhouses. The only problem was that I had to share a room with a policeman from the SPB, the guy who is still after me. I have to go around armed at all times—Valdivino patted his waistband. Don't tell me you carry a revolver around, said Roberto, surprised, and cuddled up to Aunt Matilde, as ever.

I looked at Roberto and wished I had some engineer's boots just like his, not just to keep my feet from getting muddy, but also so I could feel superior to the rest of humanity. The quality of the boots unequivocally established the hierarchy. Through them, rather than the jeans and khaki canvas shirts that Valdivino also wore, I was able to distinguish between the engineers and the workers. I saw boots all over the place, the shoemakers and shoe-shiners of the Free City were all busy with boots, not shoes, and I found Roberto's boots especially beautiful, tall boots, with pleats above the ankle. A person's heart is like the world itself and can spin around time and again, I recalled the first time that Aunt Matilde and Roberto ever saw each other, at our house—him, taller than Dad, muscular, and dark-skinned, standing beside the window, a determined expression on his face, and her, cold and disinterested. Now here they were kissing and hugging, like infatuated lovers.

No, not a revolver, I don't even know how to shoot, but I always have to carry my machete, Valdivino replied, I don't even know you anymore, Valdivino, have you turned into a bandit?, asked Aunt Matilde in a jesting tone, Well the guy told everybody that he wants to kill me, and he's not the only one who's said that.

Dad finally returned. He had witnessed Dona Sarah cut the symbolic ribbon and press the button that turned on the newspaper's printing press.

Later on, along with thousands of other people, we patiently waited for the Mass that was going to be held at the altar they'd set up in the Three Powers Plaza.

What time is it?, Valdivino asked me, still wondering about his failure to meet up with the mysterious woman he was waiting for. Twenty 'til midnight, I replied. Then we heard, in both Portuguese and Latin, the brief papal statement that named Cardinal Patriach of Lisbon Dom Manuel Gonçalves Cerejeira as Papal Legate of His Eminence, the Sovereign Pontiff. She'll certainly be here for the Mass, said Valdivino.

Look at the iron cross, João, it was brought all the way from Braga, in Portugal, said my Dad, pointing it out to me when the Mass began at eleven forty-five, while the choir sang Mozart's

*Coronation Mass.* I couldn't see it, Over there! It's a really small cross, the same one used during the first Mass held in Brazil, in April of 1500.

When midnight came and the bell—the one brought from Ouro Preto, which had mournfully announced the death of Tiradentes on April 21, 1792—celebrated the city that had been born after less than three years of construction, Valdivino started to cry, to hug me, to hug Dad and the strangers around him as well. Then I realized that everyone in the crowd was hugging each other and crying. I looked at Dad; his eyes were moist with tears, too. Aunt Matilde and Roberto weren't crying, but the look on their faces was somewhere between amazed and gleeful as they looked around the plaza. I kept track of time on the beautiful watch Dad had given me, at nineteen after the hour the host was raised, then the Naval Rifle Corps Band played the national anthem, and the Three Powers Plaza, the Esplanade of Ministries, and the bus station were all lit up, right in front of us, as if by magic, under the spotlights. Dad pointed out to me that even the president was crying along with the people, I too, looking at the city all lit up, could feel my eyes well up with tears, and neither Roberto nor even Aunt Matilde could bear it any longer, I could see tears running down their faces.

It was at that moment that, out of nowhere, like an apparition, a dark-skinned woman appeared, still young-looking in her thirties, who, in a fury, grabbed Valdivino by the arm and took off with him. It took us by surprise, we were dumbfounded, and I spotted Valdivino from a distance and could see him turn his long, thin nose back toward us, but the woman pulled him along, unwavering. That nutcase is Valdivino's famed girlfriend?, asked Aunt Matilde, Yes, that's her, Dad responded, dryly, So, you already know her? Dad didn't reply. I looked at my watch again, it was twelve forty-five when we began to hear the voice of Pope John XXIII over the loudspeaker, transmitted by Vatican Radio:

From All Saints Bay to Piratininga and Rio de Janeiro, under the always vibrant influence of Nóbrega and Anchieta, and emboldened by the heroic efforts of the Southern Expeditions and the campaigns in the North, Brazil, through the daring of its president, is putting down the stakes of its new capital in the Central Plateau of its immense and rich territory, which shall stand sentry over the Nation's destiny. Brasília shall thus represent a milestone in the history of the glorious Land of the Holy Cross, opening up new channels of love, hope, and progress among its people, who, united in one faith and one tongue, shall become fit for the most grandiose undertakings. We pray that God—continuing to pour out His grace in abundance—will make Brazil into an ever-stronger, ever-grander, ever-freer nation, in the light of the Gospel and the teachings of the Church, opposed to all that might rob it of its strength, compromise its greatness, and diminish its freedom.

After the choir sang the *Te Deum* and the Papal Legate blessed the city and the Brazilian flag, we started to make our way out of the plaza, and Aunt Matilde was still looking around, to see if she could spot Valdivino and his friend somewhere in the middle of the crowd. It was one-thirty in the morning and the ceremony had just ended to boisterous applause, many people were going to stay up all night to secure a good spot in the Three Powers Plaza for the inaugural ceremonies, which would begin at eight in the morning, but we returned to the Free City. And what do you think happened to Valdivino?, asked Aunt Matilde, as if she had some foreboding, You're right, that woman is a real nutcase, replied Dad, He seems untroubled, but you saw it, he goes around armed, said Aunt Matilde, And he's also taking a risk by showing up in public like that, it's better to just stay in hiding, Roberto added, He only mentioned the policeman, but what about the landowner he owes money to, and the father of the girl he got pregnant?, recalled Aunt Matilde. Don't worry, said Dad, tomorrow you'll see Valdivino in the parade down the Grand Axis Highway.

Perhaps they put more emotion in their dialogues than I was able to capture, and it could also be that, without intending to, I have corrected the grammar of that conversation, which lasted longer than the sentences above would lead one to believe, it stretched out into other subjects, and I also can't guarantee that it corresponds exactly to my transcription of it, there were points of confusion, ellipses, omissions, and interpolated stories. From all that I can remember, I've only selected that which will give you all an idea about these characters from my childhood and also, at the request of the blog-readers, that which will give you a notion of the historical moment that we lived through.

I left out my conversation with Valdivino because it was mainly focused on the gravity of his friend's absence and various related foolish notions. I also cut out conversations with strangers, which, if I had to be precise, would take up more than a page of this story, and I don't want to force you all to read more than is necessary. I eliminated the descriptions of all we could see from the plaza, since I would have had to spill out an enormous amount of words on that subject alone. Suffice it to say that we were all amazed by the Three Powers Plaza and the space that opened up above the Esplanade of the Ministries, which was thrown into relief by the elegance of the buildings. Why should I waste your reading time on descriptions of the Planalto Palace, for example, if a mere photograph can more precisely transmit the delicacy of its columns, which seem barely to touch the ground? Above all, I don't want to tire you with the description of what I was thinking, for I was thinking a lot and my thoughts had a single focus, I was thinking about Aunt Matilde, about her enormous butt, her breasts, her breath, her hands pulling me towards her, and about her threats. I also haven't included Valdivino's Bahian accent here, nor certain words from his complicated vocabulary, which I can't even remember anyways, although I do recall that they were beautiful and well-spoken. Finally, for those blog-readers who complain about not being mentioned, let me clarify that I've decided to change tactics in this second chapter and I'll no longer mention every single person who writes to me, but, as you all have noticed, I've taken your observations into account in order to touch up a timeline, add a detail about the ceremonies, include the complete name of a cardinal, or a message from the Pope.

Aunt Francisca liked to assert, Valdivino speaks slowly and more properly than everyone else, he's an educated young man, and one time she even said that given his skills, he could get work in "something else," But I don't want to do anything but build churches, he replied.

Enough! I've written too much about April 20 and I think that maybe I'll divide this chapter in two, because starting now we're into the next day, April 21, the date of Brasília's inauguration, when, at eight in the morning, my two aunts, Typhoon, and I all sat down next to the radio and listened to the Guardian Battalion Band play reveille, in the very Three Powers Plaza we'd been in the night before with Valdivino. Aunt Francisca wanted us to stand when the radio announcer declared that JK was raising the Brazilian flag—now with one more star, he said, the twenty-second—while the national anthem was performed by the Naval Rifle Corps Band, but Aunt Matilde protested, Nonsense, Francisca! Seated in front of the radio during a large part of the morning, I visualized every one of the acts described by the announcer, the presentation of credentials by one hundred and fifty ambassadors in the Planalto Palace, the instatement of the three powers of the Republic, and the first ministerial meeting.

We were moved by the emotion in the president's voice when,

close to tears, he pronounced the final words of his speech: "On this day, the 21$^{st}$ of April, consecrated to Second Lieutenant Joaquim José da Silva Xavier, known as Tiradentes, and to the one hundred and thirty-eighth year since Independence and the seventy-first year since the establishment of the Republic, I declare, under the protection of God, that the city of Brasília, the capital of the United States of Brazil, is hereby inaugurated."

The sun was already high in the sky when I went to the Esplanade of the Ministries with my aunts, them in their best dresses and me in the white linen shirt that Dad gave me as a present.

Aunt Francisca couldn't stop praising Valdivino, lamenting the fact that he was on the run and living like a convict. Aunt Matilde described the scenes from the night before, when some shrew had cruelly whisked him away without even deigning to direct a single word to us, You'll see, it'll turn out that on top of being nuts, she's mute. I'm happy that he managed to get permission to march in the parade with the other migrant workers, let's try to get a good spot so we can see Valdivino, said Aunt Francisca.

Why all the interest in Valdivino? I imagined Valdivino sucking on Aunt Francisca's breasts, and her delighting in that act, which I didn't have the courage to do with Aunt Matilde in the wee hours of the day before. I liked Valdivino because he was affectionate towards me, but at that moment I wanted him to die, to disappear from my life, he wanted to steal Aunt Francisca from me, and I didn't think that he deserved her.

Roberto and Dad were going to march in the parade with the people from Newcap, even though Dad wasn't a Newcap employee. It wasn't easy for Vadivino to get permission to march, Aunt Francisca clarified.

It was a hot day, the sun was casting lively colors upon the city, and I was carried along, like a strand of cotton in the wind, by the rhythm of the crowd. As the blog-reader who had abandoned me but has now starting following me again pointed out, Brasília had one hundred and forty thousand inhabitants, but there were two hundred thousand people spread throughout its major thoroughfares and plazas.

Later on, the clouds began to turn shades of yellow, orange, and pink, suddenly a rainbow cut across the sky from one end to the other, planes passed overhead, sketching the outline of the Pilot Plan with their exhaust, the column of Naval riflemen who had come from Rio de Janeiro on foot presented a diploma to JK, and then my aunts and I managed to settle down in a good spot to watch the parade on the southern side of Grand Axis Highway.

As each group approached, Aunt Francisca would comment that perhaps Valdivino would be part of it. After five thousand soldiers, more than ten thousand workers passed by with the tools of their trade, then students, and miles and miles of tractors, jeeps, eighteen-wheelers, cranes, and machines made for leveling, digging, transporting, and building, but no sign of Valdivino.

The leaders of Newcap also passed by, as well as architects Oscar Niemeyer and Lúcio Costa, and Dad and Roberto marched past with the Newcap employees, as expected. We waved and yelled to them and were pleased when Dad waved back. I felt intimately satisfied that Aunt Francisca hadn't seen Valdivino march past, although it bothered me that his absence occupied so much of our conversation.

At six o'clock, while the planes from the squadron with the exhaust smoke streaked the sky with white and blue, the Naval Rifle Corps Band played for the crowd, and the athletes arrived with the "flame that symbolized national unity" together with the military columns that had come from Rio and Salvador on foot, it looked like it was going to rain, We forgot to bring the umbrellas, said Aunt Francisca, but the sky began to strip off its black garments little by little, and the weather cleared up once again.

Around seven in the evening, my aunts and I accompanied a river of people from the Grand Axis Highway to the bus station. Soon after, I'm not sure if it was seven-thirty or eight o'clock, they began to set off over twenty tons of fireworks, tracing colorful designs in the sky like I'd never seen before. My aunts sang on the Monumental Axis Highway, right in front of the bus station, and a few other people followed suit. Aunt Francisca, her dress cinched tight around her waist with a white belt, danced nimbly, comfortable in her flat-heeled shoes, spinning in her full-skirted dress with its blue pattern, which revealed the bottom of her slip. Aunt Matilde, balancing on her black high-heeled shoes, shook her large breasts, which were delineated by her lustrous dress. It was a mint-colored satin with black straps, with a narrow strip of the same black fabric at her breasts, and three buttons, also black, running down from the low neckline. The slight honeycomb pleating below the waist flattened her stomach and accentuated her backside. I also tried out some dance steps, and there we remained, in song and dance, until, at nine at night, an enormous party began at the bus station.

At that point we joined the crowd at the Three Powers Plaza in hopes of meeting up with Dad and Roberto. The two of them had been invited to a state reception that the president was throwing for three thousand people at the Planalto Palace, Dad being among the small group of invited guests from the local press. Out in the plaza it was said that "Little Tony from the Pharmacy," Antonio Soares Neto, had arrived at the Palace, the same guy who, on April 4, 1955, at a rally in Jataí, Goiás, asked then-candidate JK if, when elected, he would move the capital of Brazil out there to the Central Plateau of Goiás, thus introducing that topic into the campaign for the first time.

Before we could take notice of it, JK had already descended the ramp of the Palace and was heading in our direction. Aunt Francisca kneeled before him. JK, smiling, held out his hands to her, which she kissed, then helped her up and embraced her as if he had known her for ages. He also embraced Aunt Matilde, then left, doing the same throughout the plaza, ever smiling. Aunt Francisca even mentioned something about introducing me to the president, but the opportunity had already passed.

The three of us stayed there until two in the morning, when they announced that the president had left the party, but that there was still dancing going on inside—we later learned that it had lasted almost until sunrise. I recall that as we returned home, Aunt Francisca was still lamenting the fact that we hadn't seen Valdivino march in the parade. Do you think that something happened to him?, now it was Aunt Francisca asking this, as if she were repeating the foreboding that Aunt Matilde had felt the night before.

After inauguration day, or rather, on April 22, in the early afternoon, when Dad arrived in his Ford Coupe, I noticed that he was restless, he spent hours rooting around in the boxes where he kept his notebooks and called me over to show me the hole where he was burying all his papers. He was burying his very soul there with those papers.

He told Aunt Matilde and Aunt Francisca about his suspicions, causing much commotion. For me, it was a mystery as to why Dad himself didn't just publish what he knew about Valdivino in the *Tribune* or even in the newspaper that had just been founded, the *Correio Braziliense*, the inauguration of which he'd attended, and I was frightened by Aunt Francisca's comment days later, I think Valdivino was killed, family is sacred, you can't mix it with sex.

I imagined Valdivino with his mouth on the breasts of some aunt of his and became terrified. Could it be that the woman who came to get him in the Three Powers Plaza was his aunt? What would happen to me if what occurred between me and Aunt Matilde were discovered? Ever since then, the possible death of

Valdivino, the inauguration of Brasília, and Aunt Matilde's breasts have been mixed together in my head, along with my own guilt for having wished so intensely for the death of Valdivino, who only wanted the best for me. Ruminating on my guilt, I developed a singular fixation: one day I would discover what truly happened to Valdivino, that is, until Dad came back under suspicion.

*Third Night:*
*Landscapes with Termite Mounds*

On the third night, between four dingy white walls, Dad recalled the day that we met Valdivino, at the end of October in 1956, a month that had begun with President JK's visit to Brasília, the month in which Catetinho was built, and soon after Dad had returned from Luziânia with Bernardo Sayão, bringing back construction materials for the first building projects.

Dad sometimes took me out hunting around the Free City, and every once in a while we'd make it out to the banks of the São Bartolomeu River, but on this occasion he decided to go on an even longer expedition, out toward the Descoberto River to the southeast.

We took Typhoon, our guns, and two mules we borrowed, on whose backs we traveled for more than a day and a half, with five days worth of provisions.

Typhoon barked at the raccoons and possums, as well as the red-dirt whirlwinds that spun from one place to another. We shot a guinea pig and a giant armadillo, which was all we took on the outbound trip.

In those days, the virgin savannah was a treasure trove of animals. We smelled a skunk, managed to see a stag, a maned wolf, and a sloth hanging from the branch of a peppertree, as well as an enormous amount of birds perched up in tortuous, gnarled trees of faded colors, many of them defoliated, covered

in thick, wrinkled bark. There, in the smaller trees, as well as in
the bigger ones near creeks, and up in the jatobá trees and pacara
earpod trees, I saw every bird that perched or flew, following
them with my slingshot, though I never managed to hit them,
or else at times I purposefully refrained from shooting when I
thought they were too pretty to die. We saw green parakeets with
yellow elbows, blackbirds, saffron finches, mockingbirds, hyacinth
macaws, parrots, vultures, yellow-headed caracaras, pygmy owls, a
red-headed woodpecker, and a black ani, which Dad said ate the
ticks off of other animals. We spent the night at a spot more than
halfway to the Descoberto River.

The next day, on trails that followed along the banks of the
river, I saw, for the first time, the horned dung beetle and the black
dung beetle—on piles of animal dung—I found a grasshopper
and a praying mantis, and we came across termites and wasps.

As we rode upstream alongside the Jaguar Grove Creek toward
the headwaters, the tree frogs and cane toads began to celebrate
our arrival. It was already starting to get dark, and we found a flat,
clear spot that was open to the sky, where tons of fireflies were
keeping watch over the forest. We gave the mules corn, found a
spot for them, ate cheese, and made sure the provisions were nice
and safeguarded, then spread out our tarps on the ground and
fell asleep looking up at the starry sky, molested by mosquitoes,
horseflies, and a few leafcutter ants.

We awoke to Typhoon barking in the early light at five in
the morning, and caught sight of a slender young man, all of
seventeen or eighteen years old, up on his feet, as if he had been
keeping watch. Good morning, I was holed up here, ready to
shoot, he yelled over to Dad in his sharp voice, Why were you
holed up?, asked Dad, distrustful, I passed by here really early
and saw that there was a jaguar closing in, it was a good thing
she didn't have cubs, and wasn't in heat, and wasn't with a male,
I managed to scare off the damn thing, pumas, panthers, and

ocelots all pass through here, they come to drink water from the creek, I was worried about you two, so I kept watch, since another one could pass by, right? You can't sleep out in the open out here, they don't like my meat, since I hardly have any meat at all on my bones, and what I do have is too tough, but they'd have a field day with you two.

That's how the conversation began, his name was Valdivino, he'd become separated from his traveling companion, a woman, and had been walking all night long, but that was normal for him, he often stayed up all night, walked without stopping to rest, listening to the babbling of the rivers and learning about plants and animals, his greatest passion. He concealed his slim body in an oversized shirt and pants, and his round, shifty eyes radiated sincerity and friendship. He told us that he'd come out here with a group to help Master Yokaanam found the city of Universal Brotherhood, for the master had created the Eclectic Doctrine of the Americas, which opened the way to the Just and Brotherly Unification of All the Religions and Schools of the Planet, and he, Valdivino, had come to work on the construction of the city, or, more precisely, on the construction of the church, for it had come to him in a dream that it was his destiny to build churches and cathedrals. Construction was going to start on November 4, upon the arrival of the Caravan of Pilgrims. The pilgrims were coming on a special train that would stop for the night at Leopoldo de Bulhões, then continue on to Anápolis. From there to the Campo Limpo farm—a little to the south from where we were, close to Santo Antônio de Montes Claros, where they were going to set up over seventy tents—the pilgrims, with Master Yokanaam at the lead, were going to travel in six open-backed semi-trucks, as well as a bus for children and the elderly.

Valdivino and his friend had initially left Bahia for Rio in the back of a flatbed truck, along with hundreds of their countrymen, and there they'd joined the Eclectic Universal Spiritist

Brotherhood and learned the rites of Spiritism and *umbanda*. When, soon after, the Brotherhood decided to found a holy city in the Central Plateau, the two of them obtained authorization from Master Yokaanam to come along as pioneers, to assist him in his mission of the moral and spiritual salvation and renewal of humanity before the end of time, For the Eclectic City shall be the New Jerusalem, and Yokaanam prophesied: all shall come to an end when the star passes by, said Valdivino, What religion do you all practice?, asked Dad, It's not a religion, it's a mixture of the best of all religions, so that there can be universal harmony among them.

Valdivino helped Dad start a campfire, which they used to grill up the guinea pig we'd brought with us and two field doves that Valdivino had shot. He had also brought cassava flour and a block of raw brown sugar, and Dad laid our provisions out in dishes on the ground, which included some jerky that Aunt Francisca had made. I made the trip by train, one of the first to come from Rio to Anápolis, accompanied by my only true lifelong friend, and we set ourselves up at the Campo Limpo farm, before everyone else arrived. The two of us and twenty or so other people have already set up the first tents, explained Valdivino.

When we spotted a jararaca viper coiled up on a rock, Valdivino armed himself with a stick, but eventually decided that it wasn't necessary to kill it, since it was far enough away from us. There are also vine snakes, rattlesnakes, and bushmaster vipers out here, said Dad, yellow-headed caracaras and other kinds of falcons, as well as the greater rheas and seriemas, are the animals that prey on those snakes.

Still grilling his field dove, Valdivino explained, This friend of mine is much older than I am, but that doesn't matter to me, I just don't know if I want to live forever with her in the Eclectic City, she gets on my nerves but I think I'd be lost without her.

He was religious, but didn't attend just one church, because

God was present wherever there was kindness, and there was kindness in all the churches, All faiths and all religions are true, to which Dad objected, How can all religions be true if each one considers its God to be the only true God, if one faith is true, then the others have to be false, Are you Catholic, Mr. Moacyr?, I used to be, But you, Sir, must believe in God, because you can be sure of this, Sir, that there are many gods and one God who is above all others, the creator, And who created that God?, asked Dad, you must agree that he would have to be more complex than all of creation, so then how could he have come into being?, What are you saying, Mr. Moacyr?, In your commune, how are you going to treat those who don't believe, like me?, You're a good man, Mr. Moacyr, that's easy to see, I'll convert you yet, Sir.

Dad just smiled, and the irony in his smile was clearly visible, Sir, have you ever heard of the City of Z?, asked Valdivino, No, Well it's a lost city that's somewhere in this region, near the Araguaia River, where there was once a great civilization, and it seems that the explorer who came out here to discover this city founded a theosophical community where, like ours, there is respect for all religions, one day I'm going to find that lost city.

Valdivino accompanied us on the stretch along the creek and for a part of the return trip, always smiling, there was no malice, or distrust, or irony in his smile, it was a sweet smile, which perhaps concealed many difficulties and afflictions, Are you married, Sir? No, and João is my adopted son, But did you have a special woman in your life, Sir?, I've already forgotten about that, You should get yourself a beautiful woman, Sir, a woman that you really want to love, Too many people compete for the affections of beautiful women, they just end up leaving you for someone else, No, you're mistaken, Sir, they're faithful because they learned from an early age to defend themselves against the seductions of men, Alright then, I'll see if I can't catch hold of one, but it's not easy, Valdivino, what beautiful woman is going to want to live out here in the Wild West?, Mine came out here, if you ever saw her you'd fall in love with her, but I don't want that to happen, you can fall in love with any woman you want, Sir, just not her, because if I didn't have her, I don't know what would become of me, women are our future and our salvation, Mr. Moacyr, don't you think? The conversation was painful for Dad, who had been through an extremely bitter romantic experience, But there are women of all kinds, and sometimes there are great disappointments, Without women we're not very interesting, Aunt Matilde is going to come here from Rio, I said to Valdivino—I either said it just to say something or simply because we were talking about women.

Every once in a while Valdivino would spot a flower and leave the trail to pick it, later he classified them by colors, gathering together yellow ones of different shapes and sizes, like the yellow rhubarb and the *pau-terra-da-folha-larga*, or the ones with a yellow center, like the wolf apple (violet, with a little yellow wiener in the middle), the *santa rita* flower (pink, with yellow fuzz), the *candombá* (white, also with yellow fluff), and the *canela-de-ema* (light violet with a yellow bud), and to these he added whites ones, the white *ipê*, the velvety *flor-do-pau*, and the *Cerrado* orchid, as well as violet ones, the *roxinha*, the arnica, and some morning glories.

I'm going to give these to my friend, he said, she likes white, yellow, and purple. Then he also picked a mimosa (a downy, pink ball), a heart pea (which also blossomed spherically, but was a reddish-orange color), and mixed in some burheads. Take these for yourself, João, he tousled my hair and put his arm around my shoulders as if we were already old friends, later he snatched up a chamomile, which was a dingy off-white color—as well as some showerhead and clitoria flowers—and wanted to give them to Dad. Give them to João, Dad told him, You can make a bouquet of dried flowers with these, said Valdivino.

My hands were already full of flowers, so Dad found a place

for them on the back of one of the mules, The Descoberto River flows into the Corumbá, which, just like the São Bartolomeu, empties into the Paranaíba, which then descends into the Rio de la Plata basin, explained Dad, It's very beautiful here, but the soil is no good, said Valdivino, Dad replied, Mr. Israel Pinheiro is going to bring in some Japanese who will take care of that.

Valdivino not only knew plants like nobody's business, he knew birds as well. While we walked along, he pointed out to me the nightjar, the kingfisher, the umbrella bird, the bellbird, the tyrant flycatcher, the ovenbird with its nest in a gnarled rosewood tree, the song thrush, the tooth-billed wren, the carrion crow, the lapwing, and the white-naped jay.

We saw another termite mound, One day all of this will be gone, it will be covered with houses and people, the river will be full of garbage, and there won't be so many animals, like there are now, even these termite mounds will disappear, said Dad, Don't talk that way, Mr. Moacyr, or God will punish you, replied Valdivino, Well, I'm just being realistic.

Typhoon was barking nonstop. I told Valdivino that out behind our house, one of his favorite pastimes was to bark at white-breasted swallows that perched on the eave I'd built, Oh look at the white-bellied toucan!, said Valdivino, pointing. For me, it was the most beautiful thing we'd seen the entire trip, the toucan perched on a wine palm. I didn't have the courage to shoot at it with my slingshot. We stopped to show respect to that ten-meter tall palm tree with its fanned-out leaves, Dad said that its trunk could be used to make sturdy houses and its leaves were as good as the best roof-tiles, that you could make palm wine from its fermented sap, which the Indians used to drink, You should never cut down a wine palm, because the wine palm attracts water, it's the tree of life, explained Dad.

Typhoon was lagging behind, whether out of exhaustion or laziness, I'm unsure. He only looked alert and courageous when he caught the scent of another guinea pig, which was all we got on the return trip.

At one point on the way back, Valdivino turned south, heading towards the Campo Limpo farm. With an arm around Dad's shoulders, he bid us farewell, saying, Mr. Moacyr, when the path becomes clearer, I'll finish telling you my story. Dad wished him good luck, and we didn't suspect that we'd ever see him again.

After a long and exhaustive return trip, already nearing the Free City, we spotted one more termite mound, a red clay sculpture in a spot that was almost devoid of vegetation, This will all be paved over one day, covered with buildings, not a single termite mound will survive, the city is going to be planted here and then more city after that, that's what the future holds, Dad said to me.

Upon arriving home, it seemed like we'd seen quite a lot, but Dad had promised me much more, we hadn't come across any tarantulas, centipedes, striped hog-nosed skunks, coatis, or anteaters, which Dad had assured me inhabited the Plateau, nor otters, giant otters, peccaries, or tapirs, which could be found in the rivers or on their banks.

We discovered that we were covered with ticks. Dad and I had some small ones on our arms and legs, and there were some large ones stuck to Typhoon. It took us two days to remove them all carefully, with the help of some rubbing alcohol.

A little over a week later, Aunt Francisca told us, There's a handsome young man at the door, charming and polite, who says he knows you two. It was the first time that Aunt Francisca had ever seen Valdivino and she took a liking to him, I'm not sure whether because of his intelligence or his fragility.

Back in those days addresses weren't necessary, we had moved into one of the first houses in the Free City, and it wasn't hard for Valdivino to find us. He proved himself to be the same talkative young guy from the hunt. He had also returned home covered in ticks and his body still itched. He talked about the founding of the Eclectic City and narrated the arrival of the pilgrims in great detail. No, he hadn't become separated from the woman who was his traveling companion, she was very temperamental and had decided to abandon him all alone out on those footpaths because of a disagreement they'd had, she didn't support the idea of him leaving the Eclectic City to dedicate himself to the construction of Brasília.

Full of theories and imagination, Valdivino had, in his simplicity, a refined mind that was attentive to those sorts of details about banal facts that were far from obvious, through which Aunt Francisca discerned in him a sensitive profundity. He's a prodigy, she used to say, he learns things easily.

That isn't what Dad, and much less Aunt Matilde, thought about him, for them Valdivino had a talent for talking endlessly and could recognize plants and animals, but nothing more, they didn't see genius in the art of sprinkling vague thoughts with strange details, but we all agreed on one point: that he was what he appeared to be, averse to all forms of hypocrisy, sincere even while agreeing with everything and everyone, as a result of which it was often necessary to pull off mental contortions that contained flagrant contradictions. He didn't hide anything, except for the woman who was the love of his life, who always remained shrouded in a mysteriousness that aroused our curiosity. His desire to do the right thing at all times led him to confess his mistakes and attempt to remedy them, to behave in a humble manner that was appreciated by all, and almost always to put other peoples' opinions ahead of his, as if he preferred to have others think for him. He didn't act this way out of fear, on the contrary, he was willing to face any dangers he happened to encounter, but was under the impression that he hadn't encountered any yet. Since he needed very little to be content, he was convinced that the world had, up to that point, treated him well. Sometimes he was unsure about what was right and what was wrong, and was always happy when someone cleared things up for him, although he always considered it wrong to lie, to be cruel to animals, to hurt others, and even to be jealous . . . People were good, it was the world that was cruel and changed them, and only kindness and politeness were able to overcome the cruelty and violence of the world. Valdivino combined ignorance with an enormous desire to learn, grand ideas with minute day-to-day ones, passion with indifference. The impression that I had of him back then was created over the course of many years of familiarity, an impression that lacked the complete sentence that I'm only now able to compose. These days, I understand how Aunt Francisca felt. How could you not feel compassion and affection for such a person?

You're right, Mr. Moacyr, to want to be a great man and do so many things; you have so many plans, Sir . . . I only have one plan and I'll be content if I'm able to achieve it, said Valdivino, while all of us were gathered in the living room, for me it's like this: choose something and remain faithful to it, You're right about that, Valdivino, replied Aunt Francisca, but what sort of plan is it?, To keep to myself, content with what I have, he confessed, a beatific expression on his face, and out there, in the world, to dedicate myself to one thing, carry out a mission that will be useful to others, Nonsense, that's just being resigned, it's conformism, no one can get ahead with that kind of thinking, advised Aunt Matilde, It's not very easy to be content with the little you've got, is it, Valdivino?, replied Aunt Francisca in refutation, There isn't much that I can do in this world, Dona Matilde, money would only make a difference in the world if I had a lot of it, and my talents aren't many, the important thing is to have someone beside us that we really like and find the right mission to carry out. He thought that helping to build churches in the new city was the mission to which he'd been called, he had dreamt a beautiful dream in which he was building Brasília and the city had begun with the construction of a church, I want to keep building new churches.

Because of the interest displayed by Valdivino, Dad promised to take him to Newcap and, just the next day, introduced him to no less a figure than Bernardo Sayão. Sayão, without skipping a beat, took him to one of the camps of the workers who were building Brasília, where more than two hundred and thirty migrant workers had already settled down, and where a few days later, on November 10, 1956, beneath an enormous downpour, JK paid a visit. Do jaguars prowl around here?, asked the president, to which Valdivino replied, raising his chin, They don't bother us: the meat of migrant workers is too tough for jaguars, according to what JK himself transcribed in one of his books. Sayão, who was there at the time, told Dad that he liked the young man's attitude.

To the blog-reader who asked that I cite him as my source, I should make it clear that it's recorded in one of Dad's "Onward" notebooks and in various other books that it was also on this occasion that JK asked Bernardo Sayão to move to Brasília definitively, What day would you like me to move here, Sir? Sayão is said to have asked, Yesterday, JK is said to have replied. Early the following day, at six in the morning on November 11, according to how the story goes, as well as what Sayão recounted to Dad, Sayão arrived at Catetinho in a semi-truck, with his wife and two daughters, Where are you going to live?, asked the president, Under that tree, to start with, and after that I'll set up some kind of shelter.

He needed someone to help him set up the prefab Eucatex boards he was going to use to build the house that ended up on Sossego Street, in Candangolândia, and then he recalled the young man that Dad had brought to him and his attitude from the day before, He's a good kid and did really good work, he later told Dad. Sayão obtained a lot for him in the Free City, which had only started to take shape with the construction of a bakery and a few other houses. On that lot, Valdivino erected a shack made of wine palm fronds, scraps of boards, leftover Eucatex from Sayão's house, thick cardboard, and empty cement bags, all of which, according to him, was enough to shelter him from the torrential rains that had already started, planting a physic nut tree—which was willing to die defending him, and whose prickly barbs absorbed any glance from the evil eye—right by the front door.

A friendship soon developed between Valdivino and all of us, but especially between him and Aunt Francisca. He acquired a habit of stopping by our house on his way to or from work and would talk with us as he folded and unfolded his arms, full of admiration for Aunt Francisca. He looked at her as if she were a saint upon an altar, to whom he asked enigmatic questions and requested advice. My opinion doesn't matter, Valdivino, you're the only one who can say for sure, she'd reply. He was interested in the books on display on the shelves in the living room. No, she didn't know much about books, Valdivino should ask Aunt Matilde about them, Aunt Francisca would tell him, and then he'd leave with a book that Aunt Matilde let him borrow. Perhaps because Aunt Francisca, simple and spontaneous like him, naturally understood the things he said, he was extremely courteous towards her, took pleasure in the favors she asked of him, and, when she didn't ask anything of him, reminded her that he was at her disposal for whatever she needed. For Aunt Francisca, Valdivino made the house—which received very few visits—a cheerier place, and she filled their conversations with inquiries about Bahia, as well as the Eclectic City, which he'd helped build. I listened to those prolonged dialogues without asking any questions, for I was more inclined to observe than to question. But Dad, especially at the beginning, felt uneasy about the friendship between Aunt Francisca and Valdivino, There's no such thing as friendship between a man and a woman, Francisca, be careful, don't lead that boy on.

If I'm not mistaken it was January of 1957 when, one day, Dad, Aunt Francisca, and I—as well as Aunt Matilde, who had already arrived by then—were out walking in the vicinity of Valdivino's shack and came across him hauling a little table and three low stools in a pushcart. A little before Christmas and after an entire day on a Real Airlines flight—which, after leaving at seven in the morning, had stops in Três Pontes, Vargínia, Belo Horizonte, Uberaba, Araguari, Uberlândia, Goiânia, and Anápolis—Aunt Matilde had arrived from Rio, where she'd been living for the last ten years. We were with her, returning from a restaurant that had just opened for business, which belonged to an Italian, Vítor Pelechia, in the area near the wooden bridge over Deep Creek, and had the idea to get coffee at the Confessor Café in the Free City, which back then was just a sparse cluster of houses with about three hundred residents, almost all of them men, and, along with the Candangolândia camp, the only new population hub in the region of the new capital.

Valdivino told us that he made a living as a scribe, writing letters that were dictated to him, and that he'd also worked on the construction of the first church in the Free City, smack in the middle of the rainy season, perhaps the rainiest season in the entire history of Brasília—there still were no decent highways, and the semi-trucks that hauled construction materials to the worksites slid and shimmied all along those sludgy roadways—But at the end I felt very satisfied when I saw the finished church, he said, Me, too, said Aunt Francisca. She had taken me to that church, its simplicity visible in the horizontally rectangular side windows with their white frames, and its solitary tower, only connected to the nave by a canopy that was held up by brown pillars, which matched the color of the mud in the city.

Aunt Matilde just listened, silently, examining with an

impatient stare that young man who was both tranquil and talkative.

Dad informed us, in a jesting tone, The first hotel is also being built now, The Brasília Hotel; after a building for confessing, another one to sin in, Behave yourself, implored Aunt Francisca, Seriously, after you build a church you can then build a hotel, Dad proposed, No, after one church, then another, replied Valdivino, A construction worker shouldn't pick and choose the jobs he takes, Dad advised, But Valdivino isn't just any old construction worker, he's an idealist, said Aunt Francisca, defending him.

Valdivino just smiled, the smile of a person who doesn't take himself too seriously and knows what he wants.

Aunt Francisca told him that the president was going to come eat in the SWAS restaurant sometime soon, You should show up, it's going to be a special day. Since December of 1956, Aunt Francisca had worked in her new position as caterer and also helped out in the kitchen of the Social Welfare Alimentation Service restaurant, although it would only be formally inaugurated on February 21, 1957. Up until the Japanese arrived in August of 1957 to create a greenbelt in Brasília, it was difficult to get tomatoes, bell peppers, cabbage, and other vegetables. The menu she prepared never varied and included beans, rice, potatoes, chayote, cassava, and—for the engineers—boar, which she bought in Luziânia.

When Dad informed her that Sayão had confirmed JK's visit to the restaurant, Aunt Francisca figured out all the things the president liked to eat: steak, pork loin or *molho pardo* chicken, accompanied by—depending on the main dish—rice, beans, cassava flour, okra, French fries, vegetables, cassava-flour porridge, boiled or fried cassava, or even *tropeiro* beans with kale. As for fruits, jabuticaba fruit, tangerines, mangos, and for dessert, chunky guava jam or dulce de leche with Minas-style cheese.

However, she wasn't allowed to prepare any special dishes for the president, since he wanted to eat what the workers usually ate. So, for the long-awaited lunch—at which both Dad and Valdivino showed up—she managed to get a one hundred and eighty kilo boar.

JK seemed content to eat alongside the workers, struck up conversations with them, and joked around with one guy after another. When he shook hands with Dad, Dad reminded him of their encounter at Catetinho and his desire to contribute to the historical record of the construction of the city, Well, don't miss the opportunity to cover the first scientific summit of Brasília, said the president, on August 6 we're going to have a conference here with more than one hundred doctors from various states around the country—for Dad, these words seemed to confirm for him, once more, his status as official recorder.

I wasn't there that day, and Dad didn't write anything about their conversation in his notebooks. Even so, it's possible, with what I've heard, with what Dad later told Aunt Francisca, with what Aunt Francisca later mentioned to me, and even with what Dad revealed to me, enclosed within four walls, to reconstitute the dialogues, as biographers and fiction writers sometimes do. As such, I wouldn't be inventing anything if I were to say that, during that lunch, Dad told Valdivino that Bernardo Sayão had staked out the location, along the trail leading out to the Paranoá waterfall, of Brasília's first chapel, the Don Bosco Hermitage— named for the saint who had prophesied the founding of the city— for that really was the main subject of conversation, If you want to keep building churches . . . I know you don't believe in it, Sir, but religion is the first necessity of those who are going to arrive here, I will do everything I can, really, to work on the construction of this hermitage, because, as I told you, Sir, I mainly want to help with the building of churches; a new city needs churches, there's nothing more important than churches, Valdivino repeated, and if the location was chosen by Mr. Bernardo Sayão, then the construction is blessed by God even as it begins.

I'll say in passing that Valdivino certainly didn't speak in that orderly a manner, nor did he just stick to this one subject, he zigzagged off into other conversations, asked silly questions, told stories about his life in Bahia, talked about Bernardo Sayão, and other subjects still, which I left out in order to simplify the reading and get right to the point. He recounted that his friend had found it necessary to leave the Eclectic City, for a reason that he would rather not mention, and that she was nowhere to be found, When my path becomes clearer, I'll finish telling you my story, Mr. Moacyr, Sir, You said that to me once before and you've still never told me anything, replied Dad in a recriminatory tone of voice.

To tell the truth, I'm not sure if it was then or a few days later that Valdivino promised Dad that he'd one day tell him his story, what matters is that Dad replied that he was curious to hear it and on more than one occasion thereafter reminded Valdivino of the promise he'd made. Each time, Valdivino asked Dad to be patient and eventually even confessed to him, with his customary candor, that he could only be completely open with him once they became friends. We still need to get to know each other better, but it will happen one day, Mr. Moacyr, we'll be great friends, Don't you trust me, Valdivino? I don't know if you'd understand me, Sir.

Valdivino looked out the window with the fixed stare of a drug addict, and then, as if he had suddenly woken up, explained that as long as he couldn't find another job, he'd continue his work as a scribe in the Free City, he liked to put the things the migrant workers dictated to him on paper, letters of joy and sadness, of love, of sorrows, of longing, and of mourning, Put this, they'd say, and then they'd tell the story that they wanted transcribed, they send greetings or set a date for the family to be reunited. Valdivino took pleasure in helping to reconnect those family ties, since the

Free City was being populated by separated families, especially men without women, children without parents, parents without children, and fiancés without their brides-to-be. In this function, he also discovered many indiscretions and secrets, Because of this I've realized that I'm not alone in the world, I'm not the only one who makes mistakes, because I make mistakes, too, but I know that God forgives me, yes, one day I'll finish telling you my story, Sir.

In his edit, João Almino suggested that I should include here some of Valdivino's stories in order to captivate the reader. The problem is that we went several months without seeing Valdivino, so how can I invent something out of nothing? Sometimes Aunt Francisca asked Dad about him or said, Oh, he really has disappeared, until we ran into him at the first Mass held in Brasília, on May 3 of that year, 1957, a day that began with an argument between Dad and Aunt Francisca about the resurrection of Christ. The debate confused me, and, without uttering a peep, I intuitively took Aunt Francisca's side. It's not true that Christ died to save us, because, if he was resurrected, then he didn't actually die, said Dad, provoking Aunt Francisca, You're going to hell, she replied, Religion is the true hell, if you study history, you'll see how much violence and crime religion has caused, Then just stay home, don't go to the Mass, because it'll be a sacrilege, I'm going today because of what it symbolizes. And then he explained to us that JK, who would be present at the Mass, had chosen May 3 because of its proximity to the anniversary of the first Mass that Pedro Álvares Cabral ordered to be held, which marked the discovery of Brazil, and this other Mass, four hundred years later, represented, according to the president, the true appropriation of the national territory.

All of us—me, Dad, Aunt Francisca, and Aunt Matilde—headed out to a spot near the large cross, where more than fifteen thousand people had gathered from all over Brazil, traveling in open-back semi-trucks, hundreds of automobiles, and around forty airplanes. I had never seen so many children in one place. I was fascinated with the Carajá Indians who were wearing feathers and the women from Rio in their long dresses, which went only halfway down the shin. Those dresses were designed in Paris, commented Aunt Matilde, who herself was showing hips that were almost bursting out of her tight blue dress, which was, according to Aunt Francisca, also indecent, mainly because it didn't have sleeves, You can't show up in front of the Archbishop like that, he'll send you straight home, Matilde, predicted Aunt Francisca.

Aunt Francisca wanted to see the image, brought for the occasion from São Paulo, of Our Lady of Aparecida, Brazil's patroness, who had also been, for less than six months, or rather, since November 14, the patroness of Brasília, per the suggestion of then-bishop Don Hélder Câmara. As she tried to get closer to Our Lady, she spotted Valdivino and waved to him from afar, and he waved back with the gestures and giddiness of a child.

We listened to the sermon by Don Carlos Carmelo de Vasconcellos Motta, Archbishop of São Paulo: " . . . we shall all rejoice, because we're living through one of the three greatest events in the glorious history of our homeland. In fact, the discovery of Brazil in 1500, Independence in 1822, and—in the present day—the founding of this new Metropolitan Capital, in the middle of the country, are the three crowning landmarks of the life of the nation," and with each phrase Valdivino nodded his head in approval.

Dad jotted down Don Carmelo's words, since he wanted to collect as many arguments as possible against the caustic critiques of the construction of the city.

After the ceremony, while the Carajá Indians—transported there from Bananal Island by the Brazilian Air Force—paid homage to the president by presenting him with spears, war clubs, cudgels, and arrows, Valdivino came running over to meet up with us. He had worked on the construction of the enormous improvised awning over the altar, he told us, and a few days earlier he had worked on the Don Bosco Hermitage, which would be inaugurated the following day, May 4, he had applied some of the last coats of white paint on the building, which was all white, a white that sparkled against the landscape, the first finished building in Brasília, he said, it wasn't just any old chapel like all the rest, since it would be on the shores of the lake, once the lake was filled in, and its location, together with its sharply angular pyramidal shape, which pointed to the heavens, would attract powerful energies, his girlfriend was the one who showed him that. Hadn't she disappeared?, asked Dad, No, she's coming with me tomorrow.

Valdivino wanted to know if we'd seen Bernardo Sayão, I'd really like to meet up with him again, maybe he's here somewhere in the middle of this crowd, but there are so many people ... And then he offered us the invitation, I'd really like you all to come to the inauguration of the Hermitage tomorrow.

Faced with Dad's silence, Aunt Francisca promised that, yes, we would go, all of us. You shouldn't have spoken for us all, we're not going to that piece of shit Hermitage, no way, Dad said later, visibly angry.

Still that same day, Valdivino showed up at our house in the Free City, disappointed because, three hours after the Mass ended, they had torn down the awning that he'd helped build. Was that a premonition? Could it be that the things he built wouldn't stand the test of time? Just remember that the awning was temporary, said Aunt Francisca, calming him down, the churches you build are the things that will remain standing. Are you all really going to come to the inauguration of the Hermitage, do you think you'll have enough room in the jeep for me?, asked Valdivino, Unfortunately, we can't go, explained Dad, dryly, But

don't you want to record all the important events?, demanded
Aunt Francisca, nothing could be more important than the
inauguration of this Hermitage.

Valdivino kept insisting that we come, but we missed
the inauguration of the Hermitage, despite Aunt Francisca's
entreaties.

You can go if you want, said Dad, and Aunt Francisca
responded that she wouldn't be able to make it there by herself,
Go with Valdivino, In the back of a truck? and plus his girlfriend
won't like that.

*Fourth Night:*
*Lucrécia*

On the fourth night, Dad, locked up between four dingy walls, told me that some of the most lucrative business ventures in the Free City were the brothels, where, in their free time and on the weekend, the workers spent the money they'd earned from their excessive hours of work. Dad remembered the bars, the drinking binges, and the district of bohemian lifestyles, gambling, and prostitution—the red-light district, called Placa da Mercedes—that were responsible for turning Brasília into a "licentious and immoral city," as *The Globe* newspaper asserted on June 16, 1958. There were prostitutes all over—hundreds of them, in whorehouses, bars, and cabarets—because the market was thriving: a lot of men had come to work construction and hadn't brought their families. There were so many prostitutes that Dad even suggested to Valdivino that, if he wanted to earn a lot of money, he should specialize in fixing beds broken by overuse in the brothels, but Valdivino just repeated, No, Mr. Moacyr, my business is building churches. Women who weren't prostitutes were rare and, for that reason, highly desired. The scarcity of women contributed, in large part, to the sexual thirst among the men, and Dad was no exception.

My child's ears were attentive to the stories about this sexual marketplace, and I remember that, when the census came out in July of 1957, Dad complained that for every three men, there were only two women in the Free City, which certainly took into account the prostitutes who resided there, although a lot of them only came for a single night of work, then returned to their hometowns, Formosa or Luziânia. Look here, he said, pointing to the newspaper, In a population of two thousand two hundred people, there are only eight hundred and seventy women, I could practically get to know them all, It's wonderful, I'm not complaining about it, said Aunt Matilde, We can't even go out in the street without being harassed, the men here are brazen, shameless, complained Aunt Francisca, Men are just like that, a couple of days ago one of them grabbed my butt, said Aunt Matilde, laughing, And you aren't complaining?, said Aunt Francisca in protest, The worst is a perverted old man who chases after all the young girls with his cock all hard and then, since they all run away from him, ends up fucking a donkey right in the middle of the street, Don't talk that way in front of the boy, Matilde, Dad shouted, The only decent man that I've met here is Valdivino, a simple, bashful young man, but religious, too, and you can tell that he respects women, it's true, he's the only exception around here, he's a saint, an innocent, not brazen and obscene like all the rest of the men around here, said Aunt Francisca.

In those moments Aunt Francisca's admiration for Valdivino made me resentful, and I swore to myself that one day I'd be just like him, but I'd already see myself failing in my attempt. Out on the street the kids messed around with Valdivino, and sometimes I joined in with them and would notice Valdivino shooting me a look of disappointment. The little boys would hit him, and he never reacted, but one day he became enraged and said, You're going to regret this, I'm going to end up killing one of you. From that day on, we started to respect him, because—as one can infer from the well-known saying—the dog that never barks is the one that bites.

Aunt Francisca's conviction that Valdivino was different from the rest of the men in the Free City was strengthened, I believe, one day when I was walking beside her along a smoothed-dirt street with no sidewalks, she was wearing a checkered dress, tight at the waist and quite wide at the bottom, the type that gets blown up by a treacherous gust of wind. Some men who had galloped past us on horses, raising up a cloud of dust, turned their heads back when they saw her, she was holding her dress down, and other men, at the shops in front of us, were looking at her intensely, waiting for the chance to relish every centimeter of her dark thighs with their eyes. One of them whistled at Aunt Francisca, then another, and another, it was a whole orchestra of whistles, and suddenly one of them yelled: Let that skirt fly up! And other voices responded: Let it fly! Let it fly! At this point, Aunt Francisca ran off towards Valdivino, who was sitting at his desk out in the open air, transcribing letters, and felt safely sheltered when he considerately offered her his chair.

It was the end of winter of 1957, and Dad, playing the role of tour guide in the Free City, got the sudden idea to show off one of the city's curiosities: Valdivino, the scribe. The tourist being guided around was an engineer connected to the group that the architect Oscar Niemeyer had brought with him to Brasília, named Roberto Gonçalves, whom Sayão had introduced to Dad at Newcap headquarters. Roberto mentioned the city plan designed by Lúcio Costa, who had won the design competition for the Brasília project in March of that year, and told Dad, After coming to Brasília, I must confess that I'm sorry that I'm not an architect, engineering is prose, but architecture is pure poetry, Niemeyer— the poet of concrete—wants to create a bold city, as he sometimes says, "reason isn't just the enemy of thought, as Heidegger put it, but also the enemy of imagination," He's going to get rich with Brasília, No way, he didn't even want Israel Pinheiro to give him a commission, because he doesn't like the word, he's developing a whole series of projects for just forty thousand *cruzeiros* a month,

I know him pretty well, I've spent time with some of the people who came with him, twenty architects in all, but he also brought some people that he wanted to lend a hand to, people who are fun to have around, there's a doctor, a journalist, an official from the Aviation division, a goalie from the Flamengo soccer team ... they even started a musical group, with Niemeyer on ukulele.

The fact that Roberto had access to Niemeyer and, through him, to the president, was for Dad the greatest possible letter of introduction, as if he belonged to some special caste. I met an engineer who moves in the social circles at Catetinho and should be coming to pay us a visit, he mentioned at home one day, You're enchanted by power, protested Aunt Matilde, and her criticism was amplified by the tone in which she pronounced the word "power," That's not the reason, this guy knows the city plan of Brasília in detail, and he continued talking about Roberto, who ended up occupying a special place in my infantile imagination, that of a figure who was as majestic as a statue in a public plaza. From what Dad told us, Roberto, the right man in the right place, had taken on big responsibilities and held the key to opportunities that could be opened up to anyone who wanted to work in construction.

Roberto had explained to Dad that, according to Lúcio Costa, the sensibility and reality of Brasília were Brazilian, but had a French affiliation, Just think of the main axis thoroughfares, of the perspectives and proportions of Paris, if you draw a straight line, it's three kilometers from the Arc du Triomphe du Caroussel to the Arc de Triomphe de l'Étoile, which will be the same distance from the palaces to the television tower. I'd like to see the layout of these worksites, said Dad, Well I'd like to get to know the Free City, replied Roberto, who, living in a prefab public housing unit right in the Pilot Plan, had yet to visit the Free City, Well, come visit, I'll be your tour guide.

And that's how, on that day back in September of 1957,

Roberto came to visit the Free City for the first time—the fact that it was a day in September might be an unnecessary piece of information, but I prefer to note it here, since Aunt Matilde, during conversations and confessions about our years in the Free City, had this date fresh in her mind when she received me many years later, after I had left home on bad terms with Dad. There wasn't much to show him, the city was just a cluster of houses made out of boards and asbestos roof-tiles, with three wide and, at that time of year, dusty avenues: Third Avenue, Second Avenue, and Central Avenue, But when it rains, this all turns to mud, Dad told Roberto. And that was when, while walking along Central Avenue, Dad had the idea to show him that curiosity. Aunt Francisca had already called me over for us to leave, since Valdivino had just received a customer. Wait a bit, I insist on walking you all home, Valdivino had promised, and upon the arrival of Dad and Roberto we made a little circle around the young scribe, Roberto feeling moved not only by the skill of that simple young man in precisely and rapidly putting the dictated words on paper, but also by the observation he'd made about Lúcio Costa's city plan, The plan for Brasília is divinely inspired, so much so that the architect said that the solution wasn't sought out, it emerged, so to speak, already complete; for me it's obvious, it was whispered from above, by Don Bosco.

Since the conversation was dragging on and Dad had invited Roberto to come to our house, Aunt Francisca asked Valdivino to make good on his promise, Didn't you say that you'd walk us home?

We all walked down the avenue together. The person who can really tell you all about the Free City is João, said Dad to Roberto, explaining that in my free time in the afternoon I served as a tour guide for visitors. Roberto then asked me a bunch of questions, and I described, to his great wonder, the whole layout of the city, reciting the names of shops, bars, and hotels.

What a smart little boy, he said in praise, walking with his hands in his pockets and his eyes on Aunt Matilde, who at that point could be seen in the window of our house, like a figure in a painting. Perhaps his eyes had first been attracted there by Typhoon, who was barking from his post under the window. He doesn't bite, I said, trying to set him at ease, but Typhoon wouldn't stop barking and came at Roberto, as if he wanted to attack him. I bent down to grab hold of Typhoon, but he slipped out of my hands, took off, and went straight back for Roberto's feet, barking all the while, then eventually he responded to Dad's commands and went over to the front door of the house, but he kept on barking and was at the ready.

Aunt Matilde, impassive, displayed her *décolleté* beauty in the window. When we entered the house, she had sat down, with her hands folded on her lap, her head raised elegantly. She had an independent way about her, which included the capacity to be unpleasant as she expressed her graceful, yet sharp-edged style, if not downright aggressive.

Let's leave Aunt Matilde there immobile for a moment to say, in a brief parenthesis, that the fact that Typhoon had reacted so oddly to the presence of Roberto was a subject of conversation in our house for a long time. Dad disciplined him, but he only stopped barking when Valdivino calmed him down with his gentle voice, This engineer here is our friend, Typhoon, he said as he stroked his head.

Roberto resumed the conversation about the construction of Brasília, It's already been a month since work first started on the Monumental Axis Highway, I don't know if you all have been past there, but you can already start to get a sense of the space, Brasília's detractors don't have a leg to stand on, nobody has ever seen anything like what this city will be, the president was right when he said back in March, talking about the results of the competition, that the impact of this move will even affect the mentality and the manner of feeling of the Brazilian people, That's what my companion says, too, said Valdivino, that a new humanity is going to emerge, What attracts me most is that the city is going to be vibrant, pleasant, and fitting for intellectual endeavors, a cultural epicenter of the brightest people in the country, added Roberto, I'll have to see it first, commented Aunt Matilde, raising her eyebrows and adding a skeptical smile to her large eyes, This is already a certainty, replied Roberto, serious and restraining his irritation, And once they put in the lake?, asked Valdivino, There aren't going to be any residential buildings alongside the lake, replied Dad, It's true, the banks are going to be left intact, with groves of trees and fields, the only things allowed at the edge of the lake will be clubs, restaurants, spas . . . anything that's oriented towards recreation, Perhaps you all could take us out there, requested Aunt Francisca, Now it's my turn, I'll be the tour guide this time, said Roberto, there isn't yet much to see in the area near the lake, but we can already get a sense of what the Monumental Axis will be like.

As she listened to Roberto, Aunt Matilde affected a smile of distrust on her red lips and a certain gravity in the expression in her eyes. She, who normally sought to impress men with her opinions and feminine antics, merely examined Roberto, as if she were inspecting a product for sale, still uncertain about its possible qualities and with the air of someone who doesn't have high hopes. He seemed like an actor on a stage, but the role he was playing wasn't attracting her attention. He was charming and handsome, there was some trace of tenderness in his facial features, which contrasted with the severity of his loud, rough voice, the voice of someone who isn't afraid of what he says. It's a pity that he was pretentious.

I was telling Moacyr that he should come to my house next weekend, it would be my great pleasure if the rest of you could come as well, said Roberto, addressing all of us, yet looking solely at Aunt Matilde, from there we can walk over to a spot where we can get a extensive view of the construction sites at the Esplanade.

From that day forth, Roberto and Valdivino came over to our house in the Free City many times, and for a while the limits of the known world seemed to be the two of them, aside from my own family, a few friends, the employees of the shops we frequented, and one or another stranger I knew in passing. Roberto was the only visitor who traveled quite a distance to see us, and the most distinguished of them all. For that reason, he was always the object of special care, especially in the case of Aunt Francisca, who would prepare his favorite sweets and juices.

Aunt Matilde thought that Roberto disliked her. Aunt Francisca would ask her, What about you, do you like him? I haven't thought about it, all I know is that he doesn't like me, What did you do to make him not like you? You don't have to do anything for someone to like or dislike you, There must be some reason, Do you think there's some reason why he likes you? Me? Yes, you, it's as clear as day that he likes it when you're cheeky with him, So you're jealous, is that it? I hope I'm wrong, because he doesn't deserve you.

Sometimes Roberto would show up unannounced, appearing in the windows of our house, which were always open, and we'd put another plate on the dinner table, which was in the same room where I would set up the hammock I slept in, or else he'd come later on in the evening, and Aunt Francisca would then have to postpone her praying of the rosary. On certain moonlit nights, we'd set up chairs outside in front of the house and, as we sat there, make out his slender figure from far off, Here comes Roberto, bring out another chair, João, Aunt Francisca would bid me. She maintained an expectant air about her, waiting for a man, like Roberto, who would whisk her away from her pitiable daily routine to a grand destiny, but she would never take the initiative or show any interest aside from those minor courtesies.

On the night when Roberto paid his first visit to the Free City, Dad took him out to one of his favorite bars, Carmen's bar, where Carmen herself, a sociable woman, tended bar until late in the evening, even after her husband went to bed. They drank *caipirinhas* and competed with the workmen over the few women in the place, to dance body-to-body on the wooden dance-floor, which was set apart by a lattice-work partition and surrounded by drunks swilling beer, rum, and *Cuba libres*.

During a break in the dancing, Roberto introduced Dad to three friends, all of them engineers, who were talking about a certain Lucrécia. That Lucrécia you introduced me to is an amazing thirty-something gal, said one of them, who was tall and dark, addressing the man next to him, who was carrying his hat under his arm. Lucrécia? I also know a Lucrécia, affirmed the third man, who had a square face and green eyes. Don't even start, what do you know about her?, demanded the first, the tall, dark one. And what if I know a lot about her? Then it must be some other Lucrécia, she wouldn't give you the time of day, replied the tall engineer. That is, unless Paulão introduced you to her, he's over there in the back, said the second man, the one with the hat under his arm. They all looked at the man in the long-sleeved white shirt, who stood out because of his size and the size of his moustache. He knows how to make money with construction sand and women, said the tall, dark man, lowering his voice. His brothel must be a gold mine, confirmed the man with the hat under his arm. And what if I prove that I know Lucrécia intimately?, insisted the man with the square face and green eyes. So, what is she like, then?, asked the tall engineer, with a smile on his lips, as if he were testing the other man. She's knowledgeable, although crazy, she's probably about forty years old, but she doesn't look it, and she's nothing like these young, inexperienced whores around here, she's highly sought after because she's mastered all the techniques.

A blog reader who used to know Lucrécia started an argument about her age, saying that she was thirty-five back then. Others, however, claim that I'm correct, that she would have been at least forty. In order to calm down the heated discussion, I thought about meeting in the middle: thirty-seven and a half, but I ended up just opting for forty, after employing some deductive reasoning and a mathematical calculation or another. For those who prefer precision, I must confess that I still don't know her exact age. That heated exchange demonstrates the simultaneous usefulness and uselessness of a blog, which allowed for a laudable exchange of ideas, yet diverted my readers' attention to a detail of minor importance and took all of us away from Carmen's Bar. Aside from the addition of this paragraph—which would be a disposable one if I didn't take advantage of it to beg the pardon of Lucrécia's admirer, who wished to reduce her age—I've maintained my original text without adding or subtracting anything, which is happening more and more often. Let's quickly return, then, to the conversation at the bar.

I can't believe that you know so much about her, how is it that he knows all these things?, said the engineer with the hat under his arm ironically, Well, this guy knows it all, said the tall, dark one.

At that point the one with green eyes decided to tell them everything that he knew, You know the story, right?, he brought Lucrécia here from Bahia as some sort of high-class whore, set her up in a house that was separate from the brothel, and in time started to develop feelings for her, he practically became her lover and wouldn't let her receive guests or go out with anyone else, but they say that now he wants to get rid of her, since he's going to marry some other Bahian woman who insists that he let go of Lucrécia before the wedding; he takes Lucrécia out to the movies and everyone stares at her and says "what a beauty," I think he does that just to show off, and also advertise her, but I can tell you a true story, which happened to me: one day I was walking here in the Free City, I saw her get out of Paulão's car and was immediately smitten, then Paulão came over to talk to me, all dressed up in a white suit, like a movie star, Don't be cheeky, he said, she's not for people like you, she's a princess, but by chance I ran into him the next day and, to my surprise, he hinted to me that I could see her at the movies that night and added, If you want more, bring me three thousand *cruzeiros*, Are you nuts?, I replied, but then I still went to the movies and saw Lucrécia and was unable to sleep all night long. The next day I bought her a pretty necklace, covered with gemstones, and decided to be bold and went straight to her house with it.

The man with the hat under his arm said, Maybe it's true that he doesn't let Lucrécia go out with just anybody, but I don't know, that guy would make any deal if the price was right, She's a really high quality woman, says some curious things, and what thighs!, added the engineer with green eyes, Yeah, but nothing compares to her ass, added the man with the hat under his arm, I agree, that woman's got some ass, responded the man with green eyes.

Roberto, who up to that point had been talking to someone beside him, joined the little group, Whose ass is it? he asked, Lucrécia's, replied the engineer with green eyes, A high-class whore here in the Free City?, there's no such thing, said Roberto, You just say that because you haven't met Lucrécia, she's a true beauty, said the one with green eyes, And what an ass!, repeated the one with the hat under his arm.

That was all Dad heard. He didn't know who Lucrécia was and only knew Paulão by sight, even though he frequented his brothel.

Roberto took his leave, since he didn't want to get home too late, Come over to the house this weekend, and bring everyone, we'll go take a look at the construction sites.

Much later that night, Dad—sitting at a table by himself, drinking beer and looking out at the dance-floor—heard a voice, Have you already met Paulão? It was Carmen and, at her side, Paulão. Pull up a chair, Dad said to Paulão after the initial introductions were made.

Paulão knew who Dad was and thought that he was well connected to the inner-circles of the president and Newcap, an impression that was reinforced when he saw him with Roberto. At a certain point in the conversation, which was getting increasingly lively, he revealed that he planned to sell the brothel in order to dedicate himself to more lucrative ventures, Here in the Central Plateau there's a lot of money going around, Mr. Moacyr, you just need a few bucks to invest and then they multiply all by themselves, it hasn't even been a year since I arrived here from Bahia and I'm not complaining; look, Mr. Moacyr, there's a lot of money circulating throughout the Central Plateau, and we can't miss the opportunity to bite off the chunk that belongs to us, isn't that right?, the money that the government is bringing here alone . . .

Dad thought about the piles of money that he'd seen a little earlier at the Ipê Grange Hall, spread all throughout the immense window-filled hall, money that had been brought out of the safes and placed in the sunlight so that it wouldn't get moldy. It was true, there was a lot of money going around the Central Plateau, money from Newcap, money from social welfare institutions, money from the construction firms—which never stopped arriving, one after another—and Paulão was right, he couldn't miss the opportunity to get his hands on the chunk that belonged to him. The words he wrote didn't generate income, and he would earn very little if he just kept selling commodatums, he had to invest in land and construction, this is what was going through Dad's mind.

They keep saying that it's dirty money, Mr. Moacyr, but here you just can't afford to be scared of dirty money, all the money here is dirty, really dirty, because it's money that's as red as the dirt here, everywhere else in the country they immediately know when they get money that was made here, it's money that's covered in dirt, in dust, but it's worth just as much as clean money, and if they have a problem with it, we'll just run some soap and water over it, right?, I wanted to talk to you about some ideas I have, Mr. Moacyr.

Dad looked at Paulão, but all he could think about was Lucrécia, whom he still hadn't met. He was tired of all those second-class whores. Was it true that Paulão only introduced her to certain people?

Paulão wanted to specialize in being a tomcat, that is, a third-party contractor for the construction firms, That way I gain an advantage, Mr. Moacyr, unlike the firms themselves, I won't have to offer workers the benefits that come with a signed worker's ID card.

They talked until late at night, I'm going to screw Carmen today, Paulão announced at a late hour, Her husband is right there inside, warned Dad, Well, I'll find a way.

That weekend, we all went to Roberto's house, packed into the jeep, Dad, me, Aunt Matilde, Aunt Francisca, and—at Aunt Francisca's invitation—Valdivino, too. We advanced across the terrain with difficulty. Crowning our excitement about this new discovery, the afternoon descended in red over the valley's vast, rough, imposing nakedness. At one end of it we caught a glimpse of the house on a dirt road that had recently been cleared out. There was something poetic about that outpost, where the first residents of the city of the future lived. As soon as we arrived, Roberto offered his hand to help Aunt Francisca and Aunt Matilde down from the jeep. After that he walked up front with Dad, and we followed the two of them up to the living room of the small house.

Roberto, whose eyes were as agile as his words, looked like some large bird with a long head, a long body, and a long nose. In beautiful boots and khaki pants and shirt, he had the mannerisms of an educated person, both in his gestures and in his appealing and good-humored conversational manner. Later on I learned from Aunt Matilde that that appearance was hollow. After the military coup in 1964, he became violent in his outbursts of jealousy, trying to control her and forbidding her to go out at night to spray political graffiti on walls or even simply to meet up with friends. But at that moment I knew nothing of the future, except that it was going to be grand.

This house is more than enough for me: a living room, two bedrooms, a bathroom, and a kitchen, said Roberto, as he showed us into the house, Niemeyer's house is just like this one, no better and no worse, it's nearby, at the end of W-3 Street, I've been over there to play cards and play drums; in the living room there's a small field radio, and in the bedroom there's a cot, a temporary wardrobe like this one, and a stool for a nightstand.

From there we took two cars and drove out as far as we could. Then we went on foot, and Aunt Francisca, wearing a blue dress that went down to the middle of her shins, held on to Valdivino for support and held out her hand to him whenever she had the chance, so she could step over holes in the ground. The temperature was pleasant, and the sun, with its soft light, projected our enormous shadows onto the ground, on which we could freely make our own path.

We went past the wide Esplanade, which they'd just started to clear out. Watch out for holes, advised Roberto. Aunt Francisca held ever more closely to Valdivino, who complained about the dust staining his white pants. At least it's not raining and your boots aren't all muddy, said Aunt Francisca.

There's nothing picturesque about this place, if it at least had mountains, like Rio . . . said Aunt Matilde critically, This is meant to be a modern city, open to the world, it doesn't need to be picturesque, replied Roberto, who then explained that he knew Lúcio Costa's plan in detail, the bus station was going to be over there, by the Rabelo Overpass, and next to it would be a center of entertainment, a mixture of Picadilly Circus, Times Square, and the Champs-Élysées, with galleries, wide sidewalks, patios, and cafés, as in Europe, the theaters will be next to each other along alleyways, the way they are on Ouvidor Street in Rio and in the narrow streets of Venice, or along covered walkways, like arcades, and these alleyways will give out onto courtyards with bars, cafés, and loggias with views of the park.

I'll have to see it first, repeated Aunt Matilde, adjusting her long, tight pants, and I, without saying anything, took part in her skepticism, because out there in the landscape before us, aside from the parts that had already been excavated, we could only see the outline of crooked, rickety trees and some termite mounds, aside from the flowers, which, as always—once the depths of winter were over and it started to warm up again—blossomed even if there hadn't been a single drop of rain.

Valdivino picked two velvety flowers. He gave one to Aunt Matilde and the other to Aunt Francisca.

Without paying Aunt Matilde's comment any mind, Roberto continued, They're also going to build two big plazas here, one beside the Opera House and the other in front of a pavilion, which will contain a restaurant, a bar, and a tea house that gives out onto the gardens of the cultural sector, and over there on the southern and northern sides, there between the residential areas, he said, pointing it out to us, there are going to be rows of shops and, in front of the shop windows, covered walkways bordering the tree-lined sections of the city blocks.

We looked out at the excavated holes and the mounds of dirt, trying to imagine what he was describing to us, like tourists listening to a tour guide give a description of majestic cities that have barely survived in ruins.

I heard that near the residential areas there's going to be a plot reserved for planting flowers, vegetables, and fruits, said Aunt Francisca, It's true, but that's in another sector.

When he found out that they planned to build a chapel next to the Palace of the Dawn—construction on which had yet to begin—Valdivino became interested in working there, That's what I want to do, more than anything else: build churches, that's my earthly mission, Ah, what a noble gesture, said Aunt Francisca, with her sentimental kindness, which bothered Aunt Matilde, I wonder if Mr. Bernardo Sayão remembers me, I bet he could help me get a job there.

A red ball of fire was disappearing on the horizon, and soon the golden hues began to take on a grayish tint. The colors of the immense valley were likewise cooling down, and the outlines of the hills were being erased from view, in a harmony that would have been perfect if it weren't for the gusts of wind, which carried dust into our nostrils.

I'm not sure about Matilde, but I feel like you enjoyed coming out here, whenever you'd like to come back, just let me know, said Roberto to Aunt Francisca, as if he owned the landscape himself.

When we arrived back home, Aunt Francisca commented, Valdivino is such a sensitive young man, You're easily enchanted, said Dad, objecting, And you're practically drooling over Roberto, what a pretentious ass, needled Aunt Matilde.

I was lying on the floor at the entrance to the room so that I could catch a glimpse of Aunt Francisca's striped panties, and I felt jealous over her because of Valdivino. Why was Aunt Francisca interested in Valdivino? It must be because she had heard Dad say that Valdivino liked older women. Typhoon, seeing me on the floor, came over to sniff at my face and frustrate my intentions.

I told Valdivino, said Aunt Matilde, I know a lot of women

who would be wild about dating you, don't you like Francisca?, and he got all . . . , You didn't do that, not even as a joke, are you nuts!, protested Aunt Francisca, but he's not like the other men around here, they're crude, and he's not like that, she added, while I remained lying on the floor, regarding myself as just as crude as the men of the Free City. Get out of the way, little boy, she ordered.

A few days later, after running into Dad by chance at the Oasis Bar, on Central Avenue, Paulão asked him to have a beer with him. He'd had to flee from Carmen's house naked, because she'd heard her husband coming and threw his clothes out the window. The next day, a pair of underwear was found in the street and word got around, Didn't you hear about this, Sir?, I like my women just like that, a little mature, like a delicious fruit, or at just the right age, like a fine wine. I heard that you only like women in their thirties, said Dad. No, it's just that Carmen is something special, an amazing woman, Well, I've heard tell of a different woman, Ah, word of Lucrécia's fame has gotten around to you, too, has it? Is she your girlfriend? No, I brought her here from Bahia, or rather, I didn't bring her, she was already here when I arrived, but she had worked for me back in Bahia, So, she's available? That's a subject we've got to handle with care, but for you, Sir, yes, she's available, When? Give me a couple of days, it's worth the wait, she doesn't like to meet up at the brothel, you can invite her to some hotel, I guarantee that she's the best in all the Central Plateau, but I've got something more important to discuss with you, Mr. Moacyr, I wonder if you would like to form a partnership, you'll just make the contacts, arrange for us to provide the service, and I'll take care of the rest; once you have some money put away, we can start buying more sand, trust me, we'll make a huge profit, Let me think about it, replied Dad, who was more interested in Lucrécia than any business deal.

The next day, as it started to get dark, Dad was strolling along

Second Avenue when he walked past a plump, dark-skinned, thirty-something year-old woman, who trailed in her wake a bitter perfume that mixed with the smell of gasoline from the cars. Dad turned about face and followed her distracted gait, as she zigzagged her starched and lustrous backside through the avenues. He kept on following her, strolling throughout the city, and then a few drops of rain began to fall, the first of the "cashew showers." Dad sat down, dazzled, at the table of some bar and stayed there, watching the raindrops fall and imagining Lucrécia in wet clothes, Lucrécia's wet, naked body, imagining Lucrécia in bed, Lucrécia, who had mastered all the techniques, as the engineer with green eyes had put it.

On the agreed upon date, Paulão introduced her to Dad in Olga's Bar. Dad immediately invited her to accompany him to a party, for which Roberto had managed to get him an invitation. It was to be held at the recently inaugurated Black House, a temporary structure on the south wing of the Pilot Plan. If you want, said Lucrécia.

Lucrécia had sharp eyes and revealed a specialized knowledge of useless, absurd things. Did you know that there's already a Brasília? she asked Dad as they headed out in the jeep, Yeah, that's where we're going, replied Dad, Brasília is asteroid number 293, which, if you count backwards from 1956, was discovered sixty-six years ago; that's the number six, two times, six and six, and that's not by chance; it's fifty-five kilometers in diameter, five and five. She paused, and all that could be heard was the sound of the jeep's engine and the tires in the potholes of the highway. Do you know that on the Veadeiro Plateau, in Paradise Heights in Goiás, there's a base for interplanetary spaceships? Really?, says who?, asked Dad, smiling, Why are you taking me so far out here on this road full of potholes? I thought we were going to do something else, I even brought a surprise for you, You'll like this, the president himself sometimes attends the parties at the Black

House, because the people who live there are engineers from Minas Gerais with connections to him, explained Dad, I want to meet the president, he is the Egyptian Pharaoh Akhenaten, of the eighteenth dynasty, Lucrécia claimed categorically. JK is not going to build just a city, but a civilization. The Pharoah, who governed between 1353 and 1335 B.C., created the first master-planned capital out of nothing, just like Brasília, and it was called Akhetaten.

Lucrécia's ideas aren't unfounded, thought Dad, someone had told him that JK had visited Egypt in 1930 and mentioned to some friends that the admiration he felt for Akhenaten in his childhood could have nurtured his ideal of building Brasília.

The wooden house, painted black, occupied half of a big, fenced-in lot on what would come to be Block 309 South. The doorman checked credentials through a hole in the gate and only allowed entry to those on his list.

As they went through the front door, Dad and Lucrécia saw people dancing to the sound of raucous music, as well as a dinner table overflowing with food and a chef in a tall, white hat. Roberto hadn't arrived yet, and Dad asked an engineer if he knew if JK was coming, If he shows up it won't be before one in the morning.

Lucrécia didn't want to stay, I've had enough, she said, I don't want to meet the president, That's not what you said a little while ago, I changed my mind, am I not allowed to change my mind? But after such a long trip out here . . .

On the way back, Dad put his hands on Lucrécias smooth thighs, which were smoother than anything he'd ever felt. All of her skin was just as smooth, he noted, and he had the urge to run his hands over other parts of that body. No, said Lucrécia, forcefully, and then started to cry, What is it, Lucrécia? Why does every man who lays eyes on me immediately think I'm a whore?

They were silent for the rest of the trip, with Dad not knowing how to act, until Lucrécia stopped crying. When they got close to the Free City, Lucrécia kissed Dad's face and then lowered her right hand down between his legs like a professional.

It was already past eleven when they arrived at the Brasília Hotel in the Free City. She said, Brasília will only be built once the spirits of the past decide to take part in it: Pedro Álvares Cabral, Dom Pedro I, Dom Pedro II, Epitácio Pessoa . . . All the spirits of every place and time can assemble here, did you know that? Zumbi of Palmares, Tiradentes, Getúlio Vargas, Machado de Assis, Tarsila do Amaral, Camões, the Marquis of Pombal, Fernando Pessoa, Freud, Marx, Nietzsche, Alain Kardec . . . but there must be criteria for choosing who should and who shouldn't come down here, the soul becomes adapted to the necessities of the times, and it's essential that there be a host who is already dead, someone the other souls can trust.

And who would be this host?, asked Dad jokingly, Dom Pedro II, she replied, seriously and categorically, all these spirits can come down here during a séance to guide our future.

Dad took her up to a room, and she didn't offer any resistance, just took off her clothes, without Dad even asking, and lay down on the bed, I told you, I brought you a surprise, And what is it? Not yet, come over here. She cried out in pleasure throughout the whole time they screwed. Then she cried, sobbing loudly. Again, Lucrécia?, what is it? Then she began to laugh, then laughed louder, bursting with laughter, That's just the way I am. She pulled Dad toward her, got him aroused again and opened herself to him. While Dad bent his body over hers, slowly penetrating her, she cried out, unrestrained, Give me more, give me more, Quiet, Lucrécia, don't yell so loud, In the commune I'm going to establish, there will be a new commandment: make love, as long as it doesn't cause anyone harm, said Lucrécia, instead of Mass, we should have purification festivals, like a fertility cult, don't you think?, the way the Bantu people do, You're thinking about creating a commune? I've already been a part of one, but it was strictly Christian, its members weren't willing to explore Spiritism, that's why I left; one thing's for certain, the visible world is part of a spiritual universe.

After a moment of silence, during which barking dogs could be heard, Lucrécia, still naked on the bed, resumed the conversation, Do you know what the great snake is? Dad tried to pull one of Lucrécia's hands onto his penis, This here? She pulled away, giving Dad's hand a delicate little slap, No, it's a snake with magical powers, silly, I don't know if you've ever heard of Colonel Fawcett, the man who killed the great snake and founded a community that accepts all religions, near the City of Z, between Araguaia and Xingu, the capital of civilization in Amazônia, one of the most ancient cities in the world, over seven thousand years old, a city with plazas, canals, highways, bridges, and even an astronomical observatory, did you know that Amazônia was the first region in the Americas to produce ceramics?; I've spoken with Colonel Fawcett, By telegraph or by phone? Dad asked mockingly, The colonel dematerialized at the age of ninety, Lucrécia replied sorrowfully, it would be best to attract the survivors of his community to Brasília, because Brasília is special, do you know that on the route of the extraterrestrials, Brasília Station is the seventh stop? The day you come across an extraterrestrial, introduce me to it, said Dad, still poking fun. I came here because I have been called, this is going to be the capital of the third millennium and the Aquarian civilization, Where did you learn these things?, asked Dad, who was starting to lose desire for Lucrécia, even while whetting his curiosity about her. Lucrécia merely replied, I bet you don't know that the solar system was already turned inside out when it was formed more than four and a half billion years ago, there was a movement of matter from the inside out, to a frozen region out past the orbit of Pluto, and more than a tenth of the matter that comets are made of comes from this inner region of the solar system, where the Earth is located. Lucrécia covered herself with the bed sheet, Today is special, she said, and then asked Dad to leave the room, to wait at the door until she called for him.

When he came back in, she was still lying on the bed, covered by the sheet, Come here, uncover me. As he pulled back the sheet, Dad saw Lucrécia's body, and there were large white flowers on her mons pubis, What is that?, said Dad, laughing, They're angel trumpets, *datura suaveolens*, they're the surprise I was telling you about.

She grabbed Dad's head, pulled it toward her, and put his mouth near her pubis, I just rubbed it with the nectar of joy, she said. Then she completely lowered Dad's head between her legs, and Dad just lay there, inert and intoxicated, enjoying the touch of Lucrécia's pubic hair and the wetness of her pubis, That nectar is a balm made from a mixture of herbs and angel trumpets, boiled in oil; those flowers, when they're hanging from branches, look like miniature chandeliers, but be careful, they can kill you; I'm going to teach you to lick them and they'll bring you wisdom, a different way of seeing things and a knowledge of the sacred, because you still need to learn that we must worship all the gods, as well the Earth, other heavenly bodies, time, the planets, and animals.

Dad felt uncomfortable, he couldn't screw while thinking about sacred things, screwing had to be dirty, it was filthy, and didn't have anything to do with the worship of gods or heavenly bodies, but the flowers must have had some effect on him, for he began to feel, as he entered Lucrécia, a pleasure unlike any he'd ever known.

Then a profound fear came upon him, he felt chills and considered bolting from the room, as if he were escaping a prison, How much do I owe you?, he asked Lucrécia, You're a sensitive man, I don't want your money right now, I'll need you in another cycle of the cosmos, I want to count on you for that, do you promise? Depends, what is it about? No, it doesn't depend on anything, promise me or you'll never see me again, I promise, but what if I'm unable to pay? You'll be able to, you just have to want to, so tell me that you want to. Dad said yes, knowing that he wasn't taking on any obligation and had nothing to lose.

For the hasty blog-reader who would like to skip ahead in the story, I must clearly state that it isn't yet time to rush that far ahead, for now we'll just move along to the next day, when Lucrécia crossed paths with Dad on Second Avenue in the Free City. She pretended that she didn't know him, which he thought proper, he didn't want to be familiar with her in public right there where everyone knew him.

Dad walked past banks, the offices of airlines, stores that sold wooden wardrobes, ones that sold new furniture and others that were packed with second-hand furniture, pension houses, dormitories, hotels, bars, restaurants, and small shops with window displays filled with shirts, pants, blouses, dresses, and pink and blue panties, he heard a phonograph from inside a shop that was blasting a well-known English-language song, he looked at the houses of every size, color, and shape, buildings placed snug one beside the next, right at the edge of the wide avenue, he stared at the plastic belts, bags, buckets, and washbasins hanging in front of another store, and felt that the world was going to be made of plastic, but also that wealth was definitively arriving in the Free City. He didn't have anything to lose by becoming partners with Paulão, Dad concluded, he just didn't want to have anything to do with the business of brothels and prostitutes.

*Fifth Night:*
*Building the Mystery*


On the fifth night, enclosed within four dingy white walls, Dad was inspired, and we almost didn't sleep at all. Neither the disgust I felt from being in that fetid place, nor the awful smells that invaded my nostrils hindered me from remembering many things from the year of 1958, which he reminisced about with intense emotion. Back then, the Free City and I were both growing bigger, and I'd go on walks with Typhoon throughout the entire area delimited by Vicente Pires Creek to the east and Deep Creek to the south, by the three rows of four long rectangular blocks of houses, which were separated by the avenues, and by the three blocks to the south, which formed a curve around the plaza of the Don Bosco church.

Dad was becoming wealthy through his partnership with Paulão and, in proportion to how much wealth he accrued, he was able to become wealthier still. He went on business trips to Rio, Belo Horizonte, and São Paulo, shopped in sophisticated stores, brought presents back for me, Aunt Francisca, and Aunt Matilde, and gave money to Aunt Francisca so she could replace the baubles on the tables in the living room with something nicer. On the other hand, wealth brought him more worries and responsibilities, and he became circumspect, perhaps because he couldn't fail in his objective to make profits, which demanded concentration, I only had one hundred and twenty thousand *cruzeiros* in the bank, he told me, shut in between four walls, that's what I started with, I figured out how to quickly multiply that money through work, through imagination . . . Think about that: your house and all that you'll inherit, Francisca as well, came from that first hundred and twenty thousand *cruzeiros*.

I didn't yet know that I would also inherit his enormous debt, nor that one day I would lose the house where I'm currently writing, before I was ready to move. I even started to believe that money, which shapes behavior, and the social status Dad was able to attain before the disaster that confined him within those four walls had added some sweetness to his character. I didn't want to start another fight with Dad, to remind him that perhaps imagination—not just his, but also, and above all, Paulão's—more than work, was what made him rich, If I could have seen the future, of course, there are things I wouldn't have done.

I didn't sense any repentance or preoccupations of a moral order in this observation, Dad was merely lamenting the fact that he had lost a part of the money he'd earned as a result of the manner in which he'd earned it, But one thing is certain: I knew where I wanted to get and I worked hard to get there, overcoming all obstacles in my way; the trick is to start earning decent money, after that everything falls into place, he continued, you can take risks, the bank will give you a loan, people trust you, you establish a name for yourself, you start to get commissions, you're praised for being a bold entrepreneur, politicians come calling, if there's a lot of money no one is going to notice your mistakes, and, when they do, you can neutralize it with charitable works; I was very successful, and what eventually happened to me was the dirty work of one of my enemies.

Everything began with his partnership with Paulão, I thought, just as his relationship with Lucrécia had started with Paulão. He would get together with her every so often and had begun to develop feelings for her. One day, he had the crazy idea that he should set her up in her own house and make her into his exclusive lover. I needed a stable relationship, Dad told me between four walls, I wanted to get married, it was a notion that suddenly occurred to me, I felt alone, but there was a lack of women. One woman I dated seemed too nutty—although she was a young lady from a good family—and less trustworthy than Lucrécia, I even started to think that she might be a streetwalker herself. Another was too modern, part of the subversive youth culture of that era. There was Mr. Ferreira's daughter, always admired as she walked into church in her flashy dresses, but her eyes were too big, she always looked as if she was frightened, and she was kind of a dummy. There were others who were even respectable, but they were all plain, poorly dressed, or just downright ugly.

There was only one who was, perhaps, worth it: Aunt Francisca herself, but she would never accept a proposal from Dad; no, Dad had already blown that chance. He tried to imagine a woman who would give him pleasure, who was good company, who could lift him out of his melancholic daily grind, and surprise him with interesting stories. The only one left was Lucrécia, whom it was inadvisable to marry. He carried out his plan by building, on the other side of the city, a second house. He'd go over there every once in a while, dreaming his dreams of grandeur, and then he also started to take Lucrécia there. The first time, he asked her to bring her tarot cards and read his palm, You'll go far in life, very far, said Lucrécia, And in love?, he asked, There's a woman who is waiting for you, Couldn't it be you, wouldn't you like to come out here, settle down here, so we can meet up every day, without anybody bothering us? Lucrécia didn't respond. He didn't want to let go of her, he liked Lucrécia's soft skin, Lucrécia's smell, Lucrécia's wackiness, which drew him out of his seriousness and the world around him, and sometimes he desired her so intensely in the middle of the night that he could no longer stand to be apart.

I knew of the existence of Lucrécia and discovered the house where Dad took her. I used to look at Dad and Aunt Francisca on the couch in the living room, both of them sad and silent, Aunt Francisca knitting, concentrating on the movement of the needles, and Dad reading his newspapers or else leaning his head back and closing his eyes. I always saw them like that, and it never crossed my mind that something might be going on between the two of them, not between him and Aunt Francisca, Aunt Francisca was no Lucrécia. That's why it was so shocking when, one day, I arrived home from school and saw—through a crack in the bedroom door—Dad on top of Aunt Francisca, her struggling at the edge of the bed, still dressed, with her thighs spread open, him stumbling around afterwards, his breath smelling of alcohol, kicking the door open right into my face.

I thought that I should protect her by telling what not only I, but all the neighborhood kids knew, that Dad met up with Lucrécia in that house on the other side of town, and the sense of power was stronger than the regret I felt when, to my relief, Aunt Francisca definitively broke things off with Dad after an enormous argument, the reasons for which I didn't understand completely, but certainly Lucrécia must have been behind those motives that weren't quite clear to me.

From what Dad told me within four walls, I suppose that, if he wasn't kicked out, he at least felt as if he'd been kicked out of the house, and so he went to find Lucrécia, he wanted her to move definitively to the house where they had their *rendezvous*, but she seemed different, distant, receiving his visit as if she were a psychologist in her office, attempting to analyze him, explain his behavior, and, refusing his pleas, telling him that no, she wasn't the woman who was waiting for him. Devastated, Dad didn't give up, he spotted a ray of hope when she said, Let's spend a week apart, then come get me one night, I want to know if you love me, because I feel like you don't really love me, like you just want a woman who will keep you company at times like these.

He came to get her, took her to the house that he'd built for their trysts, and, under the faint light from the gas lamp, Lucrécia's body grew larger as she took her clothes off layer-by-layer, her breasts swelled, her buttocks were like two great arches, still firm and nicely-shaped, Dad felt fragile in front of that majestic flesh, but Lucrécia knew how to rekindle his desire, and he gave himself over to the heat of her body and her skillful fingers and lips, and moments later he was gliding inside her, exploring and abusing the possibilities of that body in all its furrows with complete freedom, the way she arched her back and swayed her hips and the flexibility of her joints made it seem as if she'd gone mad, the spring mattress never stopped shaking, whack whack whack, impacts of desire hammering away at that body, harder, ever harder, and faster, tender filth spoken in whispered, vulgar words, which further aroused Lucrécia's mouth, hands, and thighs, between which flowed a slippery pleasure, and he wanted to squeeze her, fuse his body to hers, all other bodies were contained in hers, Aunt Francisca's, Mr. Ferreira's daughter's, and he powerfully hammered away at all of them at once, heedlessly and without fear of injuring her, he sunk his fingernails into her until her bounteous flesh began to bleed, he sucked hungrily at her breasts, bit her nipples, she screamed, screamed louder, he figured that all of the Free City could hear them, but they didn't care, he was sweating, disoriented, lost, broken, almost unconscious on the bed.

That night Lucrécia opened up to him, about how she'd been raped as a little girl, how she ran away from her home in the *sertão* region of Bahia to end up in a red-light district in the capital city, Salvador, how she had given up that life and now only made dates with him, and Dad replied that he wanted her forever, that she should move into the house, that they'd be happy.

Those big belly laughs of Lucrécia, those crying outbreaks,

none of those took place that night. Dad thought that he had finally found serenity in his relationship with Lucrécia, that tranquility was possible in the love between people who were merely lovers, that below the turbulent waves of passion there lay waters that were denser and deeper, wherein the heart could still beat, We have a little place of our own here, I want to be here with you everyday.

It was a Tuesday, and he didn't see Lucrécia again the whole week. Dad looked everywhere for her, in Placa da Mercedes, in the little house that Paulão had bought for her . . . He walked along the avenues, hoping to come upon her the way he had before, going from one side of the city to the other, and spent a number of nights waiting for her in vain, alone, in the house that he had planned to share with her.

One fine day, Paulão brought him a note from Lucrécia and the news that she had gone back to Bahia, of her own accord. The note simply said, I don't deserve you.

Dad felt as if the ground beneath his feet had been pulled out from under him and that he might suddenly fall into an abyss. Wandering the avenues, he no longer looked like the superior man that he had been before. Paulão had perhaps been the one responsible for Lucrécia's departure, and it was possible that she hadn't even left, Dad didn't trust him, he thought that he should dissolve his partnership with him, but he feared that his own business ventures would deteriorate. He suffered from insomnia, and in his sleepless nights Aunt Francisca appeared to him as his salvation.

To the devil with you, Mister, Aunt Francisca told him when he tried to come back, What do you think I am, you think you can come sniffing after me just because some hussy abandoned you, everyone in town knows about that, And Francisca was completely right, Dad confessed to me between those four walls.

What sustained Dad during that difficult time—or so

I deduced from what he told me on that fifth night—was his dream of greatness, a dream that had one side planted on the ground and the other elevated in the air, and if the ground happened to become unstable and no longer supported him, well, he'd fly, he would get back to his first and foremost mission there in the Central Plateau, the door that Bernardo Sayão had opened for him back in those very early days. He hadn't been able to accompany visitors as he would have liked, not even Júlia Kubitschek, a teacher and the mother of the president, who was to arrive that January, in 1958, but when he found out that Sayão had just been asked by the president to build the Belém-Brasília highway, he offered to accompany him for the start of the work, and not only because he was in need of a spiritual retreat. He missed Sayão's high spirits, his constant activity, and Dad knew that he was the right person for that undertaking, since he was the one who had made, back in 1949, the first sketches for the highway that would connect Anápolis to Belém, in the state of Pará, and he also knew that the president, according to what people were saying, chose Sayão for impossible tasks because he considered him naturally good and instinctually courageous. He had listened with admiration to the account of a conversation between the president and Sayão, Let's tear down this jungle and unite the country from north to south, JK is to have said, This is the happiest day of my life, after I build this highway I can die, Sayão is said to have replied, and he even repeated, On the day that the highway is finished, I can depart forever, for I will have given my best effort to our cause. Like Sayão, Dad also had a liking for great challenges and danger, he would swim across rivers with him, like Sayão he would drive tractors at the edge of a cliff, with him he would make hedgehopping inspection flights above the jungle in his single-engine plane, and would tame the wild forests at some point along the 2,240 kilometer trajectory of the highway that would connect Brasília to Belém, in the state of

Pará, a thruway that would make up part of the Trans-Brazilian Highway, which started in Santana do Livramento, in the state of Rio Grande do Sul. Dad asked to accompany Sayão on the construction of the highway, not because he wanted to usher in progress, bring about agrarian reform, or colonize the interior with agricultural settlements, as Sayão did, but because he wanted to record the endeavor for history, and he arrived in time to witness Sayão set up his trailer near Porangatu underneath an enormous pequi tree, light a campfire, and put some wooden boxes out front as a place to receive visitors.

A reader of this blog asked me, along these lines, if it is true that Dad accompanied Sayão on the day when his single-engine plane lost altitude after taking off and got stuck in a treetop. Dad said that he had and told the story often, adding the detail that he and Sayão easily shimmied down the trunk of the tree, and that, once on the ground, Sayão merely inquired, unconcernedly, How am I going to get that damned thing down from those branches? I have no doubt, however, that herein is revealed my Dad's mythomaniacal side, and that the true source of this story was JK, in one of his books, in which I found the same version of the story.

I'm not going to narrate in detail the three short trips that Dad made into the jungle, because it would take me too far away from the Free City, as well as from Lucrécia, Valdivino, Aunt Matilde, and Aunt Francisca, the main characters, without whom this narrative could not proceed. Nor do I intend to analyze Dad's feelings as he went into the forest, or count his heartbeats as he encountered wild animals in the foggy night, ever lamenting the falling-out he'd had with Aunt Francisca and thinking of how much he missed Lucrécia. Suffice it to say, for now, it felt good for him to meet up with Sayão again and be a witness to one more important creation: the birth of the highway that would cut the map of Brazil from north to south like a sword. He had always liked geography, and geography itself was out there in the density of the forests and abundance of rivers, but, more precisely, the geography of the country was being redrawn out there. He had always admired the great conquests that he read about in history books, and the highway was no less a feat than any of them, not even those of Alexander the Great. That was what really moved him, and what even allowed him, after a few weeks, to forget about Lucrécia and Aunt Francisca. Those who first met him out in the jungle—like the blog-reader who, up to this point, is the only one who identified himself as being a native of Ceres—got the impression that he was a taciturn, circumspect man, a man of few words, but with enough courage to confront the jungle, without fear of mosquitoes or snakes. He felt that he was doing something fulfilling and carrying out a mission as true as Valdivino's, a double mission, because if Valdivino had the sole mission of building churches, Dad had two: bear witness to those beginnings and record them for history, and get rich with the opportunities that presented themselves—he told me that very thing between four walls. He had gone through many difficulties, life hadn't been easy for him, but a highway was now opening up for him, a highway for his life, one that was long, but true, just like the Belém-Brasília. Pain and satisfaction, fear, shock, and attraction to the unknown were all mixed together in his conscience, and this admixture was provided to him by the forest; the atmosphere that was enveloping him completely, affecting both his mood and emotional state, was the atmosphere of the forest itself.

I didn't know whether Dad would ever come back home or if, upon returning from the jungle, he would go on living in that other house. If you want, you can go live there with him, Aunt Matilde told me one day, or you can live in both houses and spend one day here and the next over there. It rained a lot in the Free City, and Aunt Matilde reminded me that it was probably raining much more out in the forest. How could the thunder and lightening be any bigger than they already were? How could there be more rain than all that rain that was beating down on us? I imagined enormous running faucets in the sky above the jungle, above Dad and Bernardo Sayão, and the two of them having to escape from all that water in canoes. The days were drawing out, gladdened here and there by frequent visits from Valdivino and Roberto. Aunt Francisca had long conversations with Valdivino, even longer than when Dad used to be there, Valdivino lamenting the fact that he hadn't gone into the forest with Dad, since he wished to meet up with Bernardo Sayão again and missed Dad.

Both Aunt Matilde and Aunt Francisca started to have more to talk about after Dad left, or perhaps it was Roberto and Valdivino who became more inspired. I do know that the conversations lasted longer, and that I didn't always manage to hear them as well as I wanted. Sometimes, even in the rain, Aunt Matilde would go out with Roberto, with no set time to come back home. When they went out on foot, with umbrella in hand, I would follow them from afar, watching the movements of their bodies, their embraces and kisses. The city had its own smell, the smell of damp earth after the heat of the day, a fresh smell, of the wood of the houses, of the foliage of the shrubs. It's better like this, this way the house doesn't get so dusty, Aunt Francisca would say. But when the rains came, Aunt Francisca—if she wasn't working, that is, since she still held the position of caterer at the SWAS restaurant—became a prisoner of the house. I'd often see her figure fixed in the window, or else she'd spend hours on the accordion or with her crochet, displaying her great skill with the needles. Sometimes we'd go out with an umbrella to do the shopping, and I'd accompany her along the avenues, keeping us clear of the enormous puddles and the mud that was splattered by passing cars. We'd come back home satisfied with our little adventures, clean off our shoes when we arrived, and

Aunt Francisca would make me a snack while we discussed what we'd seen out in the streets and shops.

Aunt Francisca paid close attention to the sunsets whenever the rain let up and would point out to me all the colors that filled the sky, as if she had painted them herself. At night she'd sit down with her accordion, and I would silently listen to her, sometimes her only spectator, other times with some of my friends, who also listened with awe as she played, considering her to be a great musician and putting off the intelligence and humor of our conversations until later.

Unlike Aunt Matilde, Aunt Francisca never raised her voice. Her politeness and good manners had been with her from the crib on, it was something that came natural to her, that didn't seem to have been learned, that didn't arise from rules, but rather from her temperament alone. She didn't think she was better than other people, nor did she have the pretence of originality. She was conventional in the way she dressed, thought, and spoke, which, at the time, seemed to me like lofty qualities—the opposite of what I later came to believe. If she suffered, she suffered silently and extracted lessons and wisdom from her suffering. If the incident with Dad had troubled her or even devastated her, she didn't show it. I saw her as a beautiful crystal vase that had shattered, but whose pieces were put back together in their rightful places in such a way that the fissures couldn't be seen, and, yet, in spite of that, all you had to do was shine a little light on the crystal to realize that it was in a fragile state.

She was not as extroverted as Aunt Matilde, who seemed only to live through her relationships with the radio and with other people. I won't go as far as to say that Aunt Matilde was superficial, dissolute, or that she lacked firm principles, since just because a surface is full of colors doesn't mean that that's all there is to it, and also because I'm not going to restrict what I write to the mere perceptions of the child I was: I gradually came to understand Aunt Matilde's nonconformism and, from my point of view today, even when applied to the past, I am incapable of painting her portrait in dark tones.

When he returned from the forest, Dad would sometimes come to see me and ask after Aunt Francisca. I don't want to see him, not even from afar, not while he's still conducting business with Paulão, she said to Aunt Matilde one day. But when I'd catch her at the window or lost in thought, or even playing solitaire with a deck of cards, I imagined that it was because she missed Dad, and I began to feel guilty for telling her about Dad's second house.

On his next trip out to the jungle, at the end of May, Dad helped open up a small clearing, where they built a little shelter next to a tiny cassava patch, which had been planted by farmhands from the Northeast, and a well, where they could get drinking water and rinse off using a hollow gourd. Dad felt suffocated by the trees around the shelter, but this time he worked up the courage to go out into the jungle, taking footpaths that the highway workers had blazed, accompanied by one of their number, a guy from Ceará who already knew those woods well. Dad noted that sometimes there were enormous tree trunks blocking the paths. They toppled over right there, dead, and remained there, to be consumed by time, yet tufts of green were already emerging from them, life in constant renewal.

Was there some order in that chaos of trunks and leaves, with such varying distance from one to the next and so many different species? The trees were gathered there like confused giants, on whose legs hung parasites and webs of branches, like curtains that filtered the already weakened light through layers of leaves. The sun could barely be detected, hidden behind those lush, green structures.

If the trees of the Central Plain only knew the rainy season and the dry season, the trees in that forest, permanently covered in their verdant vestments, knew nothing of the desert or the dry season, nor even of the changing seasons. Beneath the carpet of dead leaves, down where the snakes slithered about, the green extended over the ground and out to every side, dense and vibrant, in stark contrast to the dryness of the savannah, to which Dad had already become accustomed.

They had to be on the lookout for snakes. When he saw his first one, Dad thought about Valdivino, but the one we'd seen on our hunt near the Descoberto seemed harmless compared to the ones they came across in great number out there in the jungle, twisted around branches like rings or curling up in the leaves, compared with the deadly bushmaster or the giant sucuri, the "great snake" that Colonel Fawcett had killed, the one that Lucrécia had described as having magic powers, and which, as Dad came to learn out there, could swallow a man, squeezing him and crushing his bones to dust before eating him piecemeal. As he hiked, he always kept in mind the possibility that he would be forced to take an antidotal serum or simply burn the location of the bite without remorse.

If in the Central Plateau he felt abandoned by the vast horizons, out there he thought himself crushed by their absence. Instead of getting lost in a boundless nothingness, his range of vision only reached the vines, which served as a trampoline for capuchin monkeys and woolly monkeys. On a rare occasion, the light would appear on high, filtered by leaves and branches, vaporously projected on the trunks of the trees, giving life to the colors of the orchids and butterflies. On a rare occasion, a majestic palm tree would reveal its clusters of açaí. We have to be careful not to catch the *chagas* disease, the *barbeiro* bug lives here in these branches, said Dad's companion, taking all the lyricism out of that poetry. Then came insects in great quantity, hordes of mosquitoes ready to attack. Dad was bit by a midge. If it's not *chagas*, it'll be malaria, he thought. Caravans of ants cut leaves and carried them single-file to their ant mounds in incessant toil, like the workers of the Belém-Brasília.

He had always felt at ease with geography, his favorite subject in school, he'd studied rivers and their watersheds, forests, memorizing the names of their fauna and flora, and traveled all over the surface of the Earth in his imagination, but nothing that he had imagined compared with what he saw in the forest in reality, which surpassed all intuition or knowledge.

Nobody here has enough memory to store that many names of trees, fruits, and animals, said the guy from Ceará. They saw a giant anteater and coati, Don't you like to hunt, Sir?, because out here there's no end of things to hunt, there are tapir, paca, agouti, deer, and armadillo, you just have to watch out for the jaguars. Dad recalled the first time that we laid eyes on Valdivino. Could it be true that he'd saved us, that he'd scared off a jaguar? Jaguars are dangerous when they're with their cubs or in heat, going around with the male at their side, said Dad, as if he were a specialist on the subject, remembering what Valdivino had explained to him, Ah, so you already know about it, right?

Dad couldn't stay away from his business interests for a long time and didn't want to miss the inauguration of the Palace of the Dawn, at which hundreds of illustrious visitors would convene.

When he got back from his trip to the jungle, I noticed that something started to happen again, I guess distance serves to separate those who aren't destined to stay together and, in other cases, brings those who can't stay apart back together again. Thus it was that Aunt Francisca didn't refuse Dad's visits this time, she even served him sweets that couldn't have been prepared the night before just by chance, and she didn't object to him leaving a pair of macaws and a monkey in our backyard, with the condition that he wouldn't just abandon them there and that he'd stop by every day to take care of them.

A day before the inauguration of the Palace, Dad managed to

get into the lobby of the Tourism Hotel, where JK was listening to the championship game of the World Cup on the radio. I'll never forget that day, June 29, 1958, when Brazil became the world champion for the first time, beating Sweden 5-2. I remember the broadcasters calling each goal and each firework that went off, at which Typhoon barked endlessly. I remember the dribbles and passes of the players, of Garrincha, Didi, Pelé, Vavá, I remember Gilmar's defensive stops, which I visualized through the lively descriptions of the radio announcer. On the radio, the game always seemed faster and more chock-full of dribbling than any game seen in person.

The next day, Dad got his hands on a copy of the telegram from the president to the new champions and soon copied it onto the first page of one of his notebooks:

> It was with deep emotion that we received, in Brasília, where we just finished listening to the dazzling performance of the Brazilian team, the great news of the victory, which was anxiously hoped for. I would like to confess the joy that at this moment is sweeping across the entire nation . . . Please accept the warmest congratulations from the president of Brazil and send our greetings to the valiant Swedes, who conducted themselves with such gallantry and hospitality.

Remember this date, João, Dad told me, and not because of the World Cup, but because of all this that's being inaugurated in Brasília, and then he mentioned the Avenue of Nations, the Monumental Axis Highway, the Brasília Palace Hotel, which had already accommodated President Stroessner on May 2, as well as the paved highway from Brasília to Anápolis, whose construction Dad had hoped to accompany, not as an engineer, nor as a doctor, but as a note-taker, at the side of Bernardo Sayão. And there was also going to be the first transfer of diplomatic credentials, to the Portuguese ambassador. The date should be remembered chiefly because of the Palace of the Dawn, the only large building, together with the Brasília Palace Hotel, that had already been completed, a building that should have been finished in March, but which was going to be inaugurated on the day after the World Cup victory, that is, on June 30, 1958.

Years later, in 1966, when I left home on bad terms with Dad because of the stories I'd heard about him and Valdivino, because Aunt Francisca didn't want to believe me, or even because I had taken after Aunt Matilde in my political affinities, in opposition to the rest of the house, I recalled what Dad had said about the Palace as I read a sentence from Toynbee: "The creation of Brasília is an act of human affirmation that constitutes an event in the history of humanity . . . The Palace of the Dawn broke with all of the traditional columns of the last five thousand years."

Aunt Matilde was critical of all those inaugurations, I'm growing more and more convinced that this Brasília project is useless, a brutal waste of money, Then why did you move here?, Aunt Francisca would ask, Just for the money, look, I won't deny it, but this is certainly a waste of resources in such a poor country, and on top of that they're building everything out of the most expensive stuff they can find; just imagine how many hospitals and schools they could build with the money that was poured into that Palace of the Dawn, the capital should really just stay in Rio.

As a result of these opinions, Aunt Matilde had some quarrels with Roberto, and also disagreed with him about the choice of the new Treasury Minister, although they agreed in their criticism of the previous one. It's been twenty-eight months since the president appointed this José Maria Alkmin as Treasury Minister, and the economy has gone from bad to worse, she said, I agree with that, it's fiscal chaos, the deficit has increased on the balance sheets, he said, strengthening her argument, It's a disaster, concluded Aunt Matilde, And another thing, said Dad, joining the conversation, a dollar used to be worth seventy *cruzeiros*, now it's worth a hundred and forty-seven, But with the appointment of Lucas Lopes, things are going to change, asserted Roberto, he believes in foreign investment to increase revenues, the country needs industrialization and development, then the automobile industry will arrive here, He sold himself to foreign monopolies, that part's true, said Aunt Matilde in disagreement, he should be strengthening domestic industries, not bringing foreign capital into the country.

Aunt Francisca sometimes listened to these arguments and would get so upset about the disagreements that she'd use any pretext, skillfully deviating the conversation, to achieve harmony among them all on the topic of how the dessert tasted or the beauty of the full moon or even the possibility that it would rain the next day.

Closed in between four walls, on that fifth night, Dad told me that he hadn't been able to get invited to the inauguration of the Palace of the Dawn, but that days later the president had some friends over, including the small group surrounding Niemeyer, and Roberto, who was connected to that group, extended invitations to Dad and Aunt Matilde. The blog-reader who had previously insisted that I include a few more names and dates has now informed me, citing well-known sources, that Milton Prates, as well as Rochinha and Juca Chaves—who were frequent guests of the president—would certainly have figured among those present, in addition to Dilermando Reis, who brought his guitar to the Palace and played his old waltzes, Bené Nunes, who performed his melodies on the piano, and César Prates, who intoned sentimental songs. I'm not certain about this, and I recommend that the reader who is interested in this type of detail consult those well-known sources.

In that relaxed atmosphere, in which JK even danced a samba to the rhythms of guitar and piano, Dad once more spoke to him about the notebooks he was working on so that they might serve as a source for the history of the construction of Brasília, And, if you prefer, Sir, even as a source for your Golden Book, and then he told the president that, during that very month of July in 1958, when the writer John Dos Passos—who had written about Bernardo Sayão in 1948 for *Life Magazine*—came back to Brazil and was searching in vain for him in Brasília, he, Dad, had been one of the sources that passed along new facts to Dos Passos about the expeditions of that modern pioneer into the Amazonian jungle. And then JK promised him, I'm going to request that you join my press committee this August, during the visits of José Mora, the Secretary General of the Organization of American States, Foster Dulles, the American Secretary of State, and also a legation of members of the Japanese parliament.

Come August, seeing as no one ever came to get him, Dad resolved to introduce himself to the press committee, and by chance he ran into an acquaintance there, Miguel Andrade, from Minas Gerais, a short, skinny old man, with big ears and sad eyes. Since the chair of the committee wasn't there, he settled for telling an advisor to the advisor to the committee chair that he had come at the recommendation of the president himself. No, there was no record of the president proposing that he accompany any of the visiting authorities, and some of the visits that Dad mentioned had already taken place. Miguel Andrade then mentioned to Dad that he had been put in charge of picking up the poet Elizabeth Bishop from the airport, but that he'd failed to meet up with her, But tomorrow the writer Aldous Huxley is going to arrive here with a number of other people, and they're all going to stay at the Brasília Palace Hotel.

It was an opportunity sent straight from heaven. Around noon on Saturday on August 16, 1958, a date recorded in one of the

"Onward" notebooks, a hot, clear day during the dry season, Dad witnessed the arrival, at the Brasília Palace Hotel, of a number of cars carrying more than forty men and women, and the lobby of the hotel, which had been deserted up to that point, was filled with laughter and conversation, with women in sack dresses of the latest fashion and men in dark pinstripe suits, who had all come in on a chartered flight from São Paulo, invited guests for one of the almost weekly banquets and balls thrown by the president for groups from Rio, São Paulo, Belo Horizonte, Porto Alegre, and other cities. The president was also set to arrive for the party, someone mentioned to Dad—one of the two hundred and twenty-five trips he would make to Brasília in 1957 and 1958, almost ten a month, first in a DC-3, then in the spacious, comfortable four-engine Viscount.

Ten minutes after the group from São Paulo, Huxley arrived. Elegantly tall and slender, so white he was almost yellow, in a white sport coat that contrasted with the dark suits and ties that the Paulistas were wearing for the winter in Brasília, he was accompanied by his Italian wife, Laura. Short and blonde, with greenish-gray eyes, a Polaroid camera slung over her shoulder, and nicely made-up, she looked to be much younger than him and, in fact, Dad later found out that she was twenty years younger. They were later joined by the writer Antonio Callado, the Polish-Brazilian architect Maya Osser, an employee from the Ministry of External Relations, and, soon after the others arrived, the poet Elizabeth Bishop.

Dad wondered whether he should introduce himself right away, but when he learned from the Ministry employee that they were going to visit the Palace of the Dawn after lunch, he stuck around to accompany them. The Huxleys and writer Antonio Callado left in the Lincoln convertible that the president had made available for illustrious visitors.

Identifying himself as a member of the president's press

committee, Dad was able to climb aboard the cream-colored minibus that had come to take the rest of the group, including the poet Elizabeth Bishop, but a guard at the entrance to the Palace consulted a list and refused them all entry. They had to go back to the hotel to sort out the confusion, before being driven back to the Palace. Dad preferred to wait for them at the hotel, for he knew that his name still wouldn't be on the list of people authorized for entry.

It was the first time that he'd explored the interior of the Brasília Palace Hotel. If instead of Dad, Roberto had been there, I would certainly have to include here a detailed description of the Palace of the Dawn, but Dad only glimpsed it from one angle, and from afar, and, therefore, I don't need to jot down anything more than his perception of the play of light and shadow on the bold, white shapes, intensified by the afternoon sun, and of the columns that he so admired. At the back of the Brasília Palace Hotel, there was space for a still nonexistent garden, bordered by some shoddy buildings used by the hotel employees. Dad went up to the dining room, at the end of which one could see an enormous swimming pool, which was still empty at the time; a photograph of that pool was sent to me by a blog-reader and serves to help me complement Dad's memory with details about its oval shape and blue tiles. On the same floor, behind a black wall, there was a bar and a lobby, where noisy background music could be heard.

By chance, Dad ran into the Countess Tarnowska there, as well as her beautiful dark-eyed daughter, who was in blue jeans and a khaki shirt. The countess, with a straw hat on her head and white scarf wrapped around her neck, was also wearing blue jeans. They talked about the fires in the Free City. A day earlier, a bank next to the countess's movie theater had caught fire. She'd been scared at first, but fortunately the fire hadn't spread. I went there to see *And God Created Woman*, with Brigitte Bardot, said

Dad, to which the countess replied, Picture this, one day during a showing of that movie, when it got to the nude scene, Brigitte had barely unbuttoned a button when the projectionist stopped the film and announced: We request that women and young ladies please leave and wait outside. That's the way it is, only men can look at naked women in the Free City, joked Dad.

The Huxleys and their entourage finally returned from the Palace of the Dawn. One of them mentioned that they'd seen the magnolia tree, still just a meter tall, that Foster Dulles, the American Secretary of State, had recently planted in the gardens in front of the Palace.

Happy and charming, the countess greeted Maya—the young Polish woman—effusively, spoke to everyone else in English that sounded perfect to Dad—who could barely make himself understood in that tongue, which all the others there had mastered—and later invited the whole group out for a drink at her hotel, the Santos Dumont, in the Free City. Why don't you come along, too?, she said to Dad.

It was starting to get dark when they arrived in the Free City. Since he'd only seen it from the outside, Dad had never taken notice of how elegant the Santos Dumont Hotel was. It was a short building, like so many others in the Free City, with metal chairs along the narrow cement entryway, but its interior elegance filled with joy the eyes of those who entered. This looks like a Greenwich Village bar, said Elizabeth Bishop, referring to the ample, ten meter-wide room, with a bamboo bar, vibrant, fresh colors, scarlet red tablecloths on the tables, black chairs, and red and green frames around the windows, and atop the hi-fi, which was playing classical music, records by Villa-Lobos, Stravinsky, and Bartok.

Tables were pushed together. Countess Tarnowksa, who had arrived a little earlier and had quickly bathed, appeared in a patterned Indian dress with a rolled-up bandana around her neck, offered us whisky sours and orange juice, and introduced us to a Polish guest, who was stout and blonde, My daughter and I went hunting with him, the trip lasted three weeks, Where did you go?, asked Huxley, To the west of here. Then Dad said, I go hunting sometimes, too, out to the São Bartolomeu and near the Descoberto, Oh, no, we went much further out, we wanted to hunt jaguars, but we ended up getting deer, it was the first time my daughter had ever been hunting, and she also managed to kill a dozen caimans, we just adore living in this place, you know? I was out in the middle of the jungle with Bernado Sayão, but that place is frightening, I still haven't built up the courage to hunt out there, said Dad, Are there snakes around here?, Elizabeth Bishop wanted to know, They've seen two-headed snakes in Feia Lake, and even boa constrictors, but anacondas are only commonly found out by the Samambaia and São Bartolomeu rivers, Dad informed them.

Later, they walked through the Free City and went into a narrow, empty bar, where a lone customer was drinking beer, I've never been to this one, said Dad. Dad related these details to me, enclosed within four walls, but I, too, vaguely remember those figures that arrived there, because I lingered in the entryway of that bar until Dad told me to go back home. All of them took notice of the young woman with Renaissance features, bleach-blonde hair, and an audaciously low-cut black sweater, sulking in a corner of the room. She looks like a mermaid coming out of her grotto, said Elizabeth Bishop.

Near her, on the counter, two little rosy-cheeked children looked at the group with curiosity, and every now and then the young woman's husband took a look around the room, sticking his head out between the flowery curtains, as Elizabeth Bishop pointed out. The young woman didn't speak English, but she could stammer out some French. She was the daughter of Lebanese immigrants, she said. *Aimez-vous vivre ici?* Laura Huxley asked her, *Je le déteste! Mais mon mari, oui, il l'aime bien.* They were both from São Paulo, the husband had adapted to life out there, but she was dying of longing for her hometown.

On the way back to the Brasília Palace Hotel, Dad, who had caught a ride with the group, asked: So what do you all think of Brasília? It reminds me of those depressing landscapes around Madrid, replied Elizabeth Bishop—mentioning that it wasn't her opinion alone, but that other members of the group thought the same—and doesn't it seem ironic that the first buildings to be constructed are palaces, while those that belong to the workers are these temporary wooden houses?

Not wanting to seem like an interloper, Dad left the group while they had dinner, but remained in the hotel, where he ran into Miguel Andrade and invited him for a drink at the bar, where some of JK's invited guests were also milling around.

He was surprised to see Valdivino, dressed in white, with a black bowtie, come up to greet him. He was working as a waiter there in the Brasília Palace. He'd heard about Dad's trips from Aunt Francisca, wanted to know about his adventures in the jungle, and asked after Bernardo Sayão, Boy, what a good man, don't you think?, I'll never forget that he was the one who helped me when I first arrived here, who asked me to work on the construction of his house. He later mentioned that he'd brought his brother down from the Northeast, with whom he was living in a nearby village. The situation is dark in the Northeast, Mr. Moacyr, a lot of people are fleeing the drought, coming to Brasília from all over the place, by bus to Governador Valadares, then by train to Belo Horizonte, then on to Anápolis, or else by semi-truck through Paraopeba and Patos de Minas and São Gotardo and Paracatu, crossing the Paracatu River on a ferry, There are so many people coming here that they've started to restrict the entry of workers, said Miguel Andrade in agreement.

It was so true, in fact, that, if I were interested in doing so, I would accept João Almino's suggestion that I write and include here a dense Northeastern regionalist novel in which the watering holes are all dried up, the ground cracked, the plants turned gray, the rivers are highways made of sand, the carcasses of animals signal more deaths to come, and the migrants flee in caravans, bringing their dramas with them, in search of the promised land. We'll talk more later, Valdivino, suggested Dad.

Miguel had come to the hotel to confirm the details of the Huxleys' return to the airport the next day, This time there's not going to be any mix up. He had been charged with accompanying the group to Xingu in a Brazilian Air Force plane.

I need to get a statement out of Huxley, Dad mentioned, I want to make a collection of comments about Brasília in a structured way, with the name of the visitor at the top of a note card, then a record of their first impressions of the city, and one day these collected statements will be in a museum, Seems like a magnificent idea to me, said Miguel, That's why I've got to come here tomorrow and wait for you all to get back.

Valdivino reappeared, balancing a serving tray on his hand. He then resumed the conversation, as if he had forgotten to say something, When I arrived with my brother, Mr. Moacyr, I got rid of my shack in the Free City, I thought it better to live here close to the Bananal Creek, in the Bananal Village, which we all call Amaury Village, but I'm worried that the village is going to get flooded, Why didn't you look for housing in the workers' camp?, asked Dad, Well, I had already stopped working construction, Mr. Moacyr, and, even when I was working construction at the Palace, as you know, only the engineers got houses in the camp, me and the other workers all lived in sheds, where there wouldn't have been any room for my brother, and plus I like to be independent, living out at the Amaury Village, and working as a waiter, the only problem is that they say that around September of next year, in 1959, when they build the dam and stop up the waterfall to fill the lake, the village is going to get covered up by all the water, It sure is, affirmed Miguel Andrade—emphasizing his words with his index finger—the lake is going fill up and spill over its banks, it will spread out to five kilometers in width and forty kilometers in length, with a circumference of more than 100 kilometers— he was tracing circles on the table with his index finger—there will be around thirty-eight square kilometers of lake, and it will be thirty-five meters deep . . . But some are saying, like the famous thinker from Rio de Janeiro, Gustavo Corção, said Dad, interrupting, that the soil here is so dry that the lake will never fill up, the water will all get sucked up by the subsoil, and if that happens, you and your brother will be saved, Valdivino.

When Valdivino went on his way with tray in hand, Miguel Andrade mentioned that the Amaury Village had been named after a Newcap employee called Amaury de Almeida. At the beginning of that year, 1958, with the arrival of so many people to Brasília, there were some twenty thousand people without a place to live, and so Amaury, whom Miguel Andrade knew well, managed to set up a camp for them on the lands that would later be flooded.

Two men passed by in dark suits. I saw them when they arrived, said Dad, they've all come from São Paulo, No, there are also people from Rio and Belo Horizonte, seems like the actress Tônia Carrero is here, and there have been whispers about the possibility that another very elegant woman is here, by the name of Maria Lúcia Pedroso, who was recently seen at the president's side in Rio.

Huxley and his group came down for dinner. An older Italian waiter was serving them, Dad noted. The writer was now wearing a beige suit and a silk tie with Persian horses on it, which descended disproportionally far below his waist. From afar, Dad witnessed the gestures of Laura, Elizabeth, and Huxley himself, who seemed disturbed by all the noise, Why don't you ask Huxley to write his comments now?, asked Miguel, No, he's having dinner right now, and I don't have a note card . . . it'll be better closer to the end of his stay.

After Miguel Andrade left, Dad tried to get into the ball, but was refused entry for lack of an invitation. So he returned to the bar, where three young women had arrived, who, judging by the cut of their long gowns and the quality of their make-up, were certainly among the night's invited guests. He remained there observing them, working up the courage to strike up a conversation.

Seeing Dad all by himself, Valdivino returned, I'm going to tell you something, Mr. Moacyr, I sold that shack in the Free City to pay down my debt, but the buyers were just some poor Northeasterners, just like me and the others, and they still owe me more than half, and what I did get from them I decided to give to the woman that I've already told you about, Sir, who is my ruin, it went to a work of divine inspiration, but I might have made a mistake, because she's being difficult these days, complicated, and she didn't like it one bit that I brought my brother down here. She demands things of me, Mr. Moacyr, I have to prove that I love her, but that proof is never enough, she's always unsatisfied, it's a woman thing, you know how it is, Sir, happy on the outside, sad on the inside, thinking that I don't really love her, that no one loves her, lying on her bed, waiting for the world to end. Everything's all well and good, it seems, and then all of a sudden it isn't, the world is about to end, and then she lets loose crying, feeling a deep sorrow, she doesn't let me come near her, demands that I do things for her, that I cook, take care of her, tidy up her room . . . I wouldn't complain if she'd let me sleep with her, And why are you still with this woman, Valdivino, dump that crazy lady, I can't, Mr. Moacyr, it's just that you don't know my whole story, Well tell me that story once and for all, man, I don't care if I live in a house, not at all, Mr. Moacyr, if I could get a new construction job, I'd find some place to live outside of the Amaury Village, it's just that I can't manage to get one, I read all the signs on street corners, asking for bricklayers, laborers, carpenters, joiners, indicating the offices we should report to, I listen to all the announcements from the loudspeakers on the light-poles in parks and on top of cars, telling construction workers to report to the camps, I also see the announcements at the movie theater in the Free City, and it's true that they need workers, the announcements even say how many they need, they advertise the firm and then the registration trucks arrive, but I don't want to work on just anything, in any place, do you know, Sir, when they're going to start building the cathedral?

Dad drank one whiskey, then another, and another still, and worked up the courage to sit down at the table with the young women, who showed some curiosity about what he did for a living, and especially about life in the Free City. Dad pointed out Huxley to them. The three of them immediately took their menus, which had beef stroganoff at the top of the list, to be autographed by Huxley, and Laura as well. Then they went into the ball.

The Huxleys' dinner came to an end around eleven, and Huxley and his entire group went up to their bedrooms, but the ball was still going, and at midnight the loud music and lively conversations could still be heard.

Dad hadn't stopped drinking whiskey and was now alone once again. He felt ill, a sensation of nausea, and had to go to the restroom. That's where Valdivino found him, stretched out on the floor, You hardly ate anything, Mr. Moacyr, that's why. Valdivino took care of him and offered to serve as his chauffeur that night, driving him back to the Free City.

Dad didn't explain to Valdivino that he no longer shared the house with us, nor did Aunt Francisca refuse to take him to his bedroom when he arrived with Valdivino, You don't have a way to get back at this time of night, she said to Valdivino. So a second hammock was set up, and Valdivino slept in the living room with me. That night, Typhoon, who had already grown accustomed to spending the night in the backyard, whined so much at the backdoor that we had to let him in, and he ended up sleeping beneath Valdivino's hammock.

Early the next morning, a Sunday, Valdivino wanted to know how Dad was feeling, Just a bit of a hangover, but it'll be gone soon. Then Valdivino went to the grocery store to get some *boldo* tea for Dad, and later he accompanied Aunt Francisca and me to Mass. When we returned, he wanted to see the macaws and the monkey, and he stayed out at the back of the house, talking reservedly with Dad, to whom he revealed one more secret about his mysterious friend, She likes me, she has always liked me—not only does she like me, she's in love with me, the way I am with her—but there's another guy who's in love with her too, and she allows herself to be influenced by him; I don't have the courage to complain about it, because she's very strong willed, when her spirit revolts she knows no bounds, she doesn't think twice about any danger, one second she's calm, even overly calm, as if she'd been sleeping while still awake, but then her disposition just does an about-face, she becomes the complete opposite and is worse than a viper.

Whenever Aunt Matilde and Aunt Francisca came near, Valdivino would change the subject, Mr. Moacyr, it's like I told you, I want to get a new construction job and move out of Amaury Village, I can talk to Roberto, Aunt Matilde offered, if he could get you a job at the Congress building . . . I'd take it then and there, Dona Matilde, it's not a church, but it might as well be, What?, don't go thinking that it's a house of God, no way, said Aunt Matilde, it's very much the opposite, it'll be more brothel than church, Don't talk that way, Matilde, show some respect, objected Aunt Francisca, The quality of politics is going to go to the pits once Congress is transferred to the interior of Goiás, if it's already bad in Rio, just imagine what it'll be like here, insisted Aunt Matilde, What matters is that Valdivino find a good job, right, Valdivino?, said Aunt Francisca, with a maternal air.

That night, when Dad went to the Brasília Palace to await the arrival of the Huxleys, Miguel Andrade, at the front of the group, announced, You're not going to be able to talk to him, he's exhausted, but there's no need anyway, I got the statement that you wanted. They went up to the bar, where Miguel Andrade told Dad about his trip in the Air Force DC-3, We flew over the region of the lost City of Z, I've heard about that, said Dad, The one who really knew the story well was Antonio Callado, who had even written a book, called *The Skeleton of the Green Lake*, based on the expeditions made by Colonel Fawcett to discover Z, I met a woman who believes that that colonel died there last year, said Dad, That British explorer, Percy Harrison Fawcett, his twenty-one-year-old son, Jack, and his son's best friend, named Raleigh Rimell, continued Miguel, disappeared in 1925, when Colonel Fawcett, who had begun his search in 1906, made his eighth expedition to Brazil in search of the City of Z, the lost city of an ancient and advanced civilization, a story which inspired the novel *The Lost World*, by Arthur Conan Doyle, a friend of Fawcett, But did you all see anything when you flew over that area?, asked Dad, Every once in a while, in the middle of the forest, we'd see some rocks that were in the shape of buildings and jagged or crumbling fortresses, and later, when we arrived at the Posto Capitão Vasconcelos, on a tributary of the Xingu River, to visit the Uialapiti tribe, we were received by Claudio Villas-Boas, who told us that his brother, Orlando, had found a pile of bones in 1952 in the Xingu region, which appeared to belong to Fawcett, and that he'd heard the Kalapalo confess to killing him, but according to Callado that was all disproven later on when Fawcett's dentist examined the skeleton's dental arch, and years after Fawcett's disappearance there were people who swore that they'd seen him, a Swiss hunter spotted him out in the forest in 1931, and in 1937 an American missionary ran into Fawcett's grandson, the son of Jack and an Indian woman, but look, Moacyr, I know that this is what you really want to see. It was Huxley's statement on a piece of paper clipped onto a clipboard: "I came straight from Ouro Preto to Brasília. What a dramatic voyage across time and history! A journey from Yesterday to Tomorrow, from what has ended to what has yet to begin, from ancient accomplishments to new promises."

I did as you said, explained Miguel, up here at the top, as you can see, I printed, in capital letters, "Aldous Huxley," and then I asked him what were his impressions of Brasília, told him he could write anything he liked, he was surprised, obviously he wasn't expecting that, and I clarified that it was for a collection of statements from illustrious visitors, to be displayed in the future museum of Brasília, exactly as you had suggested. He took his pen out of his pocket right away, turned to the next page, and started to scribble, then scribble some more, he tore out one, two, three pages, then finally composed these sentences.

Enthusiastic, the two of them agreed to take that statement to JK's press committee early the next morning, it was Dad's first triumph as the president's note-taker, albeit an imperfect one, who had to resort to a third party.

Two days later—I remember this well—Dad showed us, triumphantly, that the words that he'd helped obtain from Aldous Huxley appeared in all the newspapers, as if they were a telegram that JK had received from Huxley, I knew right away that it didn't have the feel of a telegram, said Aunt Matilde.

Less than a month had passed when Valdivino showed up in the doorway of our house, on a day when Aunt Francisca was taking care of me. I didn't like being sick, but I have fond memories of my illnesses, for through those memories I can see how tenderly Aunt Francisca treated me. A wave of affection swept over me whenever I heard her footsteps, the door to the bedroom would open slowly and silently, and, from the other side, her sweet figure would appear, she came to check if I was running a fever or not, if I was feeling any pain, if I'd been able to sleep. I'd lie there waiting for her, looking up at the ceiling. I would wake up when the first light of the morning came in through the window and the cracks between the zinc roof-tiles, waiting for her to come see me, for I always felt better once I saw her. She would put a chair beside the bed and stay there, passing her small, delicate hands over my forehead, squeezing my hands, sometimes soaking a cloth in alcohol and wrapping it around my throat. She'd sit on the mattress, directing her loving eyes towards me, which tore me to pieces inside, and then, like a gentle welding torch, they would put my broken body back together. If I could have, I would have asked her to lie down beside me, I would have shrunk myself down and nestled on her lap, I would have gone back to being the small child that she had taken in when my parents died. And other times she'd bring her accordion and play a soft song—which produced waves of sweet emotion—to cheer me up. Then she'd carefully tuck me into the bed sheet and kiss me on the forehead.

On that day I had chicken pox. There were blisters on my body and my face. Aunt Francisca, always by my side, suffered for me, and was touched, as if I were on my deathbed. She brought me hot soup that had been made especially for me and carefully brought the spoon, which caressed my lips—with just the right portion so that it wouldn't spill on me—up to my mouth. She took me into the living room and gave me a present: a journal, where I could write whatever I wanted—and in which, though I didn't know it then, I would later commit indiscretions that would cause her harm. The window brought me renewed and joyful light, a landscape filled with houses, and sounds from the streets, even the mud outside seemed new to me. I rested my head on Aunt Francisca's lap, closing my eyes, and she would look down at me and we'd smile at each other, looking into each other's eyes, her lips would come near my forehead, her long hair caressing my face, and she would sigh into my ear, telling me that I'd feel better soon, very soon. I had never loved anyone as much as I loved Aunt Francisca and I was frightened by the thought of losing her, of her running off with Valdivino, and Valdivino had come to spoil the harmony of that afternoon, I came out here to deposit my salary and I couldn't leave without stopping by to thank Dona Matilde.

The job, with the Pacheco Fernandes Dantas construction firm, really was on the construction of the Congress building, I receive my pay in cold hard cash, always on Sunday, and I come out here with some co-workers, who fill up on booze out at Maracangalha Bar, they even drink it in coffee mugs, but not me, I still don't drink, or smoke, I don't see the fun of it, I deposit almost all of it at the Caixa Savings Bank, That's the way to do it, said Aunt Francisca. Dad, who at that point ate all his meals at our house, but still wasn't sleeping there, asked him, How do you like the work? I can't complain about the work, Mr. Moacyr, it's really great, I like the Planalto Village, and I get room and board for free, but I have to share a room with a policeman from the SPB, one of the few who live there, I don't know why he doesn't move to the wooden barracks out in Oldcap, like all the other policemen, he's a brawny, broad-shouldered guy, by the name of Aristotle, always wearing his yellow uniform. Typhoon snarled, which he rarely did. Valdivino said, You see?, Typhoon already understands it all, His name is Aristotle?, asked Aunt Matilde, I know it doesn't fit him, but that's his name all right, he's from Paraíba, They reused the old Air Force uniforms to make the SPB uniforms, explained Dad.

I asked Aristotle: what are you all doing here, doesn't the

construction company have its own security? I thought that you all mainly patrolled the Free City, and he said: We're the ones who watch over the companies' building materials. And how many of you all are there?, I asked him. Just a year ago there were only fifty of us, but now there are three hundred of us, well-chosen, fearless guys, suffice it to say that, aside from a few chiefs and commissioners from police departments in Minas Gerais and Goiás, the rest of the team is made up of tough guys from the Northeast, like you and me, aside from the commander, who's a retired colonel from the Rio police. I wouldn't be fit for that kind of job, I explained. True, when you really think about it, you wouldn't pass the test, he quickly replied to me, we don't have rickety little guys like you there, nope; for the exam I had to lift a seventy-kilo sack, he told me this right there in our first conversation, Dona Matilde. I knew about the reputation of those guys in the SPB, they'd beat the workers with nightsticks, and women and children as well. In the Amaury Village they accused my brother of theft, and dragged him in chains to the police station, and he got off easy, 'cause I heard that a year ago they even poked out a worker's eyeballs, and they didn't get punished for it or anything. This guy complains about everything, Mr. Moacyr, the cold showers, the fleas, the rats, the bedbugs . . . All the pests bother me to, especially those bedbugs that suck your blood during the night, but what is there to do? They're everywhere. So why waste time complaining about it, instead of just focusing on your job and doing good work? He's supposed to be in charge of controlling the entrance of liquor into the village, which always causes fights among the workers. But no, he just lets it pass through, because he wants to be able to drink his booze, too. Even the main guard of the camp, who inspects the workers, looking for big knives and booze, is bribed with a bottle of the stuff, so that he'll let in all the bottles that are for the engineers, administrators, and even this guy, my roommate.

Although I received many comments on the blog about this dreadful police force, the SPB, I'd rather leave them alone and focus here on my own recollection of that conversation, which I listened to the way someone watches a movie they're not really interested in, waiting for Valdivino to leave so I could have my accordion lesson with Aunt Francisca. But can't you just change rooms and tell that guy to buzz off, Valdivino?, asked Aunt Matilde, I'm wondering whether I should just leave there for good, once and for all, 'cause I've heard that they're about to start work on the cathedral, No, no, don't be in such a hurry, don't lose a good job over some nonsense, Dad advised.

When Valdivino left, Typhoon followed after him, and that day I had a really hard time bringing him back, because Aunt Francisca wouldn't let me leave the house on account of the chicken pox, and Typhoon only obeyed me after a lot of whistling and promises of cookies, the delicious cookies that Aunt Francisca had made for me.

*Sixth Night:*
*The Field of Hope*

On the sixth night, surrounded by four dirty white walls, Dad acknowledged that his success as an official note-taker had been insignificant and temporary, as I myself had confirmed through my reading of the "Onward" notebooks. In one of them he had transcribed the assertion of the Italian president, Giovanni Gronchi, from September 8 of that year, 1958, that the construction of Brasília was "an endeavor worthy of the Roman era," and he'd recorded that, following the example of Foster Dulles, Gronchi had also planted a tree in Brasília, this time an Italian cypress, but it was nothing more than facts taken from the newspapers. Even though he'd insistently sought out JK's press committee, he still wasn't receiving invitations to accompany visitors. Aldous Huxley had been an exception, thanks to Miguel Andrade. So Dad dedicated himself even more to selling plots and commodatums and, with the profits gained, he invested heavily in his partnership with Paulão.

I went up with Dad into one of the Ministry buildings that was under construction and looked down at the construction sites that stretched out into the vastness of dirt and building plots of the Esplanade. In the distance we could see low hills and cloud formations. The lines of trees descended the valley and ascended those hills, until their colors faded into a soft blue. The outlines of walls, pilasters, staircases, doors, and windows stood out against the horizons, where, above the blue, brushstrokes of yellow and pink could be seen. The tiny forms of fifty thousand workers, like ants, endlessly mimed the chaotic dance of hammer strikes between cement slabs and steel rebar that striated the sky. Beyond those horizons where I glimpsed such beauty, Dad saw mountains of money, and he was right, for the city was being erected at a frantic pace due to the circulation of government money and the investment that social welfare institutions made in buying up whole city blocks so they could quickly build their respective apartment buildings. It's utter nonsense, it's absurd, protested Aunt Matilde. Dad silently agreed, but the absurd yielded profits, and without profit the greatness of the endeavor was lost.

There was something magical about the transformation of emptiness into something concrete. If there was a lack of money, then they printed more money. Out of that invented money, that nothingness, buildings sprouted from the ground, like plants that didn't even need water to put forth shoots. Money circulated from hand to hand, and the faster it went around, the more likely it was to raise up from the earth cement and steel forms, which, like mushrooms, came into being overnight. And the money circulated to the turbulent rhythm of the city. The Free City was being built from nothing—from the selling of titles for structures that would later be destroyed. Brasília was being built from nothing—from money that was issued without a gold reserve. For Aunt Matilde, this was proof that it was all the same whether you made the economy grow out of something or out of nothing, out of something useful or something useless. The unnecessary could become an engine of wealth. Don't say that building Brasília is unnecessary, argued Roberto, So, what is necessary?, there are very few necessary things in this world, so tell me exactly what is necessary! Brasília, he replied, No, if you had said food, I would have understood, but even so there are Indians who find food without growing a thing, and here in Brazil, in this climate, if you really think about it, not even clothing is necessary, almost everything in the world is unnecessary, Well I don't understand where you're going with this, said Roberto.

It's my way of agreeing with you, my love, for it's better to build Brasília than an atomic bomb, dreams are more valuable than fear, rivers of money are wasted on atomic bombs, and do you think it's necessary to build an atomic bomb? A necessity that only comes out of fear? And why is wasting money out of fear any different from wasting money because of a desire, a dream? What I'm trying to say is just that, that we can construct reality, and wealth, that we can put money into circulation from nothingness, from emptiness, from the fictitious, from the useless and the unnecessary, and Brasília is all of those things, or rather, it is nothing at all.

And it's better than an atomic bomb, said Dad, ironically, completing her line of reasoning. He thought it was an odd theory, but he was pleased that he could extract from it what interested him most: the construction of Brasília was making him wealthy. He already knew the details of his partner's quite unlawful transactions, but Paulão was the one getting his hands dirty, Dad merely handed over the money, and sometimes asked for Roberto, who was already Aunt Matilde's boyfriend at this point, to intercede on their behalf. Paulão had a special talent for obtaining three or four receipts for the delivery of a single truckload of construction sand, gravel, or cement. He'd weigh the truck on the scales, get the receipt for having loaded up the truck, leave, but not unload it, and enter the scales again, multiplying this operation again and again, like a magician at a circus. After a few months, he had racked up invoices for six or even eight thousand cubic meters of construction sand, although he'd only delivered two thousand cubic meters. At 760 *cruzeiros* per cubic meter, the net monthly profit could surpass a million *cruzeiros*, with Dad receiving half of that. Another of his clever operations was to put the names of migrant workers from other worksites on their payroll, pay them a salary, then get most of that money back from them. When payment was made per kilometer driven, Paulão would put the semi-truck up on wooden beams and let the wheels spin all night long. It wasn't right, and Dad knew that, but there were so many people around him getting rich ... With the money he earned selling commodatums, the construction of houses on the land he owned, the resale of lands that had increased in value, and the highly profitable business partnership with Paulão, he saw his reputation grow, not only in the Free City, but also in Brasília, which was starting to take shape.

One night we heard screams and woke up with a start: Fire! The city's catching fire! I quickly got dressed and went out into the street. The fire was at a store that Dad had opened with Paulão, an enormous warehouse that sold everything. The atmosphere out on the street was festive, inspired by fear. People were moving about, forming groups, and conversing excitedly. The blaze threatened to spread to the wooden houses, and Dad and Paulão were among those who took action to put out the fire. Flames filled the sky. The walls of the store had disappeared. You could see the remains of some furniture, various kinds of wardrobes, tables, and beds catching fire. In what was left of a window, the flames were growing larger, thick ones flared up, smoke billowed out, and the smell of burnt cloth spread all around, from all the mattresses, bedspreads, and towels, the glass in the windows shattered, resulting in delicate little sounds. Many people came up to Dad to express sorrow about what had happened, and he replied, with great dignity, that the important thing was to save the other buildings, These things happen, it was just a spontaneous combustion. I heard, They're saying it was done on purpose, for the insurance—and I never was able to figure out if Dad really had told Paulão to set the building ablaze. I know that

Dad didn't sleep that night, and that it wasn't out of worry—he was counting the money he'd earned and running the numbers on new investments.

However, his glory could not be complete unless he explored his other calling, which was like a virtue to ease his conscience, to compensate for his vice and give his life a spiritual dimension that he wouldn't find in any god or religion. In December of 1958 he made the decision to return to the jungle and join Bernardo Sayão's team, which had continued its work without rest and refused to be intimidated by the hundreds of kilometers of wide forest trails and service lanes left to clear out, now that they were nearing the end of the Belém-Brasília, which was expected to be completed on January 31, 1959. You're going back out to that jaguar trail?, asked Aunt Matilde, using the term employed by the enemies of the highway, who were also the enemies of Brasília.

On the eve of Dad's departure, on Sunday afternoon, payday for the workers, Valdivino came looking for Dad with a worried look on his face: Can you take me with you out into the jungle, Mr. Moacyr? What's the meaning of this, Valdivino? Mr. Moacyr, you're like a priest to me, a priest I can confess to, but one that gives me solutions here on earth, there's something I wanted to talk to you about, alone, Sir, Go ahead, Valdivino, I'm going to get married, Mr. Moacyr. Typhoon lowered his head between his stretched out forelegs and looked askance at Valdivino. Well then you've got to stay here, is it that young woman you like so much? They heard a noise from the kitchen. It was Aunt Matilde. Mr. Moacyr, I don't want anyone to hear, said Valdivino in a lowered voice. Dad suggested that they go out.

In contrast to the rhythm of the construction sites, time was passing slowly on that payday, when the population seemed to multiply by at least four, the avenues filling up with workers from the construction firm camps and nearby towns. Valdivino looked from side to side as he talked, lowering his voice whenever a

passer-by drew near, I wanted to tell you about this situation to
see what you think about it and what advice you have for me, Mr.
Moacyr, one night this guy from the SPB, Aristotle, with whom I
share a room, came up to me and asked: Do you know such-and-
such girl, who's like this and like that? And then he said right
away: She sent a message for you, she's going to be over by the
warehouse after eleven o'clock tonight. But I barely even know
this girl, I said. She always stares at you when you pass in the
street, a pretty woman who's always enticing you but you never
bite, you're not going to tell me you're a fag, he said, provoking
me.

Men in long-sleeved white shirts swapped stories in front of
shops, bars, restaurants, and nightclubs—small buildings, just one
story. Some street vendors could be seen at the sides of the streets,
and in the middle of the avenue there were lines of semi-trucks
of every make and year, buses, jeeps and more jeeps, wagons,
and horses. I believe that we're supposed to resist, continued
Valdivino, there's only one woman for me in this life, I've never
been with another, but I agreed that the young woman was cute,
the daughter of a laborer from Paraíba, her name is Carminha,
and it's true that she sometimes smiled at me, so I got to thinking
about her smile and left for the warehouse.

Dad and Valdivino passed in front of the movie theater made
of corrugated iron owned by Countess Tarnowska, which was
advertising *Rio, 40 Degrees* by Nelson Pereira dos Santos, starring
Glauce Rocha and Jece Valadão, and then went past the big red
wooden building, on the front of which, in white, capital letters,
it read "Presbyterian Church."

When I got to the warehouse, Mr. Moacyr, Carminha was
already there, I went over to her and she didn't move away, then
I got even closer and she put her hands in front of her in the
shape of a "v," as if she were protecting herself, so I put her hands
on my waist, and she let me do it, so I got a little closer, I pulled

Carminha against me, embraced Carminha, kissed Carminha's mouth, and my hands were groping all over.

They kept walking down the avenues, watching people come and go from the little markets, grocery stores, barber shops, and pharmacies, watching the cobblers and shoe-shines who at that hour were still working on boot after boot. I'm telling you this, Mr. Moacyr, because then something happened that I'm still trying to understand, Carminha suddenly pushed me away and we stood there, screwing each other with just our eyes, surprised and dizzy, so dizzy in fact that she didn't even straighten her clothes, she was leaning against the wall with her skirt pulled up, exposing one of her thighs, one of her breasts showing through her low-necked, unbuttoned blouse. I had the urge to embrace her even more forcefully, and then she yelled: Oh my God! And she turned around to straighten her clothes, ashamed. When she turned back to look at me, her breast and thigh were covered up, but her face looked even more frightened than before: What now, Valdivino?, she said, saying my name like that, and then she started to cry with such emotion that her crying really touched me, and I felt regret for touching such a pure little angel, I'd been the first person to fondle her breasts and kiss her mouth, I thought, and I was in agony: It's not anybody's fault, I said, if there's anything to blame it's our human nature, I like you. I like you, too, she replied, already wiping away her tears, come here and give me a kiss, she said, calling me over to her. I'm telling you all these details, Mr. Moacyr, because you know what goes on in peoples' heads. If you were in that situation, would you or would you not think that she was a virtuous woman? Seems like I would, Valdivino, why do you ask? asked Dad, while he observed the cracked wood of some of the buildings, palm trees planted in pots, and meat hanging in the front window of a butcher shop, where the violet light from a lightbulb buzzed intermittently. Well then, when I gave her that kiss, it was a kiss that never ended, and things started happening before I even had time to think them through, next thing I knew I had ripped all the buttons off of Carminha's blouse, and we were lying down in the weeds. Not here, she said, and then she pulled me by the arm over by a shrub in a darkened spot behind a semi-truck in the parking lot behind the soccer field—Valdivino motioned and pointed to the sides of the street as if he were looking out at the location of that secret encounter. There wasn't even enough time for me to realize how much pleasure I was feeling, because everything happened all of a sudden, Carminha, completely naked, covered her breasts, closed her thighs together, and wriggled from one side to another, but that didn't extinguish the flames, I kissed every little bit of her body, I could feel the goose bumps on her skin with my lips, I was in a trance, Mr. Moacyr, I didn't know what to do, but all of a sudden she did everything, and did it all so well that she hardly seemed like that young woman who had shed tears of shame. Someone saw us and went to tell the guard, and the guard told the head of the camp, a surly guy who goes around in a pickup truck. You shameless bastard, did you fuck that girl or not? I kept silent. Did you fuck her or not? Still nothing out of me. You fucked her and now you've got to marry her, you shameless thing. Do you think you can fuck this girl and then just abandon her? Her dad's furious. You've gotta get married now. So, are you gonna marry her or not? I still kept quiet. There's no use in trying to escape. We know everybody around here. If you run off, we'll catch you. So, are you gonna marry her or not? I didn't think I had any way out, so I said: I'll marry her. This was the day before yesterday, Mr. Moacyr.

Dad lowered his head, giving the impression that he was examining each speck of dirt below. He seemed as worried as Valdivino, or even more. The two of them walked for a few minutes in silence, listening to the sound of music coming from one of the shops.

I don't like her enough to marry her, Mr. Moacyr, that's the plain truth, and I don't know if I actually even screwed Carminha, it's possible that she's still a virgin, because we did everything, but at the last moment . . . I'm sad, Mr. Moacyr, this is what I wanted to talk to you about, I'm really sad, I've even started to think about things that I shouldn't, because to go on living like this . . . I know that you're a brain doctor, if it were you, would you marry her or give up everything and escape to somewhere far away, hiding out in the forest? They were passing in front of a small shop where they could see black umbrellas and colorful parasols hanging on the walls, as well as baby clothes, crocheted booties, and white, embroidered baptismal gowns. Dad noticed that Valdivino was staring intently at those tiny clothes. I don't know, Valdivino, only you can decide what to do. And could I go with you, Sir? You're going on a trip, aren't you? Francisca told me.

Calm down, think it through, talk to the young woman, It's not something that can be talked over, Mr. Moacyr, her dad is fuming mad, Well, I can see if they have any use for you out on the highway, but I can't promise anything, construction is almost done out there.

I don't know what women see in him, Dad said to Aunt Matilde when he arrived home. Typhoon barked three times, as if in protest. He's simple-minded, naïve, but he really is a sensitive young man, and it's not just Francisca who thinks so, replied Aunt Matilde.

The next day, as expected, Dad took off in a twin-engine plane and after a couple of hours arrived at the construction site of the Belém-Brasília highway. We're ready for this challenge, Moacyr, said Sayão, wearing khaki canvas pants, boots, and a long-sleeved white shirt that was open at the chest, the sleeves rolled up over the elbow, displaying his muscular arms, we have a helicopter and a mail-plane, and once we're finished with all this customs bureaucracy, fifty-four machines are going to arrive here from Santos.

Dad felt buried by all the vegetation, his sweat flowing in rivulets in that humid, end-of-year heat. In the jungle there was an intensity and density that contrasted with the emptiness of the Plateau and it instilled fear in him. He always expected some surprise as he walked around, a falling branch, the appearance of some animal, some movement that would shatter the mysterious permanence of the jungle. He heard the constant rustling, an atonal symphony pierced through by various melodies of whistles and warbles, of sounds that buzzed in his ears or softened almost to the point of silence, and he could smell the humidity, the rotting wood and animals, the scents of flowers, fruits, and other essences that were still unknown to him. The diffused radiance of a sunbeam would twinkle, then all of a sudden thunder would roar, and the rain would begin to pour forth. Stream upon stream of water would descend between the leaves like transparent curtains, cleaning the forest with their wet, heavy sadness, and once the rains made their way to other regions, thick drops would continue to fall for some time, one by one, rhythmically, like monotonous notes. The darkness of the night was blacker than Dad had ever seen before, it swallowed up the trees, erasing the contours of objects out there where the curious or impatient eye of an animal would sometimes shine. The forest was his enemy, Dad concluded, the enemy of all those who were there, it needed to be fought against and defeated by the highway.

Dad stayed out in the jungle a little over a month, time enough to witness the terrible accident. It was January 15, 1959, and they were smack in the middle of the jungle in the state of Pará, thirty kilometers from the border of the state of Maranhão, between Imperatriz and Guamá, at a spot where they were finishing work on a camp where, on February 1, the two highways would meet up, the one from Belém, in the north, and the other from Brasília, in the south, and Bernardo Sayão, fifty-seven years old at that point, was in the door of his tent, which he had relocated the day before so that he could be closer to accompany the work in progress. A little before noon, Dad made his way up there, together with a topographer and an engineer, and around one o'clock, as they were watching the felling of a gigantic tree that was stuck to other trees by vines and parasites, a dry branch, weighing forty-five kilos and about two meters long, broke free from a nearby tree, fell ferociously through the air, and hit Bernardo Sayão's head as it came down, as well as his left arm and leg.

There was little to be done for Sayão out there in that region. They had to wait until three in the afternoon when an airplane spotted the commotion below and sent a helicopter out to them a few hours later. Sayão was transported to Açailândia, in Maranhão, and died on board the helicopter around seven in the evening.

Dad had the lumberjacks help him erect, at the spot of the accident, a large cross made with the murderous branch.

Only the next day, January 16, did the body arrive in Brasília. In the Free City, where the commotion had spread throughout every house, there was a candlelight vigil in the Don Bosco church.

That branch that killed Sayão, Aunt Matilde explained to me, is "the enchanted stick," a vengeful stick that is mentioned by a character in a book by Monteiro Lobato, I'm going to give you a copy of the book *Urupês* as a present, so you can read the story called "The Revenge of the Peroba Tree." She had a space set apart on one of the shelves in her room for about a dozen books, which I would see her leaf through on the weekends. She was the only one in the house who read works of fiction, a quality that I only came to value when, as I was just getting started with my professional life, I met up with Aunt Matilde again many years later.

Valdivino came by the house, with dark circles under his sad, sunken eyes. For him, it was as if Brasília had died before it was even born.

On that day, Typhoon whined because he wanted to go with us to the wake, and I wanted to take him, but Dad was categorical, There's no place for a dog there. We leashed him to a post at the back of the house, where he kept the monkey and the macaws company.

After we set off for church on foot, Dad accelerated his step, distancing himself from me and my aunts, and Valdivino ran up to him to talk about Carminha, to say that Carminha is beautiful, yessir, Mr. Moacyr, she's really young, but she has the body of a grown woman, with lots of curves and tricks, which he should have realized right from the start were the tricks of a woman who attracts a lot of men and isn't satisfied with just one, someone who's excessively desirous, with a very feminine way about her, daring and impertinent, unable to conform to the rigidity of morals and religion. Only later did he realize that her gaze wasn't all that innocent, nor were the smiles on that dark-skinned face, her shapely arms, or those breasts that were almost spilling out of her blouse. She flaunted her beauty, she would run her tongue over her lips, lower her eyes to the side and bat her eyelashes, smile bashfully as if cloaking herself in modesty and shyness, the costume of a virginal, virtuous woman, but her shamelessness still shined through in her gestures and skillfulness, in the desire that overflowed from her entire body, that heat that couldn't be contained, in the heaving of her breasts. She was a woman who'd been with many, capable of orgies even. Carminha is pregnant, Mr. Moacyr, and a laborer friend of mine told me that she goes out to the warehouse almost every night, that he himself knew a number of guys who used to go meet up with her there, she'd even given it up to five guys at once, and had given it up to Aristotle, that guy from the SPB I share a room with, it turns out the whole thing was a set-up concocted by Aristotle, the purpose was to get me to marry her, to help the guy rid himself of that low woman, I thought about denouncing that lowlife, but to whom,

Mr. Moacyr?, there's no justice there, justice is meted out by the SPB themselves, I'm thinking about fleeing, I just don't know where to.

They were already nearing the church, and Valdivino began to cry. Dad put his hands on Valdivino's shoulders, We'll find a way out of this, he said, You tricked me, I said to Aristotle, you got Carminha pregnant—Valdivino was now sobbing—and then he threatened me, Mr. Moacyr, he told me: Now don't go around making up stories, you shameless bastard, you don't know who you're dealing with here, you think you can fuck that girl and just get off scot-free? That you can just weasel out of it by lying? If you start to spread that story around, the guys around here will cut your balls off, and I'll take you straight to jail.

They'd already arrived in front of the church, which was full of people, and Aunt Francisca, Aunt Matilde, and I joined them. Upon seeing Valdivino cry, Aunt Francisca's eyes filled with tears, but she wasn't the only one, for, as we managed to make our way through the crowd to attend the wake, I noticed that almost all the residents of the Free City were crying.

Following the wake, we left for the Pilot Plan in a caravan, for the funeral Mass was going to be at the Sanctuary of Our Lady of Fatima, between blocks 307 and 308, the first completed architectural work of the Pilot Plan. Since you like building churches so much, Valdivino, you should have worked on this one, said Aunt Matilde as we arrived there, I had to decide, either stay on at the Palace or work on this little church, and, when I went to inquire about it, construction here was almost done.

It was the first time we'd visited that sanctuary. We admired its delicacy, its roof slab held up by only three pillars, its shape, which looked like the habits worn by the Daughters of Charity, and some details that Roberto had once mentioned to Aunt Matilde: images of the divine dove and the nativity star, which were repeated on the exterior blue and white wall tiles designed by Athos Bulcão, as well as the painting by Alfredo Volpi on the interior walls—angels, multicolored pennants, and Our Lady with baby Jesus on her lap, both of them without faces. It was the first Catholic sanctuary of the future capital, built in a hundred days and sanctified on June 28 of that year, 1958, in accordance with a promise made by the first lady, Dona Sarah Kubitschek— and the place where Friar Demétrio, a Capuchin monk with a goatee who always arrived on his motorcycle, would say Mass in the years that followed.

Valdivino cut through the crowd with his slender body—he wanted to see Bernardo Sayão's body—and soon returned, upset because it wasn't an open-casket.

At first we thought that Sayão was going to be buried in the Planaltina cemetery, as was done, up to that point, with the dead from Brasília and the Free City. Later we found out that Israel Pinheiro, the president of Newcap, intended to bury him in Goiânia, but the news was eventually confirmed that President JK, who'd just arrived in Brasília, had given the order to bury him in the parcel of land that Sayão himself had staked out, less than two years before, as the future cemetery of Brasília, the Field of Hope, which would thus be inaugurated with his burial.

Mr. Moacyr, nobody's seen what's in that casket, they won't open it, everyone thinks that there's no body in there at all, just stones or a tree trunk, Don't talk nonsense, Valdivino, his family members were the ones who decided against an open casket, It's not nonsense, not at all, Mr. Moacyr, I heard that he was abducted by Indians or that he was swallowed up by a jaguar, Those are just lies, forget about them, the only reason they won't open the casket is that, before it arrived here, the body had been deteriorating in the heat for over twelve hours, that's why the casket wasn't opened, not even by the family, And they're saying that there was no death certificate, insisted Valdivino, That's because it was dispensed with, since he died at the battle front, which is the right thing to do, because he hated unnecessary paperwork, explained Dad, But the certificate is the proof that he died, are you saying that no one wanted to confirm that?, I'm confirming it, replied Dad, I don't believe it, you're hiding the truth, too, Sir, Don't you trust me, Valdivino? I don't trust you, I don't trust you at all, Well then, you don't deserve my friendship, Okay then, I don't deserve it—and then he took off without saying goodbye to any of us, You're just upset, Valdivino, stop by the house so we can talk, we'll all go to the burial together tomorrow, Dad replied, raising his voice to be heard as Valdivino walked away.

It was the first time we'd ever seen Valdivino in that state. He didn't seem like the same tranquil, well-mannered young man that we all knew, That young man is not well, Dad said to Aunt Matilde.

The next day, Saturday, January 17, Valdivino didn't show up. Aunt Matilde decided to stay home, but I went with Dad and Aunt Francisca to the Field of Hope, where it had been necessary to have tractors working all night to open up a path through all the overgrown vegetation.

Brasília had never witnessed, and perhaps never would again, such a well-attended burial. The cemetery was a sea of thirty thousand people.

We're never going to be able to find Valdivino in the middle of this crowd, said Aunt Francisca, If he needs us, he'll find us, replied Dad, thinking of the entanglement that Valdivino had gotten himself into.

For the first time ever, my blog is filled with comments, but this isn't a biography of Bernardo Sayão, and, for me, it's sufficient to narrate the effects that his death had on my family, I'm not going to waste time saying that so-and-so has confirmed the impressions that I've communicated here about his personality, nor am I going to type out page after page of facts that will be used more ably by a historian, or even by me sometime in the future, in one of my newspaper articles. As for the other comments made, which are limited to "cool, wow, love it, beautiful, congrats," what could they possibly add to these pages?

With the death of Sayão and the sadness that took hold of Dad, Aunt Francisca, me, and even Aunt Matilde, Dad started sleeping at our house every day, for sadness is capable of bringing people together, and I believe that it was sadness that softened Aunt Francisca's heart, that made her accept Dad's return without question.

Two weeks after the death of Bernardo Sayão, when I was feeling sad and had even cried in secret because the monkey that Dad had brought back from the jungle had died of the flu, Dad came home ecstatic, bearing news that, as planned, the Belém-Brasília had been inaugurated on January 31, and that, by order of the president, it was now called the Bernardo Sayão Highway, This way his name is immortalized, it's more than just . . . Then he read us the article, on that day JK himself, beaming with pride, had knocked down an old jatoba tree at the juncture of the north and south lines of the highway, he had given the order to knock down the very first tree and was knocking down the last one himself, as the article put it. Seated in the tractor, he had carefully secured the trunk of the tree, which was still upright at that point, then engaged the tracks of the tractor and advanced on the tree resolutely, the jatoba hesitated a bit, but then the tree began to keel over, the pronouncement of its death.

I listened to the story and got scared that the next victim of "the enchanted stick" would be the president, since in the Monteiro Lobato story that Aunt Matilde had given me, I'd read the following:

> In every section of forest . . . there is a vengeful stick that punishes the evil deeds of men . . . It is the enchanted stick. The unlucky person who happens to swing an axe into the

core of that tree might as well deliver his soul over to the devil, 'cause it's lost. Whether the person gets run through with a jagged point or gets their head cracked open by a dead branch falling from on high right then and there, or, much later, gets done in by objects fashioned out of the wood, there's no escape. It's no use to be on guard, the disaster, sooner or later, will ensnare the marked man.

On February 10, the Tuesday of Carnival, my aunts and I, as well as Typhoon, were at home when Valdivino showed up looking like an apparition. The Carnivals in the Free City, as I've said, weren't as lively as the São João festival, and for that reason we usually stayed home, listening to the radio or the phonograph. Dad and Aunt Matilde, together with her boyfriend, had gone out to the balls the night before, but it was morning when Valdivino showed up, and Aunt Matilde, who had just woken up, her hair still uncombed and wearing a nightgown, was listening to the Carnival hits with me: "Mama, I'm gonna go shopping/ I won't take long/ Ha! Ha! Ha!/ Said Maria/ And every day she was late for dinner/ Riding round on the scooter seat/ Party's at Zezé's house/ Maria, dawn is breaking/ And now you're late for breakfast."

Valdivino came in from the street panting, I need to talk to Mr. Moacyr, He went out, explained Aunt Matilde, is it something urgent, Valdivino? I need to tell him I'm sorry, Ah— and this "ah" was followed by a smacking of the lips of someone who finds something to be of little importance—forget about it, Valdivino, he doesn't care about that at all, The fact is I need his help, Dona Matilde, I need to hide out somewhere, What's the matter, Valdivino, why?, asked Aunt Francisca, coming into the living room, I'm worried that my roommate, the SPB policeman, was involved in a serious crime.

Typhoon went over to Valdivino, as if he apprehended his

unease, and licked one of his hands. There wasn't enough food in the cafeteria, and when two workers from Paraíba at the firm where I work demanded food, they served them some spoiled leftovers, with dead flies on one of the steaks—spoiled food isn't uncommon there, sometimes the meat is thrown in the trash and that's why there are so many flies and dogs around there, That would never happen at the SWAS restaurant, said Aunt Francisca, And don't compare dogs to flies, Typhoon doesn't like it, said Aunt Matilde.

Valdivino didn't react to the joke, he maintained his circumspect expression and merely stroked Typhoon's head, The fight started when one of the Paraíban guys threw his plate of food at the cafeteria manager, the SPB police showed up, but a group of workers started to swing at the policemen so that they wouldn't arrest their friends, and then this policeman who shares a room with me, Aristotle, went to the barracks and told the other policemen that they should come ready for battle. My laborer friend told me all this, the same one who's been feeding me information about this guy. Well then: him and thirty or so others showed up shooting, they were machine-gunning workers in the courtyard and even in their living quarters, one bullet hit my room, and I saw with my own eyes a worker get hit in the room next door. It appears that the dead were taken away in dump-trucks to common graves in Planaltina and Padre Bernardo. I knew that Aristotle was a liar and a cheat, but now it's more serious, he's a murderer.

Aunt Francisca turned off the radio, on which a noisy Carnival song had been playing, This is a matter for the police, Valdivino, and it's not you who should be running away, it's him, Look, Francisca—he called Aunt Matilde by the more formal "Dona Matilde," but at that point he only ever addressed Aunt Francisca as "Francisca"—the criminals are precisely the ones who go free, sometimes the police arrest them and send them to Luziânia, but they just pop back up soon after, merry and content, here in the Free City. And what happens when the criminals are the policemen themselves? And of course he knows that I saw quite a bit . . .

Aunt Francisca went to the refrigerator and brought over some juice for Valdivino, Drink it, it'll calm your nerves, Ah, if only Mr. Bernardo Sayão were alive, said Valdivino, he'd find a solution, they're going to name the new railway station after him: Bernardo Sayão Station, that's what it'll be called, and it's still not enough, everything here should be named after him. I don't know what Moacyr can do to help you, said Aunt Francisca.

I won't rest until I'm able to get that guy and all the others in the SPB who participated in the massacre behind bars, I'm going to denounce them all, the only problem is that there's no judge in Brasília, only out in Planaltina, I'm going to go to their leader, the Colonel, I'll go to Newcap, I'll tell the *Tribune* everything I know, but I can't do all this while I still live there, that guy will kill me first, said Valdivino, whose eyes were filling with tears.

Come here, you, said Aunt Francisca, and she laid Valdivino's head on her shoulder, you're going to stay here, there's room for you, all we have to do is hang up another hammock in the living room, as you know, the house is yours, now let me call Moacyr.

In my journal I complained about seeing Valdivino in Aunt Francisca's arms. These days I know that I greatly exaggerated what I'd seen there: I must have made Aunt Francisca's eyes more amorous, invented malice in her tone of voice, in those hands that stroked Valdivino's head, I had Aunt Francisca sitting closer to Valdivino, to tell the truth I had her snug against him, and I mixed that together with my catechism lessons, with the obligations to God that Aunt Francisca herself had taught me, with what I'd heard in Mass about marriage—if anyone has anything to say, let them say it now—and then I vented about all that in the pages of my diary.

Aunt Francisca called Dad. He'd already heard about the massacre, but the story might have just been made up, I think we need to act quickly, argued Aunt Francisca, Valdivino can stay here for today at least, he's risking his life, That's out of the question, replied Dad over the telephone, Well then, you need to do something, talk to someone at Newcap.

Dad sensed that causing a scandal about this matter could endanger his contracts, No, tell Valdivino that he shouldn't play with fire, as far as I know no one was killed.

Valdivino understood, he thought that Dad was right to not want him to stay, I'm going to take off.

Aunt Matilde, who was normally so courageous, watched everything passively and then went to her bedroom, as if nothing were happening.

Moacyr isn't the only one who gives orders in this house, Matilde and I want you to stay, insisted Aunt Francisca, No, I don't want to disobey Mr. Moacyr.

Dad wasn't happy when he saw that Valdivino was still at our house, but he didn't say anything about it until, without my knowledge, he read those pages of my journal, You don't even have the decency to be discreet, Francisca, getting frisky with Valdivino in front of the boy—I listened to the whispered argument in the back of the house—It's him or me, said Dad, Him, then, said Aunt Francisca, I don't need you here, and if anything happens to Valdivino, it's your fault, He didn't tell you all the full story, he had a falling out with that policeman over a girl and he must have taken advantage of this story about a shootout to get revenge on him, but I doubt that he's in as much danger as he says he is, what he needs to do is just keep his mouth shut, No, you insensitive monster, Valdivino isn't one to lie or take revenge, Aunt Francisca argued further, and then frowned in a way she rarely ever did. Dad just shook his head, with an air of disbelief. And don't talk to me ever again, added Aunt Francisca.

Valdivino not only slept in our house that night, but Aunt Francisca persuaded him to stay one more day and, the day after, that he should stay another day still, It's so nice to know you, Valdivino, and it's a pleasure to have you in our home, said Aunt Francisca, challenging Dad.

I'd listened to Valdivino's story and witnessed Aunt Francisca's reaction as if I were watching a movie, but as the story developed before my ears, I became part of the movie and, attentive to the details of the plot, felt that there would be a sad ending, if not a tragic one.

Fortunately for me, Valdivino's presence didn't cause a rift between Aunt Francisca and Dad like the one that had happened before. It had been a senseless argument, it was possible to fix or amend almost anything, Aunt Francisca explained to me, without blaming me for anything, although perhaps she didn't even know that Dad had read my journal. But I could sense that she was growing increasingly critical of Dad's business deals, and especially of his partnership with Paulão.

I know why you dislike him, but look, Paulão doesn't own the brothel anymore, as I've already told you, and I don't frequent those places, explained Dad. Paulão had, in fact, closed the brothel, and Dad no longer had any interest in checking out other brothels out at Placa da Mercedes. He desired Lucrécia during his lonely nights, and even missed her craziness, the added spice to that pliant body, which exuded desire like a volcano, but Paulão finally managed to convince him that she'd really given up that life and left, that she no longer lived in the Free City, and he had no reason to suspect the surprises in store for him when he eventually saw her again.

No, it's not because of the brothel, you know what I'm talking about, replied Aunt Francisca, and Dad started to feel unsure of how much she knew about his partnership with Paulão.

Roberto came over to the house frequently and enlivened our

conversations, which at that point had transcended the borders of the Free City and Brasília. Didn't I tell you that Lucas Lopes wouldn't last?, said Aunt Matilde, triumphantly waving in his face the fact that the Treasury Minister had just been replaced that day, July 3, 1959. You disliked him for the wrong reasons, replied Roberto, Brazil does need foreign capital and to continue investing in the programs of JK's "Goal-Oriented Plan," but to get tied to the IMF right now just because of a loan … the president is right, we should cut ties with the IMF and continue doing what we have to do, But the opposition is right to object to rising inflation and runaway public spending, said Dad, They're only saying that because the electoral campaigns are starting, responded Roberto, They're saying that the governor of São Paulo is going to be nominated as the opposition candidate for president, said Dad. I trust him to get things back under control and bring morality to this country, I'd vote for him, said Aunt Matilde, It's a pity that the government's candidate is so uncharismatic, Dad commented, That general couldn't even win in his dreams, said Aunt Matilde in agreement, They're even saying that the president is going to push a Constitutional reform through congress so that he can be reelected, said Dad. Aunt Francisca grew bored with those discussions, and only participated in the conversation when the subject veered towards the singers on the radio, or the case of Aída Curi, the young woman who was murdered by playboys in Rio de Janeiro.

At this point in his edit, João Almino complained about the absence of Valdivino from the story, and for that reason I'll hasten to say that every now and then, for months, Aunt Francisca would ask after him. It's possible that he went back to the Northeast, speculated Dad, it's better for him that way, Do you have no pangs of conscience for what you did, do you have no heart?, Aunt Francisca demanded of him.

It came as a surprise to me when, in November of that year,

1959, during an enormous downpour, she came home with dramatic news about Valdivino. I had gone out into the street during the storm to join in the mirth with all the other little kids, and to build character, make myself stronger, and learn to brave bad weather. It was one of my greatest pleasures, we'd cause a ruckus running through the streets, shouting as we went, we'd argue over who got to play in the streams of water that fell from the roof-tiles—our heavy shorts dripping water onto the ground like faucets—and shudder with fear at the thunder, the way people take pleasure in watching horror films. When Aunt Francisca saw me that day, she told me to go home. I noticed that she seemed dejected and I gladly went with her, as she shielded me with her umbrella and held my wet hand. When we arrived home, she told Dad that she'd run into Valdivino in the Free City, and that he was despondent because his brother had died in tragic fashion two months earlier.

He's not upset at you, Moacyr, quite the opposite, he wants to meet up with you, he says that he still has to be careful about where he goes, that people are still after him, and that's why he's living in an isolated place, at a nearby farm. I told him that he could come visit you here next Sunday, but if you don't want to, then just leave, and we'll receive him.

Between four walls, on that sixth night, Dad related to me, with a richness of details, what Valdivino told him on that distant Sunday, I was being chased down, and still am, by Aristotle, that guy I wanted to denounce, by Carminha's dad, and even by that landowner, who is still trying to get me to pay my debt, so I had to leave my job and flee Planalto Village. When they discovered that I was living in Amaury Village with my brother, I had to take refuge in the commune where I live now. After I moved, I hardly ever saw my brother, because of the distance and also because if I ever went back to Amaury Village they would easily find me.

The shadows from the tree branches vividly striped the

ground, together with both their shadows, as they walked through a desolate landscape, on a dirt road full of deep grooves left by the recent rain.

His brother was an alcoholic and was drunk when the implacable water had risen in September, taking with it the houses of Amaury Village, setting snakes and other animals adrift, as well as everything that came out of the open septic tanks. His brother and six others had perished, They only found my brother's body some days later, floating; I made a deal with him, Mr. Moacyr, that whoever died first would send a sign to the other from the great beyond, so every day I'm looking for a sign from my brother, but there hasn't been anything yet.

The love of his life, even though she'd never wanted to meet his brother, had become really upset and cried a lot over his death, I wanted to tell you, since you're a brain doctor, Mr. Moacyr, what's been going on with me, I really want to marry her, Mr. Moacyr, but she demands that I do things for her to earn her love, and I do them, one after another, but she always finds my efforts lacking. I worked myself to death, and all the money I earned went to buy the land she wanted for her commune. I have to confess something: she doesn't give herself to me anymore, or to anybody. She'd even marry me, as long as nothing sexual ever happened between us, said Valdivino, who was breaking out in a cold sweat.

That's a nervous symptom, said Dad, diagnosing him.

You know something, Mr. Moacyr? The thing is I'm still in love with her, but now the situation's become more complicated, she only accepted me into the commune once I swore that I would stop liking her the way I do. She's really strange now, everything's very mysterious with her. I can tell you, Sir, and no one else, that there's a secret about our lives, mine and hers. Something she told me in the past, but that she now denies, and she's denying it so that we won't end up together. For her the past doesn't even exist, she believes that she's founding a new world. I have no doubt that she's virtuous, a holy virgin, it's just that she has this friend, an ill-bred sort, who doesn't like me and wants to run everything out there in the commune.

If you were a little clearer about all this, maybe I could give you some advice.

I can tell you about it, Sir, they told me that it was well-known in the Free City that she was a loose woman.

And what do you think?

It's slander, and I won't stand for such slander. What she has is a difficult temperament, and now she's having all sorts of visions and revelations, she sees spirits, Mr. Moacyr, there are even people who live with her in a cosmic world.

They could be schizophrenic outbursts.

No, they're spiritual immersions, but I'm not complaining, Mr. Moacyr, the commune is like the final church that I've helped to build, the most complete of them all, a church made up of every religion. I want to help all the hopeless people here move out to the commune, it's just that I have to be very careful whenever I go out.

But what do you want to do with your life after that, Valdivino? You have a lot of skills, you can't just stay hidden, doing nothing with your life.

Valdivino then explained to Dad, in his own words, which may not be exactly the ones that I'll use here, that he had no ambitions, only that he'd never sully his honor or lose his courage, that he'd already come close to dying, and for that reason life, for him, was a privilege, he took pleasure in the small things in life, like animals and plants, he wanted a simple happiness, harvested from the dryness of the quotidian, like flowers that grow in gray, arid, desert landscapes, his friend was reason enough to keep him interested in living, to love and to be loved were his greatest aspirations . . .

You can stay the night with us whenever you want, offered Dad this time.

Thank you very much, Mr. Moacyr, but I always prefer to make it back to the commune, it's safer that way; I only come to the Free City when I need to, and I rarely need to.

*Seventh Night:*
*The Desert and Oblivion*

On the seventh night, between bars and with one dingy white wall in front of us, which had words scrawled on it, as well as a heart, an addition problem, a division problem, and some meaningless streaks that ran up to the top of the wall, on the right side, Dad told me what he believed happened to Valdivino, and I listened to him, incredulous.

Despite my best efforts and my allegations that it was inhumane to lock up an old, sick man, Dad was still imprisoned. The most I'd managed to achieve—because of the state of his health or his age or even because the authorities respected me as a journalist—was the special permission to pay him daily visits over the course of a week.

I had spent the day preparing for what would become my last visit with Dad. Like a monk seeking out divine truths, I leafed through the last pages of his "Onward" notebooks, the ones that narrated his activities in the months leading up to the inauguration of Brasília. Dad had written about his apprehension in regard to what Don Bosco had written in 1883: "When they excavate the hidden mines amid these hills, the promised land shall here appear, a land of milk and honey."

"Only once they excavate the hidden mines, but they still haven't excavated them," wrote Dad. Perhaps he felt that it was up to him—less out of idealism than greed for gain—to help out with those excavations.

If one believes what's in those notebooks, Dad had finally managed, at the beginning of 1960, to accompany some illustrious visitors. He bemoaned the fact that when President López Mateos of México visited, received by a big crowd, he hadn't been able to accompany him, but soon after, on February 23, he had heard a speech by President Eisenhower in front of the Monumental Axis Highway: "Brasília has captured the imagination of my fellow countrymen who have visited here and who, on their return home, have been lavish in their praise of the wonders they have seen. For several reasons, Brasília fascinates the citizens of the United States . . ." Together with the quote from Eisenhower was an article, ripped out of a newspaper and already yellow with age: sixty-seven people, almost all of them members of the U.S. Navy Band, had died when a U.S. Navy plane collided with a civilian aircraft near Sugarloaf mountain in Rio.

Reading through those papers, seated by the edge of the pool beneath a rose-colored sky, which was not intimidated by the gigantic increase in the size of the city, in the house that I was going to lose in just a few days, I felt the urge to rekindle the spirit of the founding of the "Modern Capital of the World," as a professor from the University of Palermo had called it, the city that "for the inhabitants of the world" signified "hope and faith in the future," as the filmmaker Frank Capra had professed, both of them quoted in Dad's notebooks. I now looked upon that city like a child who is born into a situation of great promise, but can't even manage to grow up to be as dignified as his parents, who becomes an outcast, but who one day, through his own force of will, could live up to the calling that had given him life.

I had tried to differentiate myself from Dad, had asserted myself by denying him, and even by entering into open conflict with him, but I still recognized that I owed part of who I was to him, to all he had earned, and, now, to all he had lost—including my house by the lake, where I was leafing through those old papers. When I left home, I joined the student movement, was arrested, tortured, and, as a result of that, had a brief bout of insanity, and perhaps I would have followed another path if I wasn't my father's son, if Dad hadn't bequeathed to me, during his lifetime, a portion of his wealth and secured for me the comfort that I am now losing, also because of him. It's as if, as the Prophetess Íris Quelemém once said, we truly were just an ant on the horse's hide, believing that we are winding our own way while it's the horse that is really darting off in different directions, and yet here I am, now dreaming one dream of the future, now another, the world spins round, seemingly one place, then turning into another entirely. I left home on bad terms not only with Dad, but also with Aunt Francisca, because she didn't believe what I was telling her about Dad and because she decided to marry him despite my warnings against it. The final straw, however, was an article I wrote and never brought myself to publish.

At that time, Dad's business dealings had already extended to the wealthy areas of the capital, as had those of Aunt Francisca, who had earned quite a reputation with her cooking, which was considered sophisticated and was marketed as the traditional cuisine of Minas Gerais. I had grown as tall as Dad and was basically a grown man, adolescence had deepened my voice and turned me rebellious, just as it made me quieter: I had become reserved and serious. I had taken after Dad in one way: in my desire to record what was going on around me, believing that something grandiose was transpiring, but what I considered grandiose was the very thing he feared the most, that is, that same possibility of revolution that Aunt Matilde dreamed of. Nobody called the Free City "The Free City" anymore, and the "Pioneer Camp" had become transformed into a satellite city like many others. One day I walked up and down its main avenues, which were still the same as ever, I saw the façades of the old shops, I saw the few trees we'd planted still thriving in the backyard of our old house, which was vacant at that point, and afterwards I locked myself in my room with my books and papers, asking myself what I could make of the promise of the future of the little boy who had once lived there. I concentrated on my work, and nearly forgot to eat or sleep.

Give me that worthless article, said Dad, after reading the article without my permission, as he used to do in the old days with my journal, and, taking it from my hands, he started to rip it to shreds, which he threw in the trashcan beneath the desk. I ran over to him and managed to save one of the pages.

For the love of God, stop it right now, yelled Aunt Francisca.

I was beside myself, or rather, I had just entered my true self for the first time, Damn you and the whore that gave birth to you, you go around pretending you're a saint, but I know damn well what you did—I said to Dad—and you should be on my side, Aunt Francisca, since you were the first to defend Valdivino, but now you're just playing blind, deaf, and dumb.

Get out of this house, roared Dad, You bastard!, I replied, You're being unfair to your Dad, give me the rest of that paper, said Aunt Francisca to me, I don't want your opinion, you slut!, and I kept on raging, You're not even my dad, my real dad died a long time ago, you bastard!, you murderer!, feeling good for having had the courage to speak my mind. And I repeated it: You murderer!

Behave yourself, said Aunt Francisca, addressing me.

You miserable bitch!, I replied, and stood staring at the shredded papers in the wastebasket and the pieces that had fallen on the floor under the desk.

I think he's been talking to that scoundrel, that liar Paulão on the sly, said Aunt Francisca.

Dad was swelling with anger, it was flashing in his face, and I soon felt the sting of a powerful slap to my face, which I repaid with a punch to his face, then he pushed me hard and I fell to the floor, hitting my head against the corner of the wall. Aunt Francisca even started to come to my aid, but I left the house in a flash and never again went back.

Though I'd never felt very close to her, Aunt Matilde was the one who was there for me. Recently broken up with Roberto, she was working as a civil servant and lived in a functional apartment in the North Wing. Already in full adolescence, I desired her, recalling the night that she'd undressed in the living room where I slept. Unlike the child I'd been, the adolescent didn't fear sin and didn't think it an obstacle that she was my aunt, since she wasn't really my aunt at all. Do you remember that night, Aunt Matilde, I never forgot it, I wanted to go back in time, it's the only thing in my life that I regret not doing, you're not my aunt by blood, I don't see anything too wrong with it, it'll be a revolutionary act on our part, what are you afraid of, Aunt Matilde? Following a blunder that I'd rather not discuss, she imposed her limits and took care of me, and I truly became her friend and began to feel a true affinity for her, not like I had for Dad, or even Aunt Francisca. She sympathized with my ideas, discussed my articles with me, dreamed of socialism, and was critical of the military, like me. As I soon came to find out, she led a secret life at night, devoting herself to spraying graffiti on walls—for the revolution needed to infiltrate every corner—and she was even arrested when the police stormed her apartment and found her notebook full of addresses. Her imprisonment, along with mine, may have been the cause of my short-lived bout of insanity.

But all this happened much later on, and as these topics, as well as my falling out with Dad, still cause me pain, I'd rather return to those less bitter memories from the beginning of 1960 and to the papers that Dad buried. I read in one of the newspapers from that era, found among all those papers, that, from its inception to the beginning of 1960, Brasília had cost more than fifty billion *cruzeiros*, not counting the cost of the light and power, water, sewer, and telephone service. Twenty billion *cruzeiros* worth of building plots had been sold, and there were still billions of *cruzeiros*-worth more to be sold—which demonstrated the extraordinary possibility of riches for those who, like Dad, increasingly dedicated themselves to the buying and selling of land.

Like the countdown to a fireworks launch, Dad's box of papers proclaimed the coming inauguration of Brasília through newspaper clippings, all of them dated and numbered. On the day of its publication, January 16, 1960, Dad had shown me a newspaper report stating that the National Integration Caravan, with its four columns—coming from the north, south, east, and west, that is, from Belém, Porto Alegre, Rio, and Cuiabá—each of which was made up of fifty domestically produced vehicles, had begun its journey to the future capital, and on February 2—together with Valdivino, Aunt Francisca, and Aunt Matilde— he took me, beneath a cloudy sky, to the Three Powers Plaza, where nearly the entire population of Brasília watched the arrival of those four columns, which were going to be received by JK, Dona Sarah, and all the ministers.

Valdivino's enthusiasm was so great that we formed a little team with him, cheering on the column that received the most applause, the one from the north. It didn't matter that he was from Bahia, that Dad and Aunt Matilde were from Minas Gerais, and Aunt Francisca and I were from Goiás, we all wanted to be represented by the city of Belém, in the state of Pará. It was our way of paying homage to Bernardo Sayão.

Léa Sayão, the daughter of Bernardo, Dad informed us, took part in the caravan that was coming down the Belém-Brasília, riding in a Volkswagon bus driven by Joana Lowell Bowen, an American that I know from my time back in Goiás, the owner of a farm in the Das Almas River region, between Ceres and

Goianésia, close to where we used to live. When they got to Açailândia, the two of them and a few others prayed at the foot of the cross that I helped set up on the spot where Sayão died.

At Aunt Francisca's insistence, we moved closer to the image of Our Lady of Nazareth, the patroness of Belém, displayed on the altar next to the patroness of Brasília, Our Lady of Aparecida.

Valdivino's eyes filled with tears when JK signed the act that officially named the Belém-Brasília highway after Bernardo Sayão. He embraced Dad, overflowing with joy. Valdivino's tears were contagious, especially for Aunt Francisca, and affected us all.

At home the next day, Dad transcribed, in one of his "Onward" notebooks, the message, written on a scroll, that the poet Guilherme de Almeida had sent from São Paulo and underlined the first few words with a red pencil, as if he wished to transfer to the page the emotions of someone realizing that they are witnessing a unique, extraordinary moment: "Upon the immense map of Brazil, an enormous cross is now being drawn."

Another news item I found in the box, and which I remember Dad showing me, was dated March 27, 1960: a hundred naval riflemen and twenty volunteer marines had begun Operation Dawn, a journey on foot from Rio to Brasília which was to last until April 21. Aunt Matilde had commented at the time: Poor guys! I got to come here on an airplane, and even I regret it . . .

I also found some handwritten notes dated April 11. At the second Newcap auction, Dad had bought ten building plots, each of them measuring ten meters by forty. At the time he had to pay three million *cruzeiros* for all of them, whereas just a year before he had done the same, but had only spent two hundred and fifty thousand, which was one more indication for me that he had already accumulated enormous sums of money through land deals and construction.

Another article, which was nearly illegible, from a torn and yellowed newspaper, contained the news that, at 12:45 P.M. on April 20, 1960—thus, a day before the inauguration of Brasília—the plane carrying JK and his entourage had landed, that he was later transported to the Palace of the Dawn by helicopter, and that, on the same day—this part was underlined in ink—the one hundred naval riflemen and twenty marines of Operation Dawn had arrived on foot.

I did not, however, find anything about the possible murder of Valdivino, not even a little note or mere mention. I had suspected for some time that Dad was hiding something from me, I'd talked to people who had lived in the Garden of Salvation at the time of the incident, and, although the few people who remembered what took place were convinced of the Prophetess Íris Quelemém's version of events, one of them told me that it all started when Valdivino had a jealous outburst and attacked Dad.

On that seventh and final night, for which I had prepared by reading and rereading those papers, I confronted Dad with the version of events that had been the source of my big blowout with him and the reason I left home that day in 1966, when he was preparing to marry Aunt Francisca. Let's set aside the conjecture that was brought up years ago on my psychoanalyst's couch, that I harbored an unhealthy jealousy in regards to my aunt. In my adolescent mind, at that time, I was thinking of protecting her more than anything else, I couldn't stand to see her marry Dad, I assumed that they were getting married because Dad had had his way with her some drunken night, I couldn't accept that she, who was so very Catholic, would marry an atheist, and when I found out that Dad had probably killed Valdivino, I related the story to her, but she merely repeated what she had told me years ealier, that Valdivino had died as a result of sex within his family, Don't call your dad a criminal.

They say that Valdivino assaulted you, Dad, because he found out about your affair with Lucrécia, they think that you're the one who killed him, in self-defense, and that you later tried, unsuccessfully, to save him, to resuscitate him, Those are just stories, inventions, said Dad, who then narrated, between four dingy white walls, what had given rise to those speculations.

One day in December, Valdivino convinced him to go out to the commune with him. He was visibly anxious about the arrival of 1960: The world is going to end, Mr. Moacyr, that's one of Lúcia's secrets—he said, referring to one of the little shepherd children to whom Our Lady appeared in Fátima, Portugal—the pope never wanted to reveal this secret, 'cause he didn't want to scare everyone.

Once they picked up the highway that led to the commune, the conversation turned to the first time that they had met, out near the Descoberto, Do you want to come hunt armadillos out here with me, Sir? In addition to the giant armadillo, we also run across *açu* armadillos, six-banded armadillos, and three-banded armadillos, said Valdivino.

Armadillo hunts should take place in the winter, Valdivino, when, because of the cold, they stay underground, but come out at sunrise to hunt for worms and insects, So this winter let's go on another hunt, just like the first one, you promise? I promise, Dad said sincerely, for he still looked back fondly on the trip he'd made with Valdivino and me out near the Descoberto—but if we want to find capybara, marsh deer, red lily-trotters, garganey ducks, side-necked turtles, red-footed tortoises, and spectacled caimans, we'll need to go out to the shores of Feia Lake.

Tibouchina flowers dyed the landscape, here and there, in violet, speckled with yellow from the mimosas. Some flowers looked like snow, and on them alighted Anna's eighty-eight butterflies. Valdivino asked Dad to stop the jeep and got down to pick some of the white flowers, which he formed into a little bouquet, Isn't this pretty, Mr. Moacyr?

When they resumed the trip, he talked about the birds that

they saw out at the commune, pointing out all the ones that they could spot on the sides of the road. At this advanced point in the story, in which we are heading to meet Valdivino's mysterious girlfriend, I should say that I'm no longer interested in the blog, since no one ever provides me any useful facts or ideas, except for the author of the last comment, who suggested some names of birds that Valdivino might have shown to Dad on the side of the road, birds that are easily found in the region: masked yellowthroats, red-shouldered tanagers, rufous-collared sparrows, paramo seedeaters, white-necked thrushes, saffron finches, European goldfinches, crested oropendolas, white-tipped doves, red turtledoves, quails, and pheasants. I don't, however, have a way to fit the names of the friends of JK and Oscar Niemeyer—which another blog-reader sent me—into this part of the story.

Let's leave the birds at the side of the road and finish the trip, for Dad and Valdivino were already approaching the commune. Money isn't everything, Mr. Moacyr, I used to work myself to death and got paid well for it, and here I don't work and don't get paid a thing, but God's the one who pays me. Ah, Mr. Moacyr, it's such a great feeling to be able to walk through the fields at the commune when the weather is nice. Can you feel that little breeze, Sir? I used to have my doubts, but not anymore: life is worth living, Mr. Moacyr, even when you're trying to escape the world, like me.

When they arrived, Valdivino decided to explain further the work that his friend was doing out there. When Aunt Neiva founded the White Arrow Spiritist Union back in November, his girlfriend had wanted to pay it a visit, because she was starting to experience, more and more frequently, paranormal and extrasensory phenomena, which neither science nor religion could explain. Aunt Neiva told her that she saw dead people and the spirits of *pretos velhos*—or old black men—Indians, and friends from outer space, and one of these people, Father White

Arrow, who for millennia has sought to protect humanity during moments of transition, had charged her with a mission and helped her create a new doctrine, then she began to practice high magic and, in 1959, had even started to transport herself, on a daily basis, to Tibet so she could meet with her master, Humarram, from whom she received teachings and initiatory instructions.

I know who Neiva is, said Dad, interrupting him, I remember the bamboo shack, covered in canvas, where she lived when she first came to the Free City in 1957 to work as a Newcap-registered truck driver. I'd already heard of her back in Ceres, and Bernardo Sayão asked me, as a doctor and psychiatrist, to give her a check-up, because she had started to have visions. During the appointment, while I was explaining to her that her visions could be the result of being overworked, she launched into a conversation with someone that only she could see, behind the partition, and the dialogue was centered on my grandfather, who was already dead. I admit that it scared me and I didn't want to see her again.

Well, after that visit with Aunt Neiva, continued Valdivino, my friend started embracing some of the practices of Spiritism. Like Aunt Neiva, she began to feel the presence of enigmatic beings, who were invisible to other people, and who, to this day, guide her on her path. Also as a result of Aunt Neiva's influence, she opened the commune to the most diverse assortment of religious legacies and traditions, including those of ancient peoples, especially Egyptians, Greeks, Romans, Mayans, Aztecs, Incas, Yorubans, and Gypsies, although everything can be freely studied there: it's not necessary to obey written documents, believe in revelations, or impose rituals based on faith or fear. Everyone must feel and experience for themselves the power of their spiritual communication to truly undergo a new experience. She has also communicated with the spirit of Coronel Fawcett and says that she's going to find the City of Z.

Dad felt a strange sensation: although he'd spent so much time with Valdivino, he didn't really know him. That skinny, soft-spoken young man beside him was like that quiet, polite neighbor you see every day and then one day discover that he's a murderer. He tried to dismiss those bad thoughts, We call this place here the Garden of Salvation, said Valdivino; and one other thing, Mr. Moacyr, I forgot to tell you that I'm known as Abel in the commune.

As they went through the first of three iron gateways, they were offered a drink. It had the same smell as the nectar of joy—the balm made from a mixture of herbs and angel trumpets, boiled in oil—which Dad had inhaled on that distant night in the Brasília Hotel. It tasted just like the one that Lucrécia had made him lick on that distant night. But it was stronger, much stronger. You're only supposed to drink a little, advised Valdivino.

After that, he took Dad to a nearby hill, called Battle Hill, where his friend, surrounded by about fifty people, was preaching a sermon:

This isn't the first time that the Earth is going to be affected by an enormous comet, but the other ones were just a warning, it's been sixty-five million years since a meteorite destroyed the Earth's inhabitants, the dinosaurs, and thirteen thousand years ago a comet exploded in the heavens and rained meteorites on the Americas, to the north of here, rained balls of fire on the plant life all around, and buried microscopic diamonds in the ground, and the sun disappeared behind layers of ash and dust, that's why the human race lived through an ice age for a thousand years and many animals disappeared. The humans of that era, the Clovis culture, are no longer here to tell their story, but there are spirits from that culture that walk the earth and bring us truths from that era; we are now facing the same danger, but not those who live in the Central Plateau, where the human race established itself over ten thousand years ago and created a civilization around the city of Z, and I have received a message from the spirits of Z: the new creation emerging from the laws of the universe is that which is about to come forth in Brasília, it is that which shall come about in the new Age of Aquarius and the new millennium . . .

Dad didn't know how to react or what to say. He was in a state of shock. Was Valdivino's friend really Lucrécia, or was that just an effect of the substance he'd imbibed?

Look at how the Prophetess Íris lights up, there's some sort of light all around her body, a light that just naturally shines, said one man.

Íris?

Íris Quelemém, said Valdivino.

Íris, who was also Lucrécia, encouraged those present to make public confessions. One had been a thief, he regretted what he had done, had lost everything during his years in prison, especially his friends. He was starting over from scratch. His family had gone without basic necessities. Now his children were all grown and no longer lived at home. His wife had agreed to come with him to the Garden of Salvation.

Valdivino said, Nearly everyone here has committed terrible crimes, they're former drug addicts, repentant murderers, and there are also former prostitutes, who are starting a new life here.

Íris raised her voice, using a megaphone:

The hopeless people of the world shall find their path here in the Garden of Salvation. Our teachings are inscribed through suffering and injustice—she placed emphasis on certain words and punctuated sentences with gestures of her hands, like an orchestra conductor. It was known from our birth that we were going to sin. So much so that Jesus was crucified to atone for our sins. But all of thine imperfections can be transformed into virtues. Thine errors shall guide ye on the path of light and the creation of a new humanity. They shall be like traffic signs, said

Íris, raising up both arms and pointing them forward. Ye shall derive strength from your difficulties. Look the devils that appear before ye late at night straight in the eyes. I wish to teach ye how to transform them into guardian angels. Vice exists so that virtue may prevail. Believe in this blue sky, in the birds that are singing all around us. Love one another. Love each other truly, without envy or jealousy.

Thus spoke Íris, at the top of Battle Hill, and Dad, who could barely believe his eyes, took note of her words and concluded—in thoughts that seemed sharp and crystalline—that the Garden of Salvation was a portal to the contribution that extremists, fanatics, madmen, lunatics, the depressed, the hopeless, and the misunderstood could give to the world. There they acquired relevance. There they discovered their mission. Brasília was a refuge from hopelessness, from Dad's own hopelessness, which, though repressed and forgotten ever since he had left Rio de Janeiro to live in Ceres with Aunt Francisca, seemed to be reappearing. A feeling of distress began to gnaw at his stomach and rose up into his mouth with a bitter taste. Was the liquid he had drunk clouding his vision? No, that woman was truly Lucrécia, he recognized the look in her eye, which penetrated his mind, and her voice, which echoed in his ears.

Dad attempted to resist that avalanche of madness. He couldn't bring himself to believe in what Lucrécia was saying, although he was astonished at her knowledge, which must have come from a combination of readings and pure intuition. The words of a foreign journalist, which he had read a year or so earlier, were resounding in his head: "Brasília is something that surpasses all that can be imagined, something that would have shocked even Jules Verne, if someone were to have told him about it." The reason for such amazement wasn't the architecture of Oscar Niemeyer or Lúcio Costa's design for the layout of the city, but rather the creeds and sects that were already proliferating on the outskirts of the city, and the possibility that Lucrécia, a prostitute, had become a prophetess.

It's all written in the stars, and the future of the human race is already mapped out, said Íris.

It was that liquid that made the words spoken by Íris, who was also Lucrécia, resonate in the depths of Dad's thoughts, but he believed in the freedom to determine one's own destiny, and Brasília was a place of freedom, a place where it was possible to invent, experiment, and create something out of nothing, out of emptiness, out of the useless, the unnecessary—perhaps this was what his sister Matilde had been trying to express. All around him he saw the lawful and unlawful enrichment of so many people who benefitted from the construction business . . . He would control his own future, he would cut himself an ever-larger slice of the money that was being printed, he would be powerful, a millionaire, that was his goal.

Ye shall never be free, no one shall ever be free, said Íris. If it's money that attracts ye, by money ye shall be led.

Dad became frightened, he thought that she was reading his thoughts and, for a fraction of a second, that she was right, that he'd lost all his freedom when Paulão had shown him the easy way to make money. From that point on, he had been swallowed up into a pit of blackened gold, transported to the heavens and the bottom of the pit all at once, as if he had cheated his way into heaven and remained there in a fragile state of comfort, awaiting his downfall. It was as if Lucrécia was speaking to him and no one else, but it was another Lucrécia, it was Íris, and she truly seemed to be a saint.

It had rained the day before, and Dad could feel his feet getting mired in the mud, he noticed the expansive ground, the mirrors of water that reflected the blue sky above, the wide landscape bathed in red by the sun, and glimpsed from afar a wine palm, which, at the bottom of the hill and beside the banks of a stream, imposingly marked the edge of space.

Íris's eyes followed a bird that had taken off from atop the wine palm, You are like an ant crawling on the horse of invisible forces, forces from the deep recesses of the mind, forces from the soul, an ant that makes up stories about determining its own future, she said, once again as if she were talking directly to Dad, no longer addressing the plural and antiquated "ye" but the singular, informal "you," and, thus, just him. You don't decide beforehand, you are thrust into motion and make the decision that the motion suggests to you, you are not leading the donkey, you're merely a tick on the donkey's hide. God made men like machines, determined how they would function and what they would do, only allowing them to improvise minor variations within a prescribed set of motions. You can do whatever you want, but you cannot want whatever you want, for what we truly want comes from the outside, from God, from the devil, from spirits, and the different eras of history. I used to want one thing, but today I want something different. What we choose is the result of magic powers that come from the great beyond, that come from the spirit and pass from the spirit to our minds, to our bodies, said Íris. The greatest changes in my life happened that way, and as I have changed, so can you.

As if our conscience were unable to veto our desires, and history did not allow us to reevaluate our experiences and dream of a different future, Dad believed for a moment that Íris was right, and, thus, no one would be responsible for the consequences of their actions, or their choices. No one could stand in judgment of anyone else, nor even of one's own self. He could never be blamed for anything. It was destiny that had brought him to Paulão, and even to Lucrécia.

But there is a tiny amount of chance in the way that things come about in this world, said Íris, and cause creates the future.

Unfortunately, I have to head out, said Dad to Valdivino, But you just got here!, I wanted to introduce you to my friend, Not today, Valdivino, I'm not feeling well, let's leave it for another day, suggested Dad, not because he was starting to feel dizzy and had a headache coming on, but because he wanted to avoid any embarrassment.

The following month, January of 1960, on the night of a new moon, Valdivino urgently called Dad out to the Garden of Salvation. Lucrécia, who was also the Prophetess Íris Quelemém, appeared to have been assaulted and was confused, spouting nonsense. To his surprise, Dad encountered his partner, Paulão, there, I came out here to bring some order to this place, nobody out here has their feet on the ground, so I take care of the construction, the buying and selling, the money... she depends on me for everything.

For the love of God, do something, said Valdivino, pleading with Dad, What happened? asked Dad, This is normal, replied Paulão, she's just like that, she has these fits when she drinks those elixirs she makes; you know I like her, I already saved her life once when she hit rock bottom back when we were in Bahia.

Íris had welts on her body. Did someone hit her? Valdivino wouldn't respond to Dad's questions, as if he didn't want to reveal what had happened, She did it to herself, said Paulão.

I was relieved to see that she didn't seem to recognize me, Dad told me, looking at the white wall and the barred-up window, I wasn't ready to face her, at least not out there, in front of Valdivino.

Someone had told me that on that trip out to the Garden of Salvation, Valdivino wanted to find out if Dad had really had an affair with Lucrécia, who was also Íris, and had lost his temper. Dad had denied everything, If you're lying to me . . . , replied Valdivino, and then he made a vague threat, I'm going to end up killing someone.

Three months later I found Valdivino himself stretched out

on the ground and they told me a similar story, that he'd hurt himself, said Dad, continuing to tell me his version of the story, now that he was locked up between four walls. It had been the day after the inauguration of Brasília.

I was ten years old at the time and on that day I had asked Dad if we were going to have to tear down our house in the Free City, the Pioneer Camp; I was afraid that my short career as a tour guide, performed in my spare time on some afternoons, would thus come to an end. The city was set to be destroyed once Brasília was inaugurated, and I had heard rumors about us moving to Gama or Taguatinga, but Dad and Aunt Francisca had told me, even up through 1959, that "Saint Bernardo Sayão" would save us. Through the Merchants' Association and the Movement for the Permanence and Urbanization of the Pioneer Camp, they had joined forces with the customers, merchants, and residents of the city to change the name of it to Bernardo Sayão Quarter. Thus, instead of being destroyed, the Free City or Pioneer Camp, as it was also called, would stand as a permanent homage to the person that all of us admired as one of the great founders of Brasília. We didn't have any reason to be worried about the arsonist blazes started by those who wished to defeat the movement for the definitive permanence of the city.

Faced with the dry response of "of course not," the Free City will never be destroyed, I further inquired if we had earned the right to live there by "system of commodatum," the expression that I had memorized years before. There was no time for explanations, Dad told me, he had to make an urgent trip to the Garden of Salvation and wouldn't allow me to go with him, Go with your aunts to the Childrens' Festival, you have to tell me all about it, in detail, he ordered.

It may be that my memory has mixed up recollections from disparate time periods, but I believe that it was at this moment that I heard Aunt Matilde singing along with the phonograph as

she drummed on the tabletop:
    I'm not an Indian, nothing like that
    My ears aren't pierced through front to back
    I've got no ring hanging from my nose
    No loincloth of feathers hung 'round
    my waist, and my skin is brown
    from the sun on the beach where I was born and raised, ya
know?
    I won't go, won't go to Brasília,
    Not me and not my family, nah
    not even to get rich, 'cause I don't wanna
    Life can't be bought, just lived
    even when it's tough and expensive,
    I'd rather be poor than leave my Copacabana.
    It was an album by Billy Blanco, a present from Aunt Matilde's friends in Rio. She laughed as she listened and sang along. She later said to me, About that conversation with your Dad, don't worry, João, the Free City will never be destroyed, which to my mind is a pity, because all this is going to become the biggest slum in Brasília, you better believe it! Don't talk that way, complained Aunt Francisca, Just look, the shops are all moving from here to W-3 Street, you're going to have to open your business over there, Francisca. Aunt Francisca had lost a competition, which determined who would make the main cake for the inauguration of Brasília, to Royal Bakery, located on W-3 South.

    I remember it well, it was April 22, a Friday, and I was thinking that it had the makings of the best day ever, because the Childrens' Festival was going to start at nine o'clock, and Dad had promised to take me. Instead, he shot off in his '46 Ford Coupe, black as mourning garb. It turned into a sad day, since my aunts didn't want to take me. My only consolation was that Brasília had been inaugurated the day before, I had seen the president up close, and Dad had told us that JK had predicted that in ten years

Brazil would have a population of a hundred million and would be the fourth or fifth country in the world, in terms of economic power.

And what conclusion have you come to about what happened to Valdivino?, I asked Dad, now that he was locked up between four walls because they hadn't seen fit to pardon an inventive builder for failure to pay taxes and abide by the architects' plans.

One thing is certain, he had known Íris for a very long time. The photograph that I saw when I went into Valdivino's shack reminded me of someone, and only later did I realize . . . It was a photo of a very young Íris, a photo that she had dedicated, on the back, to Valdivino when he was just a child. After I found out about certain things, I thought that he may have really had a reason to want to kill himself, taking large doses of those liquids that Íris made. I recalled the bottle that I had seen off in a corner of the little room . . . On the other hand, Valdivino was on the lam, it might be the case that he wasn't in the crosshairs of the landowner he owed money to, but it was a fact that he was still being pursued by the father of that girl he got pregnant, and I tried in vain to get the police to investigate it. My other suspicion fell on the policeman from the SPB, who had disappeared and never turned back up, And you think that he's the one who killed Valdivino? I'm not a detective, I did what I could, the only thing I found in Valdivino's room, aside from the bottle, was a Continental brand cigarette, which could indeed have belonged to Paulão, but it didn't prove a thing, because lots of people smoked Continentals. Some time later I spoke to Íris about it . . . As you know, she couldn't be trusted. Paulão and Valdivino were competing for her, the former thinking that he owned her, and the latter bound to her by passion. Íris liked the fact that those rivals had become enemies and provided more than enough reasons for both their spirits to become routinely enraged. When I spoke with her, while she insisted that Valdivino hadn't died, but had gone off in search of the City of Z, she confessed that Valdivino had tried to kill Paulão, that Paulão had defended himself, and that in the course of the fight Valdivino had fallen to the floor, unconscious. When he halfway came to his senses, he called out for me. They went to look for me in the Free City, but only found me the next day, But there was no crime committed, there shall be no crime in Brasília, she was saying, Or the crimes just won't be discovered, I contested, No, there shall be no crime, she repeated. You know, it was hard to have a rational conversation with her.

No one knows anyone else in their entirety, we go about creating an impressionist portrait of others in our heads from elements that we gather here and there, but the painting can change when we view it from a different angle, for it is painted by our very thoughts. We knew and did not know Valdivino. I knew and did not know Dad.

But forget about the past, João, the past is long buried, he told me.

I could fit everything that I felt for him during my lifetime—hatred, affection, respect, admiration, contempt—in that sober, severe face, in that deteriorated, debilitated body, in those defiant eyes, and that tired voice, but those were feelings and impressions that were mine alone, projected onto him, and nothing more. I felt that he had figured out how to face life with greatness, and his coldness and audacity, the risks he ran, his tireless work, and the actions that landed him in prison were nothing more than the proof of this. I wasn't going to blame him for having been inflexible with his debtors and indifferent towards his creditors, but . . . a murderer? Was it possible to believe him?

I'm going to tell you what I sincerely think, continued Dad, responding to my inquisitor's silence, Valdivino revolted against his own situation, against the fact that he couldn't possess Íris and was made to witness what Paulão did to her. He was threatening to reveal to the members of the commune that Íris had seduced him while he was still a child. And neither she nor Paulão could allow that to happen. For Íris, it would mean the end of the Garden of Salvation. For Paulão, the end of a source of income. But Valdivino, if he didn't kill himself, perhaps died defending Lúcrecia's life, maybe he gave his life for her, said Dad, How so, defending her life? Paulão raped Lucrécia right in front of Valdivino, saying, loud enough for him to hear, Look at this you little faggot, this is how you do it, and yelled at her, Here's something sacred for you, you're going to feel the sacred penetrating you, you slut whore, and then he threatened her: I can reveal to your followers all that I know about you, about your time in Salvador, you weren't forced into that life, you liked it, you had a talent for it . . . You know, he was a brute, he was violent.

Readers of this blog will remember that, on this subject, there were two whole pages of insults and descriptions that were inadvisable for a book that is directed at all audiences. I can't bar the people who already read those pages from having memorized them, but I request that they do not reproduce them. The minute details of Dad's story definitively do not have a place here, after this final revision.

I asked, How do you know this? I'm not certain of it, it's what they told me, he answered, And why didn't you turn in Paulão to the authorities? Without uttering a response, and for the first time over the course of those days, an expression of anguish appeared on Dad's face. Because your hands were tied, weren't they, as a result of all the fraud he'd committed on your behalf, because you wanted to keep earning easy money . . . Don't be unfair to me, I dissolved my partnership with him the moment I found him at Lucrécia's side in the Garden of Salvation, That's not enough, not nearly enough, why didn't you turn him in? Because, as I told you, it might not have been true . . . , It was because he could destroy you any time he wanted to, and because Valdivino was just a nobody, I'm an old man, sick and unjustly punished, don't make me die of sorrow, my son, did you come here just to hurt me?, believe me, João, these were merely suppositions, and still are—and when I heard these words, I felt that I was hastening his death, and that he was already in his final throes.

For many years, I thought that, unlike the justice system, which let Dad go around with impunity, my conscience would have to punish him. Today, now that the justice system has punished him—albeit for reasons other than Valdivino's disappearance—and Dad is already dead, I think that a crime without evidence or witnesses, as terrible as it may be, should not soil Dad's memory nor drown my conscience in a sea of guilt.

I'll confess to you all something I never said to Dad: that in those bygone days, I, too, felt that I was Valdivino's murderer, a remorseless murderer. I wanted him to die, I wanted it badly, perhaps more than anyone else. On the day of April 22, 1960, when Dad told me what had happened to Valdivino and buried all his papers, my sadness at having missed the Childrens' Festival was replaced with a feeling of relief.

And why do you want to solve this problem?, not every problem has a solution, these were the last words I ever heard Dad utter, between four dingy white walls.

Our past is hidden behind barriers that are sometimes impenetrable and is only revealed by chance, here and there, when we suddenly call it forth by a token, a word, a smell, a taste, or any random detail, like someone looking at a whole landscape through tiny holes in a wall. Staring out at the pool behind my house and at Paranoá Lake, I cried and cried, copiously. The landscape of Brasília was filled with silk floss trees, bougainvillea vines, ixora shrubs, fountain trees, touch-me-nots, and nightshades. What I was looking out at was a poor imitation of what had once been, or still was, its perfection; the past was merely one possible memory, a bunch of scraps tossed to me by the people around me. My efforts had been useless, and a part of me that I had once thought nonexistent, now hurt me deeply as it was being amputated. Dad had died, and I, who had always known that I was an orphan, that Dad was not my biological father, truly felt like an orphan for the first time.

On the day of the burial, there was a curious coincidence. I felt that I knew, from somewhere, the woman with straight black hair who owned the funeral parlor close to my house in Lago Sul, with whom I arranged for the burial. Her black eyes made me remember something forgotten from my childhood, they were one more of those details that appeared like a crack in the wall, through which an entire horizon of the past could be revealed. Are you from Brasília?, I asked her, I was a pioneer, she replied with pride, lived out in Candangolândia, I went to school in Candangolândia when I was a child, I told her, Oh! was her only response, accompanied by a slight affirmative movement of her head. I left there certain that she was the girl with braids from my childhood, whom I had never seen since, the one who used to ride around on her bicycle, with whom I had fallen in love, and whose name I never knew.

Dad's burial, like Bernardo Sayão's, took place in the Field of Hope, in the presence of a half-dozen people, including Aunt Francisca, his widow. She now seemed shorter than she did in my memories of childhood, and not only because of her bowed body. Her gentle eyes were little islands of beauty and youth in a sea of wrinkles. In my mind as a little boy, I had exaggerated Aunt Francisca's affection for Valdivino and reduced her interest in Dad to almost nothing. From the fights between the two of them, I had deduced incompatibility, if not enmity, unable to discern in them the fomentation of a love that was built on familiarity, a multifaceted love, like all the loves that last.

I've never forgotten the words of Aunt Francisca days after the supposed murder of Valdivino, words that filled me with an awful fear when I was a child, because I immediately connected

Valdivino's demise with what had happened between Aunt Matilde and me. I thought about omitting this part of the story, but allow me to tell it all. I lost that fear when Aunt Matilde took me in after my falling-out with Dad, so much so that one night I dared to put my hand on her thighs and slide it underneath her skirt until I was caressing her most intimate part, my finger penetrating inside it leisurely and tenderly, until I felt Aunt Matilde's wet pleasure, I've never forgotten, I wanted to say to her, it's the only thing in my life that I regret not doing, you're not my aunt by blood, I don't see anything too wrong with it, it'll be a revolutionary act on our part, what are you afraid of, Aunt Matilde? No, I can't, was all she said, after a prolonged and pleasurable hesitation, But you're not my real aunt, That's not why, let's remain friends, I don't want to ruin our relationship—she was reluctantly and slowly removing my finger—That's just bourgeois morality, I replied, It may be, but it's stronger than I am.

Aunt Francisca, I've spent this week gathering information from Dad about those first few years in the Free City, and we ended up talking a lot about Valdivino. You used to like him ... I said, still at the cemetery.

He was a humble young man, very polite, he didn't deserve what happened to him.

Maybe you don't remember, but one time you mentioned that he died because of sex within his family.

I don't know if Íris was his mother or not, it seems that when he was a child she told him that he'd been left on the doorstep, but when she wanted to end her crazy relationship with him, she told him she was his mother.

We walked past the grave of an American—which a blog-reader informed me belonged to the same Joana Lowell Bowen that Dad knew from his time in Goiás, the owner of a farm close to where we used to live, the woman who drove a Volkswagon bus in the Belém-Brasília Caravan—and we were able to find Bernardo Sayão's grave nearby. I had never seen Sayão, but Dad would certainly be pleased to know that Aunt Francisca and I paid homage to Sayão out there, for ourselves and on Dad's behalf as well. The cemetery looked nothing like the one from Sayão's burial. In that distant past there were a multitude of living beings, and just one dead man below the ground. Now the ground was full of the dead, and we, the few living beings, were walking along it on a cold winter morning.

Back at home, flipping through my old records, I listened to the main march of the suite *On the Way to Brasília*, which Heckel Tavares had dedicated to Bernardo Sayão, the engineer who helped build an entire city by sheer force of will, an iron will, and willpower is like the strength of the wind that blows against a sailboat out on the high seas. All it takes is the strength of the blowing wind to create routes across an infinite sea. It is that strength that makes the boat glide along the water and arrive at some port, even if it's not the one we'd hoped for. Willpower alone, like a blowing nothingness, was capable of creating movement in the world.

Today, writing on the patio of the house on the lake that will soon no longer be mine, I am thinking intensely about Dad. My wife and children have already gone to bed, and the melancholy silence is only broken by the sound of a cricket. I wish I hadn't been so hard on Dad, I shouldn't have asked him such troubling questions, which turned out to be useless and might have hastened his death, because what he told me didn't solve the mystery, on the contrary, the mystery just kept growing, like a monster; I should have let him die in peace, should have sought him out only to express my affection. If I could, I would go back and do those visits differently, and then this would be a different book, although it's likely that nothing more would have been revealed about the mystery surrounding Valdivino.

In that distant era, in those by-gone days of 1960, when Brasília was just coming to life, the newspapers and the magazine *O Cruzeiro* were busy with the crime wave in Rio: the Sacopã murder, and the murders of Dana de Teffé, and Aída Curi. There was an absolute silence surrounding Valdivino and the Garden of Salvation, the case was surrounded by a fortress of purity, or merely surrounded by whispers and rumors, like those that are still passed around in the corridors and basements of the Esplanade. To this day, the mystery of Valdivino has been forgotten, and out in the Garden of Salvation, the prevailing version of the story ended up being the one in which there was no crime at all, just a miracle.

On the day of Valdivino's death, if he did in fact die, I had to stay at home the whole morning and most of the afternoon. I didn't even go out into the streets, which I assumed were deserted. I think it was on that afternoon—when Dad arrived home full of anxiety and showed me the hole in which he was going to bury his papers—that, for the first time, I thought of becoming a journalist and writing about the era of the Free City, and it was from a force of will like that of Sayão, from a wind, and from pure strength that the words with which I was able to remember those times past emerged, one after the other, torn from the silence and profound emptiness, like a creation that issues forth from zero, from uncertainty, ignorance, debt, guilt, and all that we lack. I didn't want to say anything, for memory itself has nothing that it wants to say, it merely speaks amidst oblivion and that which it seeks to hide, and for that reason there is nothing to interpret—words, like memories, are what they are, and nothing more. Looking into the mirror of the past, where at times I don't even recognize myself, I am inventing nothing, merely writing an account of what I had lived, which stands as a witness, among the many that might be in existence, that may help compose the portrait of an era.

After months of lessons with Aunt Francisca, on that distant afternoon in 1960, I was finally able to play the accordion. I took it out to Central Avenue as the large, red sun was already kissing the horizon, sat down on a bench in the open air—Typhoon had come with me and sat down at my feet—began to play, and then some people gathered around me. Some even started to shake a leg. Everyone was happy and dancing, except for Dad and Aunt Francisca. Aunt Matilde showed up, chuckled when she saw me, and said, This little boy is going to be a handful! There was a strong breeze, which made Aunt Matilde's skirt flutter, and a transparent orange hue in the air. We were still in the rainy season, and for that reason the wind was blowing from the north, and not from the east and southeast as it did in the summer, and a mixture of red mud had sullied our boots and shoes on those stretches of land that one day, who knows, would be green.

João Almino is the author of five novels, of which *The Five Seasons of Love* and *The Book of Emotions* are available in English translation. He has taught at Berkeley, Stanford, the Autonomous National University of Mexico, and the Universities of Brasília and Chicago. *Free City* received the Zaffari & Bourbon Literary Award for the best novel published in Brazil between 2009 and 2011, and was short-listed for the Portugal-Telecom and the Jabuti Literary Awards.

Rhett McNeil has translated work by António Lobo Antunes, Gonçalo M. Tavares, A. G. Porta, and Machado de Assis, all for Dalkey Archive Press.

MICHAL AJVAZ, *The Golden Age.*
  *The Other City.*
PIERRE ALBERT-BIROT, *Grabinoulor.*
YUZ ALESHKOVSKY, *Kangaroo.*
FELIPE ALFAU, *Chromos.*
  *Locos.*
IVAN ÂNGELO, *The Celebration.*
  *The Tower of Glass.*
ANTÓNIO LOBO ANTUNES, *Knowledge of Hell.*
  *The Splendor of Portugal.*
ALAIN ARIAS-MISSON, *Theatre of Incest.*
JOHN ASHBERY AND JAMES SCHUYLER,
  *A Nest of Ninnies.*
ROBERT ASHLEY, *Perfect Lives.*
GABRIELA AVIGUR-ROTEM, *Heatwave
  and Crazy Birds.*
DJUNA BARNES, *Ladies Almanack.*
  *Ryder.*
JOHN BARTH, *LETTERS.*
  *Sabbatical.*
DONALD BARTHELME, *The King.*
  *Paradise.*
SVETISLAV BASARA, *Chinese Letter.*
MIQUEL BAUÇÀ, *The Siege in the Room.*
RENÉ BELLETTO, *Dying.*
MAREK BIEŃCZYK, *Transparency.*
ANDREI BITOV, *Pushkin House.*
ANDREJ BLATNIK, *You Do Understand.*
LOUIS PAUL BOON, *Chapel Road.*
  *My Little War.*
  *Summer in Termuren.*
ROGER BOYLAN, *Killoyle.*
IGNÁCIO DE LOYOLA BRANDÃO,
  *Anonymous Celebrity.*
  *Zero.*
BONNIE BREMSER, *Troia: Mexican Memoirs.*
CHRISTINE BROOKE-ROSE, *Amalgamemnon.*
BRIGID BROPHY, *In Transit.*
GERALD L. BRUNS, *Modern Poetry and
  the Idea of Language.*
GABRIELLE BURTON, *Heartbreak Hotel.*
MICHEL BUTOR, *Degrees.*
  *Mobile.*
G. CABRERA INFANTE, *Infante's Inferno.*
  *Three Trapped Tigers.*
JULIETA CAMPOS,
  *The Fear of Losing Eurydice.*
ANNE CARSON, *Eros the Bittersweet.*
ORLY CASTEL-BLOOM, *Dolly City.*
LOUIS-FERDINAND CÉLINE, *Castle to Castle.*
  *Conversations with Professor Y.*
  *London Bridge.*
  *Normance.*
  *North.*
  *Rigadoon.*
MARIE CHAIX, *The Laurels of Lake Constance.*
HUGO CHARTERIS, *The Tide Is Right.*
ERIC CHEVILLARD, *Demolishing Nisard.*
MARC CHOLODENKO, *Mordechai Schamz.*
JOSHUA COHEN, *Witz.*
EMILY HOLMES COLEMAN, *The Shutter
  of Snow.*
ROBERT COOVER, *A Night at the Movies.*
STANLEY CRAWFORD, *Log of the S.S. The
  Mrs Unguentine.*
  *Some Instructions to My Wife.*
RENÉ CREVEL, *Putting My Foot in It.*
RALPH CUSACK, *Cadenza.*
NICHOLAS DELBANCO, *The Count of Concord.*
  *Sherbrookes.*
NIGEL DENNIS, *Cards of Identity.*

PETER DIMOCK, *A Short Rhetoric for
  Leaving the Family.*
ARIEL DORFMAN, *Konfidenz.*
COLEMAN DOWELL,
  *Island People.*
  *Too Much Flesh and Jabez.*
ARKADII DRAGOMOSHCHENKO, *Dust.*
RIKKI DUCORNET, *The Complete
  Butcher's Tales.*
  *The Fountains of Neptune.*
  *The Jade Cabinet.*
  *Phosphor in Dreamland.*
WILLIAM EASTLAKE, *The Bamboo Bed.*
  *Castle Keep.*
  *Lyric of the Circle Heart.*
JEAN ECHENOZ, *Chopin's Move.*
STANLEY ELKIN, *A Bad Man.*
  *Criers and Kibitzers, Kibitzers
  and Criers.*
  *The Dick Gibson Show.*
  *The Franchiser.*
  *The Living End.*
  *Mrs. Ted Bliss.*
FRANÇOIS EMMANUEL, *Invitation to a
  Voyage.*
SALVADOR ESPRIU, *Ariadne in the
  Grotesque Labyrinth.*
LESLIE A. FIEDLER, *Love and Death in
  the American Novel.*
JUAN FILLOY, *Op Oloop.*
ANDY FITCH, *Pop Poetics.*
GUSTAVE FLAUBERT, *Bouvard and Pécuchet.*
KASS FLEISHER, *Talking out of School.*
FORD MADOX FORD,
  *The March of Literature.*
JON FOSSE, *Aliss at the Fire.*
  *Melancholy.*
MAX FRISCH, *I'm Not Stiller.*
  *Man in the Holocene.*
CARLOS FUENTES, *Christopher Unborn.*
  *Distant Relations.*
  *Terra Nostra.*
  *Where the Air Is Clear.*
TAKEHIKO FUKUNAGA, *Flowers of Grass.*
WILLIAM GADDIS, *J R.*
  *The Recognitions.*
JANICE GALLOWAY, *Foreign Parts.*
  *The Trick Is to Keep Breathing.*
WILLIAM H. GASS, *Cartesian Sonata
  and Other Novellas.*
  *Finding a Form.*
  *A Temple of Texts.*
  *The Tunnel.*
  *Willie Masters' Lonesome Wife.*
GÉRARD GAVARRY, *Hoppla! 1 2 3.*
ETIENNE GILSON,
  *The Arts of the Beautiful.*
  *Forms and Substances in the Arts.*
C. S. GISCOMBE, *Giscome Road.*
  *Here.*
DOUGLAS GLOVER, *Bad News of the Heart.*
WITOLD GOMBROWICZ,
  *A Kind of Testament.*
PAULO EMÍLIO SALES GOMES, *P's Three
  Women.*
GEORGI GOSPODINOV, *Natural Novel.*
JUAN GOYTISOLO, *Count Julian.*
  *Juan the Landless.*
  *Makbara.*
  *Marks of Identity.*

DUMITRU TSEPENEAG, *Hotel Europa.*
*The Necessary Marriage.*
*Pigeon Post.*
*Vain Art of the Fugue.*
ESTHER TUSQUETS, *Stranded.*
DUBRAVKA UGRESIC, *Lend Me Your Character.*
*Thank You for Not Reading.*
TOR ULVEN, *Replacement.*
MATI UNT, *Brecht at Night.*
*Diary of a Blood Donor.*
*Things in the Night.*
ÁLVARO URIBE AND OLIVIA SEARS, EDS.,
*Best of Contemporary Mexican Fiction.*
ELOY URROZ, *Friction.*
*The Obstacles.*
LUISA VALENZUELA, *Dark Desires and
the Others.*
*He Who Searches.*
PAUL VERHAEGHEN, *Omega Minor.*
AGLAJA VETERANYI, *Why the Child Is
Cooking in the Polenta.*
BORIS VIAN, *Heartsnatcher.*
LLORENÇ VILLALONGA, *The Dolls' Room.*
TOOMAS VINT, *An Unending Landscape.*
ORNELA VORPSI, *The Country Where No
One Ever Dies.*
AUSTRYN WAINHOUSE, *Hedyphagetica.*
CURTIS WHITE, *America's Magic Mountain.*
*The Idea of Home.*
*Memories of My Father Watching TV.*
*Requiem.*

DIANE WILLIAMS, *Excitability:
Selected Stories.*
*Romancer Erector.*
DOUGLAS WOOLF, *Wall to Wall.*
*Ya! & John-Juan.*
JAY WRIGHT, *Polynomials and Pollen.*
*The Presentable Art of Reading
Absence.*
PHILIP WYLIE, *Generation of Vipers.*
MARGUERITE YOUNG, *Angel in the Forest.*
*Miss MacIntosh, My Darling.*
REYOUNG, *Unbabbling.*
VLADO ŽABOT, *The Succubus.*
ZORAN ŽIVKOVIĆ, *Hidden Camera.*
LOUIS ZUKOFSKY, *Collected Fiction.*
VITOMIL ZUPAN, *Minuet for Guitar.*
SCOTT ZWIREN, *God Head.*